# New Boy at the Academy

Tales from the Academy,

Book One

*Sam Hawk*

A NineStar Press Publication

Published by NineStar Press
P.O. Box 91792,
Albuquerque, New Mexico, 87199 USA.
www.ninestarpress.com

# New Boy at the Academy

Copyright © 2019 by Sam Hawk
Cover Art by Natasha Snow Copyright © 2019
Edited by Elizabetta McKay

This is a work of fiction. Names, characters, places, and incidents are either the product of the author's imagination or are used fictitiously. Any resemblance to actual persons living or dead, business establishments, events, or locales is entirely coincidental.

All rights reserved. No part of this publication may be reproduced in any material form, whether by printing, photocopying, scanning or otherwise without the written permission of the publisher. To request permission and all other inquiries, contact NineStar Press at the physical or web addresses above or at Contact@ninestarpress.com.

Printed in the USA
First Edition
March, 2019

Print ISBN: 978-1-950412-38-9

Also available in eBook, ISBN: 978-1-950412-36-5

Warning: This book contains racist, homophobic, and fat-shaming language some readers may find offensive. A warning also for sexist, sex-negative, and slut shaming language, all from secondary characters.

Timmy had no clue that the first day of 10th grade at the Academy would rock his world. He thought it would be just like last year, with its endless bullying and recesses spent reshelving books in the library with his best and only friend Carleen. The sissy boy and the fat girl had bonded over their shared outcast status. But Carleen shows up filled with sassy confidence and declares they're going to rule the school. By Christmas, the freaks and nerds would be the cool kids, and the mean girls and jocks would be the outcasts. Something had happened to her over the summer, but what?

And then, the two of them lay eyes on the new boy at the Academy. Doug has auburn feathered hair, veiny biceps, and green eyes the color of Sprite bottles. Plus, he's come all the way from exotic Los Angeles, California. He rocks out to Patti Smith while Timmy loves ABBA. How does someone so cool end up in tiny, conservative Edgewood, South Carolina?

When Carleen immediately declares Doug a fox and her new prospective boyfriend, Timmy is shocked at his jealous reaction. He's not supposed to like boys in that way, is he? Doug stirs up weird new emotions deep inside him as Timmy embarks on the adventure of his life. He and his hometown will never be the same.

For Wes, the love of my life.

# One: Unanswered Prayers

EDGEWOOD, SOUTH CAROLINA
1980

God didn't answer my prayers and bring the Rapture on Labor Day, so I had to start tenth grade after all. I stepped in front of the mirror to assess my new back-to-school outfit. I hated it. I'd begged Momma to buy me the alligator shirt from Belk's, which really cost her a lot, but did it have to hug my body so much? I tried stretching it out, but it would only stretch so far. I thought I'd look like Tom Selleck with his big veiny arms. Instead, I looked like the Pillsbury Doughboy. I was trying to flex my chest when Momma walked in.

"Honey, get a move on. We have to be out the door in fifteen minutes, and you haven't even touched your Pop-Tarts."

"Momma, I think I need to change clothes."

"What are you talking about?" she asked as she pulled and tugged on my shirt. "This is what you wanted. You look very handsome."

"But it fits so close."

"Timmy, I have told you time and again you're not fat. It's all in your head. You are absolutely average on the height and weight scale and exactly where you need to be at fifteen." She patted my tummy, causing me to suck in. "You'll lose that little bit of pudge in no time in gym class."

My heart sank at the thought of gym class, and I almost lost my appetite for Pop-Tarts. Almost. Momma smoothed down my cowlick at the kitchen table as I bit into the brown sugar cinnamon pastry.

"Thank goodness you inherited the Ashburn hair," she said. "Such a beautiful chestnut brown and such a noble hairline. It's a sign of your aristocratic heritage, you know, on my side of the family. All the Ashburn men had beautiful hairlines. Thank goodness you take after me and don't have your daddy's stringy mess."

I guessed my hairline was okay, but my new haircut was way too short. Daddy had taken me to get it cut only after Momma called him ten times to remind him. He and Momma got divorced when I was two, and it was always weird when he came by, which wasn't often. Naturally, he took me to the awful old barbershop next to the pool hall instead of the new unisex salon in the Augusta Mall I was secretly hoping for. He told the barber to "buzz it" and then went next door for a beer. I managed to talk the barber into keeping a little length, but not much.

"Now go brush your teeth quick as a bunny rabbit," said Momma. "Carleen's mother called this morning and said her car's not running and could I run by and pick her up for school. So, we have no time."

Carleen's house was across the tracks, and I knew Momma didn't like going over there, but Carleen had been my best friend since kindergarten. Actually, you could say she was my only friend. She was the only one I talked to for hours on the phone at night; the only one I hung out with after school; the only one to ever invite me to a sleepover, which Momma had never allowed me to do since boy-girl sleepovers just weren't done. I hadn't seen her all summer because she'd been working at her grandparents' peach farm. I was glad we'd be going to school together on the first day. I needed my friend with me.

We pulled in front of the house, and Carleen came right out.

"Good Lord, Carleen's put on even more weight this summer," said Momma.

Momma was right. Carleen had always been the biggest girl in class, and she wasn't getting any smaller. I recognized her smock top from last year. A smock top was supposed to fit loose, but hers pulled in all the wrong places.

"Hey, Carleen," said Momma as Carleen got in the car. "You sure do look pretty for your first day of school."

"Thank you, Mrs. Thompson," said Carleen. I waited for an eye roll, but she just smiled at Momma like she really believed it. I looked at her more closely, and there was something different about her. Was it confidence? If so, it was new. Was that lip gloss she was wearing?

"Hey, Timmy, did you hear we're getting a new boy in our class this year?"

"No," I said, dreading the addition of another redneck bubba to the roster.

"They say he's from California and he's real cute."

"Really? California?" said Momma. "What's he doing here?"

"I think his momma's people are here. He's related to all those Herlongs."

"Does that explain the lip gloss?"

"Timmy, don't be rude," said Momma.

"I just wanted to look pretty for the first day of school," replied Carleen.

"And you do," said Momma.

When Momma pulled up in front of Patriot Christian, Carleen looked me square in the eye and gave me a big smile and a thumbs-up.

"Come on, Timmy. We're gonna rule the school in tenth grade. Let's do it."

AS SOON AS she drove off, Carleen pulled me behind the crepe myrtles.

"I gotta tell you what happened to me this summer. You're the only one I'm telling, so you gotta swear to keep it secret."

"You know I don't swear, but I won't tell. What is it?"

"Brace yourself. Are you braced? This is big. Real big."

I put my hand on the tree trunk. "I'm braced. Carleen, what on earth happened?"

"I lost it. With a guy. We did the nasty."

"The nasty what?"

"The nasty. You know." She made a thrusting motion with her hips.

"You went dancing?"

"Jesus, Timmy, you are so dense. We bumped boots. Played hide the sausage. Made the beast with two backs. Ya get it?"

I shook my head in confusion. The bell was ringing, so we needed to go. "You shouldn't use the Lord's name in vain, and no, I don't get it. Just say it in plain English."

"I got screwed; now do you understand? S-E-X. His name is Juan."

Thank goodness I was braced because I almost fell over. Was that why she was suddenly so confident? Did that explain the lip gloss? Who was Juan? I didn't know any Juan.

"Carleen," I whispered. "Do you mean intercourse? We're too young for that stuff."

"*We* didn't have intercourse. *I* had intercourse, and it was great."

"I don't believe you."

Just then, Mrs. Morgan came striding down the walk toward us.

"Children— Why aren't you in assembly? It starts in thirty seconds. March!"

# Two: The New Kid

THE BLEACHERS WERE full of kids settling down for assembly, and Carleen and I were the last two in the gym. I was scanning the crowd looking for two empty spaces when I laid eyes on him for the first time. The new boy. He stopped me in my tracks. He had feathered hair, longer than any of the other boys—like Jon on *CHiPs*, only a beautiful shade of auburn instead of blond. He had green eyes the color of Sprite bottles. He wore a golf shirt with short ribbed sleeves like mine, only his had a polo player on it instead of an alligator. His biceps weren't as big as Jon's, but he had them, unlike me, and there was a little vein running through each one. He was sitting in the front row, a space or two from the next kid, and was looking straight ahead at Mrs. Holt mounting the podium. He wasn't like any of the boys around here. He wasn't like any boy I had ever seen before in my life. My pulse started pounding. I felt flushed. Why was I feeling flushed?

Carleen elbowed me in the ribs and whispered, "He's a fox." Then she pulled me over to two spaces on the front row, at the other end from the new boy. The pounding in my chest began to slow.

After the assembly started, Carleen elbowed me again because Mrs. Holt was glaring at me. I realized I was the only one not singing "Jesus Loves Me" because I was trying to spy the new boy with my peripheral vision.

I joined the singing on the last line: *"For the Bible tells me so."*

"Nice of you to join us, Timmy Thompson," Mrs. Holt said in front of the entire assembly. Everybody laughed. Only twenty minutes into tenth grade and already I wanted to crawl under the bleachers and die.

Mrs. Holt shook her head at me and addressed everyone. "Welcome back to Patriot Christian Academy, Christian Soldiers! If y'all work hard and praise His name daily, you will have a rewarding year, and we'll send another class of seniors off to conquer the world."

She paused and looked around at us, her half-rimmed glasses perched on the end of her nose. Carleen squirmed in her seat.

"All right, boys and girls, everyone proceed in an orderly fashion to your first period. Teachers? Take charge."

Mrs. Morgan stood and beckoned us tenth graders to follow her to first period. She moved in a brisk march, her crepe-soled shoes squeaking as everyone in the class sprinted to keep up.

"Move with a purpose, children."

It was her favorite phrase.

"Move with a purpose. Two by two, that's right. Keep an orderly line."

Mrs. Morgan had taught us sixth-grade English, seventh-grade American history, and she would now be teaching tenth-grade Good Citizenship. Patriot Christian didn't have a whole lot of teachers, so they had to double up. Mrs. Means taught math and art, which seemed kind of weird, and Coach Duggins taught driver's ed and South Carolina history, which seemed weirder.

Mrs. Morgan was shaped like a top and walked like a penguin. I thought if I pulled a string off one of her pastel mix and match pantsuits, she'd spin around until she fell over. I choked back a giggle.

"Did you see the new boy? He's so cute," said Carleen, walking beside me. Carleen had a way of whispering so her lips didn't move and nobody knew it was her speaking.

"We're not supposed to talk in line," I whispered.

"Do I hear talking in line?" said Mrs. Morgan, on cue. She always heard me but never Carleen.

"Old Lady's not gonna tell me what to do," whispered Carleen. I could barely hear her, but I was shocked just the same. When did Carleen start saying stuff like "Old Lady" when she was talking about our teachers? And why did I feel annoyed that Carleen called the new boy cute?

We got to our classroom, and each desk had a name written on masking tape and a new book titled *Good Citizenship in the United States of America*, published by the United Daughters of the Confederacy. On the cover were pictures of George Washington and Robert E. Lee with crossed Confederate and American flags. Carleen sat right behind me, and the new boy sat on my right.

Carleen immediately passed me a note that said, *I want to screw him.* I was shocked again. Hadn't she screwed enough? I looked up in panic and saw Mrs. Morgan was busy at the blackboard, so I quickly stuffed the note between the pages of *Good Citizenship*. When I caught my breath, I used my peripheral vision again to see what the new boy was doing. He was looking straight at me. I turned away fast.

Mrs. Morgan began speaking. "Welcome to tenth grade. You're out of the baby grades now. That means it's time to buckle down and work hard so you can graduate with the class of '83. Let's get to it. Who can tell me the answer to this question..."

She droned on with her question, but I wasn't listening. The new boy had his elbows on his desk and was looking forward. He reached his right hand over and slowly ran it up his left upper arm, under the ribbed shirtsleeve. He held it there, caressing his bicep. I couldn't take my eyes off him.

"Timmy Thompson! Pay attention," said Mrs. Morgan.

She rapped her wooden pointer on her desk.

"I don't know what you've been doing with yourself all summer, but you're back in school now. It's time to straighten up and get serious. Now that I have your attention, perhaps you would like to answer my question?"

The new boy stopped stroking his arm and turned to watch me. I looked straight at the teacher.

"Well, young man? We're waiting. I asked a question, and I expect an answer. I was addressing a very important topic."

She folded her arms and tapped her crepe-soled shoe. Since I didn't know what the question was, I sure didn't know the answer. I sat there for what seemed like forever as everyone stared at me. The only sound was Mrs. Morgan's sensible toe tapping.

Finally, Kimberly Ann Mingees stuck her hand in the air. "I know the answer, Mrs. Morgan!"

"I know you do, Kimberly Ann," said Mrs. Morgan. "And don't blurt it out. I'm sure you were listening, unlike Timmy, here. Well, Timmy? Kimberly Ann's not going to give you the answer. The whole class is waiting for you."

I had no idea what to say, so I blurted out the all-purpose answer for Patriot Christian Academy.

"John 3:16?"

Everybody laughed except the new boy who just looked confused. Mrs. Morgan threw up her hands.

"First day of school and you're already daydreaming. You'd better get your head out of the clouds and buckle down, young man. Idle hands are the devil's workshop. Remember that. Kimberly Ann, please inform Timmy what the question was and answer it."

I sank in my seat and fixed my eyes on a spot on my desk while Kimberly Ann stood up.

"The question was, what is the greatest duty of a Christian citizen in an election year such as this one? The answer is, the greatest duty of a Christian citizen is to vote for a Christian candidate like Ronald Reagan. That's what Jesus would want."

She sat down.

"Very good, Kimberly Ann," said Mrs. Morgan. "It's nice to see someone came to school ready to learn."

Kimberly Ann flipped her long blonde hair behind her shoulder and clasped her hands on her desk, a small smile on her lips.

I hated Kimberly Ann.

Then, I suddenly realized how to redeem myself with Mrs. Morgan, so I raised my hand.

"Jimmy Carter's a Christian, and my aunt Melanie is voting for him, so she's doing her duty as a Christian. Is that what you mean?"

"Absolutely not!" said Mrs. Morgan. "All those race-mixing ideas of his are certainly not Christian. Deuteronomy 7:3. Then there's all his un-Christian ideas about money and such. I know he goes to a Baptist church, or at least he says so. Maybe Georgia Baptists don't think the same way as us South Carolina Baptists, but a good

Christian politician is first and foremost a good steward of the economy. Do you know what I mean by the word steward, class? It means to take care of. The president takes care of the nation's economy for us. Wealth must be protected for those who work hard and earn it. Why, Jimmy Carter wants to give it all away to all the lazy types who expect a handout, and they'll all be voting too—don't you doubt it. And don't even get me started on that trashy brother of his, hanging around a gas station drinking beer all the time."

I sank back in my desk.

"Well, enough of that because I have somebody to introduce. We have a new boy in class this year. Let's all welcome Doug Appleby. Stand up, Doug."

The new boy stood and put his hands in his pockets. He looked around the class and met my eyes for a moment. My underarms went damp.

"Doug has come to us all the way from California."

California! But it was so far away. How did he get all the way over here? I bet California was the most perfect place to live.

Mrs. Morgan rolled down the map of the United States that was mounted above the blackboard.

"Doug, why don't you come up and show us exactly where you came from."

Doug walked to the map. Mrs. Morgan handed him her pointer, and he placed it on California.

"Southern California, LA," he mumbled, then went back to his seat, leaving the pointer on the teacher's desk.

"LA stands for Los Angeles, class," said Mrs. Morgan. She pronounced Los Angeles as "Laws Angie-lees." "It's a great big city all the way across the country on the Pacific Ocean. It's near Hollywood."

She picked up a pointer from the chalk tray and slid it across the map from South Carolina to the Pacific coast.

"I'm sure *LA*, as he calls it, is glamorous and exciting, but I know Doug is glad to be here in South Carolina with good folks and small-town values, aren't you, Doug?"

She smiled and nodded at Doug, waiting on him to agree. He stared back in silence.

She pressed on.

"He's only lived here for a week, and this is his first time ever in South Carolina, even though this is where his people are. So, let's show him what true Southern hospitality is all about, all right, class?"

She started clapping. The entire class joined in. Doug stared at his shoes while we applauded him for coming to Patriot Christian.

As the applause died off, something occurred to me: If Doug Appleby sits beside me in this class, he's probably going to sit beside me in every class. Oh my gosh, if he's going to sit next to me in every class, we could be like study buddies or trade notes or if he loses his pencil, I could give him one or if I wear down my eraser, I could borrow his or we could talk about what we're going to do next weekend or how much homework we have or we could meet up after school and plan our outfits for the week...

# Three: I Don't Think Boys are Good-Looking

THE BELL RANG, and we all gathered our books and filed out of Good Citizenship for Math. In the hallway, Jimbo Abernathy bumped me, knocking my books out of my hands.

"Smooth move, ExLax." He smelled like cigarettes and red clay.

The entire hall full of kids laughed. Carleen helped me pick up my books, and we went to math class.

"Screw those dummies," she whispered to me. "They don't matter."

It made me feel better, but I would have to have a talk with her about her new potty mouth.

In Math, Doug sat beside me, just like in Good Citizenship, but I was too humiliated to use my peripheral vision again. I just stared straight ahead and tried to make myself as invisible as possible. Even so, I couldn't concentrate on the equations Mrs. Means was scrawling across the blackboard. Doug must have seen Jimbo knock my books out of my hands. How could he miss it? Now, he knew how I was treated at school. I felt really sad he saw that before I had a chance to meet him and become his new best friend. He'd see me as a nerd and a nobody like everybody else did.

At lunch, Carleen and I filed into the cafeteria at the back of the crowd. Doug was way ahead of us in line, and I watched as he took his tray to the empty end of a long table. At the other end sat a group of cool boys from the JV football team. They looked at him and snickered, but he didn't seem to notice.

Carleen and I bought our Mountain Dews and did the same thing we always did last year: we sat at the empty end of the teachers' table and ate our sandwiches from home. I tried, but I couldn't keep my eyes off Doug for long.

"Stop it," said Carleen.

"What?"

"You're staring at the new boy, and he's gonna notice."

"I am not. I'm just looking around."

I focused on my pimento cheese sandwich, banana, and baggie of Ruffles Momma had packed.

"You just gotta be careful, or people will talk. This is tenth grade now. The big time. Senior high."

Suddenly, all eyes turned as Kimberly Ann made her entrance into the cafeteria, fashionably late, as always. She probably stopped by the girl's room first to poof her hair to perfection. She was wearing a flouncy pink skirt and a jean jacket with flower patches on it. It was a bit much for my classic taste, but it was way ahead of the fashion curve for Edgewood. I figured girls dressed like that in big cities like Columbia, which was probably where she got the outfit. All the girls at Patriot Christian would probably start sewing flower patches all over themselves now. Then Kimberly Ann would stop wearing them.

Trailing Kimberly Ann were Lisa and Kathy, who'd never been her best friends before. Last year, she was always with Patti Ann and Jaime Ann, but they were already in the cafeteria, sitting a few tables away, staring at Kimberly Ann's entrance and not touching their lunch.

"What happened to Patti Ann and Jaime Ann, and what's up with Lisa and Kathy?" I asked Carleen.

"Haven't you heard? Lisa and Kathy are new-new Anns. They want to be called Lisa Ann and Kathy Ann now, and their middle names aren't even Ann. I guess Patti Ann and Jaime Ann are now just plain old Patti and Jaime again."

"What happened?" I asked.

"I can't believe you didn't hear. It all happened at the country club dance over the Fourth of July. Debbie Abernathy, my second cousin twice removed, was bartending. You know Debbie, right?"

I nodded. I didn't like Debbie or her white trash family. She and Jimbo were first cousins, so I tried to avoid both of them.

"I know who she is."

"So, the day after the dance, Debbie came over to hang out with Momma 'cause she knows she can always find cigarettes and beer at our place, and she got about three beers in and started running her mouth. I overheard everything. It turned out Kimberly Ann started dating this boy named Kent or Ken or something. Anyway, he's a state senator's son from Greenwood and totally rich. Cute too, if you like them clean-cut and brain-dead. Anyway, all those rich kids had brought flasks from home and were getting totally wasted. Kimberly Ann was ignoring Patti Ann and Jaime Ann because there were all these older sorority girls there from Clemson, and Kimberly Ann was kissing up like crazy because she's already planning which snooty-pants sorority she's going to join when she goes to college. Anyway, some Susie Sorority took Kimberly Ann to the bathroom to hold her hair while she threw up, and they were gone for a while.

"Eww, gross."

"It's what rich girls do. They throw up. That's how they stay skinny. When they finally came out, guess who was dancing with Kent-slash-Ken? Jaime Ann. And I don't just mean dancing, I mean grinding and playing tonsil hockey. They were practically doing it on the dance floor."

"What's tonsil hockey?"

Carleen rolled her eyes. "French kissing. Don't you know anything? Jaime Ann was practically choking Kent-slash-Ken with her tongue."

"It sounds disgusting."

"It's not really, but back to the story. Kimberly Ann was so totally pissed off—"

"Carleen! Watch your mouth. You'll get expelled for profanity." I nodded toward the teachers, who were deep in conversation.

"They're not paying attention to me. Are you gonna let me finish my story?"

She didn't wait for an answer before plunging back in. "Kimberly Ann was so...*upset*..." She rolled her eyes again. "She was so pissed that she ran over to them and grabbed Jaime Ann away from that boy so hard they both fell on the floor, and Jaime Ann started kicking and scratching and pulling hair, and then Patti Ann joined in, and it took four guys to pull them apart. Then, Jaime Ann and Patti Ann started yelling at Kimberly Ann, saying she was mean to them and had ignored them all night, and they were tired of being treated like her servants."

"Took them long enough to figure it out," I said.

"Kimberly Ann stood up straight, fluffed out her hair, and declared in front of God and everybody at the country club that Jaime Ann and Patti Ann were no longer her friends, and they could no longer use the name Ann. Then she told country club security that those girls were trespassing, and they escorted them out. They had to walk miles back to town because they rode with Kimberly Ann and that boy."

"Oh my gosh. I bet they were in heels and everything."

"The next Saturday, Kimberly Ann was seen at the country club pool with Lisa and Kathy, who were her newly crowned Anns. They spent most of the summer there, fetching Cokes and suntan lotion for Miss Priss."

"Speak of the devil," I whispered as quietly as I could as Kimberly Ann and the Anns were about to walk past our table. Kimberly Ann never looked in our direction, of course, but Lisa Ann cut her eyes toward Carleen and said, "Great top. Is it from Omar the tent maker?"

Carleen flushed and said, "Hey, Lisa, why bother eating that when you're just going to throw it up in ten minutes?"

"Maybe you should try it, fatty," said Kathy Ann.

Anger flew all over me. "You're just mean. Carleen's never done anything to you."

"So?" said Kathy Ann, and she and Patti Ann laughed.

"Hurry up," said Kimberly Ann. "Quit wasting time with those two." They all sat at the table with the football players, the same table where Doug sat alone at the end. Kimberly Ann looked Doug up and down as she sat, but Doug didn't seem to notice. He was looking at me. I wished I'd come up with something smart and clever to say to Kathy Ann. Doug probably thought I was a total space cadet.

"I hate those girls," said Carleen. "They think they're so much better than the rest of us just because they're skinny and stuff. Thanks for taking up for me, pal."

"Kathy Ann used to be nice. I remember in eighth grade when we dissected a frog together and she was kind of my friend for a little while."

"It's all right. Just you wait. Those three are going to wish they never tangled with Carleen and Timmy. By the end of the year, we're gonna be the popular table. We'll be the cool kids, and those three toothpicks will be begging to sit with us."

I looked at her, wondering how on earth she thought we were going to make it happen.

"Even Kimberly Ann?" I asked.

"Screw her," Carleen said way too loud. "She'll beg all right, but I'll make her sit with the nerds."

Carleen clinked my Mountain Dew bottle with hers and took a big swig.

"Momma wouldn't like it if she knew we were talking about Kimberly Ann. She just loves her. She's always talking about what a fine young lady she is and all the good works she does at First Baptist."

"Everybody's mother loves Kimberly Ann. She snows them, but she's a real bitch."

"Carleen! You shouldn't say those words. Say a quick prayer so Jesus'll forgive you."

Carleen held her hand up, palm forward.

"Forgive me Jesus, for I spake the truth. Come on; let's go to the library. Miss Ouzts will be wondering where we are."

Carleen had been helping reshelve books since fifth grade and convinced the librarian, Miss Ouzts, to let me help out too during break. I always looked forward to break in the library with Carleen, and I wanted to talk about the new boy now that we were away from all those nosey kids in the lunchroom.

Carleen rolled up a cart of books. As I grabbed one to put on the shelf, I asked, trying to sound casual, "So, do you really think the new boy's cute?"

"You mean the one you keep staring at?" Carleen asked.

"I do not stare at him."

"You do and you're right. He's like, super cute."

"I didn't mean I thought he was cute," I said. "I just wanted to know what you thought. He seems nice, I guess. I like his hair."

"Eww. You're not supposed to notice a boy's hair." Carleen pulled Reese's Cups out of her purse.

She looked around to make sure Miss Ouzts was away from her desk, then opened the package and gave me one. There was no eating in the library, but Carleen always managed to sneak a Reese's Cup for dessert after lunch. Sometimes two.

"Why can't I notice a boy's hair?"

"It's weird," she declared.

"For the umpteenth time, I don't notice cute boys, I only notice cute girls. I only said I liked his hair because it's auburn, like my mother's, that's all. I like auburn hair. Tina Louise has auburn hair. I like Tina Louise. She's a real fox—don't you think?"

Carleen put another book on the shelf. "Tina Louise is like a hundred years old. Don't you know those *Gilligan's Island* shows are reruns? They're from like ten years ago when we were little kids. I suppose you like Mrs. Howell, too? Oh, she's so foxy."

She laughed at her own joke. I grabbed another stack of books to shelve and pretended like I didn't hear her.

"Anyway," she said, "you're just not supposed to like a boy's hair. It's sissified. You don't want people talking about you being sissified. We're in tenth grade now."

"I'm not sissified." I said, too loud for the library.

"Hurry up and eat your Reese's. Miss Ouzts will be back any minute."

I popped the whole Reese's in my mouth, and we shelved books in silence for a few minutes.

"Do you really want to screw him?" I asked.

"You mean Doug?"

"Yeah."

"Of course I do; he's sexy."

I thought about this a few minutes while I shelved some more books.

"Why do you think Doug is sexy?" I asked.

"Wouldn't you like to know..."

"No, not really," I said. "I'm just making conversation."

Carleen put down her books and turned to me. "Well, first of all, have you seen those biceps? He's got veins popping right out of 'em."

"I know. How did he get those? I bet he uses barbells and stuff."

"Then there's his hair. Wouldn't you just love to run your hands through it?"

"Yeah," I said, with a slight sigh.

"Ah-hah!" said Carleen. "You do notice cute guys!"

"I do not! I just like his hair is all."

"All right then, prove it. Name a sexy girl. Who would you want to do it with?"

"I think Kate Jackson is sexy," I said.

"Oh, gross. Kate Jackson isn't sexy. Jaclyn Smith is sexy. Why do you think they put her in the bikinis all the time while Kate wears turtlenecks? Don't you know anything? God, you're so dumb."

"You shouldn't say God, and besides, girls aren't supposed to say other girls are sexy."

"Yes, we can," said Carleen. "Boys aren't supposed to notice when other boys are sexy, but a girl can say it about another girl. It doesn't mean anything when a girl says it."

"Why not? I think Jon and Ponch on *CHiPs* are sexy," I said. "It doesn't mean I want to screw them. I only want to screw Kate Jackson or Jaclyn Smith. Tom Selleck is sexy too. It's okay to recognize that a man is good-looking."

"No, it's not. Boys can't say that. Stop saying it. Besides, Tom Selleck is too hairy. He's just gross."

I didn't think Tom's hairiness was gross, but I decided to keep that to myself.

"Well, anyway, you can't screw Doug," I said.

"Why not?"

"Because, apparently, you already have a boyfriend. What did you call him? Juan?"

"That's right. His name is Juan."

"There's nobody at Patriot Christian named Juan. Does he go to the public school?"

"He's done with school. He's twenty-five years old."

I was stunned. "Twenty-five? I still don't believe you. You're making all this stuff up."

"It's all true. We did it a lot. The first time was behind the peach shed."

"On the ground? With like ants and chiggers?"

"He put his shirt down for me to lay on."

"Well, that's just great. For a minute, I was afraid he wasn't a gentleman."

"Honey, I wasn't looking for no gentleman. I was looking for a hot guy to do it with."

"So, where is this guy? I've never heard of anybody in Edgewood named Juan."

"He's not from here. He's from Texas, and he moved on after peach season. He'll be back next year."

"He's in Texas? How convenient. Carleen, have you forgotten your boyfriend in Canada who you made up in eighth grade? Now you expect me to believe you've got one in Texas?"

"Okay, I admit I made up Barkley in Canada, but I was just a kid then. Juan's real. He writes me letters from Texas. I'll show you one sometime. He's gonna be so jealous when he finds out about Doug."

"Why is he gonna be jealous about Doug?"

"Because I'm gonna tell him about this cute new boy who flirts with me."

"Doug does not flirt with you." I said, louder than I meant to.

"He will. Just you wait. Break is almost over, and I need to fix my face before English."

I rolled my eyes as she opened her purse and pulled out a tube of Bonne Bell Dr. Pepper lip gloss.

"Does that stuff really taste like Dr. Pepper?"

"Pretty much. Want some?" She reached over like she was going to put lip gloss on me. I shrieked like a girl, and my face went beet red.

"Quiet in the library," said Mrs. Ouzts, who had apparently returned while we were talking.

"Just put some on my finger," I said. Carleen smeared a bit of pink on my finger, and I tasted it. "It tastes like flat Dr. Pepper mixed with wax. I wouldn't put it on my mouth."

"You'd be surprised what you'd put in your mouth when you have a boyfriend," said Carleen.

"Carleen, you're gross."

The bell rang, and we headed off to English class.

DOUG SAT BESIDE me again in English. I couldn't help looking at him, this time taking in the gentle waves of his hair. He had a really great cut, and I was a little jealous. It was feathered perfectly. I wondered if his mother took him to the unisex salon at the Augusta Mall, or if he got it done in California before he left. I thrilled at the possibility of a real Hollywood haircut.

By this point, I was out-and-out staring at him as Mrs. Rogers talked about gerunds or something. I only came out of my fog when he turned and met my eyes. I had never seen eyes like his before, so green and clear. Sprite bottles didn't really describe them after all. Up close they looked like peridots, my birthstone. They were green with the slightest hint of gold. They were perfect.

The bell rang and broke the spell. They were letting us out early since it was the first day. Doug walked out by himself and glanced at me once more before exiting the classroom. I walked with Carleen out to the front and looked for Momma's Catalina. Carleen's momma, Mrs. Hightower, was waiting in her dented Dart.

"I see Momma got the car running again. See you tomorrow, Timmy," said Carleen.

Mrs. Hightower rolled down the window and asked, "Timmy, is your momma here? You want a ride?"

Just then, the big red tow truck from Everette's Amoco roared into the parking lot, belching smoke and pulling an old Plymouth station wagon. It had Lil' Ole Tow

Truck painted in big old-timey letters on the side. It was Daddy. Why was Daddy here? Where was Momma? Why was he driving that contraption?

Daddy pulled up to the curb and honked. His hair was freshly buzzed, and the ever-present cigarette dangled between his lips. He was the only adult I knew who would smoke an entire cigarette without ever taking it out of his mouth. He always smelled of smoke and ash.

I looked around. Of course, Kimberly Ann and the Anns were standing nearby, staring and giggling at the rumbling wrecker. I dashed over and climbed in. The radio was blaring some sort of twangy country music.

*"She can put her shoes under my bed anytime..."*

My humiliation was complete.

I climbed in. There was a Playboy air freshener with a picture of a topless lady hanging from the rearview mirror, and it wasn't doing its job. The cab smelled like grease and sweat and cigarettes. Of course, there was no air-conditioning in the ancient thing, so I started sweating heavy in my new school clothes.

"Your momma called and said court was running late or somethin' and she had to stay at work. Said she'd be home a little after six." He was yelling over the radio and engine noise. "I told her I don't have time to do this. I have to get this Plymouth to the Amoco, and I got another call out in Modoc."

"Sorry, Daddy."

As we pulled onto the road, I could see Kimberly Ann on the sidewalk watching us. She was waving a little piece of paper in her hand as the Anns giggled. I didn't know what it was about, but I sank down in my seat.

Daddy and I rode in silence for a while. The one country song I liked, Crystal Gayle's "Talking in Your

Sleep," came on. Naturally, Daddy hated the song and mashed the buttons until he could find something horrible and common. "Take This Job and Shove It" was right up his alley, and he cranked it up and sang along.

We didn't talk anymore until we pulled up in front of the house and he killed the engine. "Your momma's afraid of you being alone in the house all afternoon. She told me to get your aunt Melanie to come sit with you. I'll call her when I get back at Everett's. I think you're old enough to be left alone for a few hours. Hell, a boy needs time alone, you know?"

I nodded, embarrassed.

"I'll call Melanie, though. I will—don't look at me like that. It might take her a while to show up, so don't tell your momma I left you alone, okay? I gotta get back to the station then go clear out to Modoc."

I nodded.

He paused and said, "Don't fill up on Ding Dongs or whatever crap your momma lets you eat. You eat too much crap. You're gettin' fat."

I told him I wouldn't. He kept staring out the windshield. I kept my hand on the door handle, unsure if I should go or not. "I bet you got some of your MeeMaw's caramel cake in there, don't you? Or chocolate?"

I didn't say anything.

"She's always baking somethin', ain't she? The woman knows how to bake."

"MeeMaw died, Daddy, last year. You don't remember?"

"Oh yeah, right, right. Sure, I remember. I just got a lot on my mind is all. Gotta go clear out to Modoc after I drop off this Plymouth."

He paused for a minute, looking out the windshield.

"Your momma doing all right? Is she missing her momma?"

"Momma's doing all right. She can bake MeeMaw's caramel cake just like MeeMaw did. Well, almost like MeeMaw did. Aunt Melanie helps. They baked one this weekend. We still have most of it. We only ate a few pieces."

Daddy turned to me. "Yeah? Your momma can bake a caramel cake?" He laughed a little. "I never would have thought it. When we was married, she couldn't make toast."

He laughed again, and I joined him. He turned to look back out the windshield.

"Don't eat all the cake just because you're on your own. Your momma let you get real fat over the summer. Now go on in, do your homework or whatever you have to do, and don't get in any trouble till I can get Melanie over here."

I opened the door and climbed down from the big cab. Before I closed it, I turned to him and asked, "You want some?"

"Some of what?"

"Some of Momma's caramel cake. There's a ton left. You could come in and have some, or I could get you some and bring it out to you."

He looked at me and then put the truck in gear. "Naw, man, I gotta go to work—don't you listen? I got to drop off this Plymouth. Now git so I can go back to work."

I shut the door and watched the Lil' Ole Tow Truck roar off.

# Four: The Hostess with the Mostest

I WATCHED DADDY'S truck until it was gone, then walked toward our red brick ranch house with banks of pink azaleas in the beds. They were so beautiful in the spring when they bloomed. Nothing was blooming right now in this heat, but the camellias would start when the weather cooled down a little.

I was on my own until six o'clock. Daddy would never remember to call Aunt Melanie. I went into the house, back to my bedroom, and took off my shoes, socks, pants, and shirt. I walked to the kitchen in my underpants and undershirt. There was a fresh pitcher of tea in the fridge, so I poured myself a glass.

I wandered into the dining room and stood before the china cabinet. Momma had inherited all of MeeMaw's china and silver, and I loved looking at it. "It'll be yours one day," Momma had told me several times. "Your aunt Melanie's never been interested in a bit of it."

She had this one really pretty silver goblet, which was my absolute favorite thing in the whole house. It was like something a king would use. It was very large with embossed grapes, and the bowl was lined in real gold. Momma always kept it polished and shiny. She said it belonged to her great-great-great-grandmother who buried it in the yard to protect it from the Yankees. I was pretty sure the Yankees never actually came to Edgewood, but I liked the story.

I reached in the drawer for one of Momma's silver cloths and used it to pick up the goblet. I examined it, tracing the grapes and leaves and vines across its surface. It made me feel rich. Holding it out in both hands in front of me, I walked formally to the big mirror over the fireplace in the living room. "I present thee with the wine of kings," I said out loud and took a long, ceremonial pretend sip. I carried it formally back to the china cabinet and put it back carefully where I found it.

Next, I picked up one of Momma's crystal champagne glasses. Momma said they were "sherbets" but I thought they looked like something Audrey Hepburn would sip champagne from, so I called them champagne glasses.

I poured my tea into the glass and wandered around the dining and living rooms.

"Hello, so nice to see you. Don't you look lovely. So nice of you to come to my cocktail party. Champagne? Why, yes, it is. It's from France, of course. Please have some. Don't you just love pink champagne from France? Oh, you're so charming."

I carried the chalice down the hall toward Momma's room.

"Do let me give you a tour of our town house. Maybe one day you could come out to our country place. Wouldn't that be delightful? Come with me down the hall. Would you like to see my boudoir?"

I went to Momma's bedroom, opened her closet, and ran my hand across her clothes. "These are my Chanels. I'm just back from Paree. Have you ever been to Paree? Dahling, you simply must go to Paree. You can't shop locally, you know, you just can't. Maybe Atlanta in a pinch."

I pushed to the back of Momma's closet, to the things she called her trousseau. There were several nighties, folded across hangers and wrapped in plastic. There were three dresses, including one of red silk, also in plastic and hanging on a soft, pink hanger. It was sleeveless with a flat bow across the front. Momma called it her Jackie dress and said she bought it because it reminded her of something Jackie Kennedy might wear. I loved Jackie Kennedy too and read everything I could find about America's Tragic Queen. I had never actually seen Momma wear the Jackie dress. Momma used to let me play in her closet when I was real little and even let me walk around in her high heels and stuff, but this one time when I was in second grade, I put on the Jackie dress and she got real mad. She made me take it off, told me I was too old to play dress-up any more and her closet was off-limits. The next day, she came home with several Tonka trucks and a GI Joe and told me to go outside and play with them.

She wasn't here now, though, so I pulled the dress out of the closet, pulled off the plastic, held it up to myself, and stood in front of the full-length mirror. I peeled off my T-shirt and slipped on the dress. The silk felt like real luxury. I rubbed it against my body, enjoying the feel of the fabric against my bare skin. It had been several years since I'd played dress-up in Momma's closet, and it felt very naughty, but in a good way.

I turned to my imaginary party guest. "I borrowed this one from Jackie and never returned it." I winked. "I hope she doesn't miss it too badly, but you know red's my color. She looks better in pastels, so I was really doing her a favor by taking it." I laughed. "I know I'm naughty, but that's part of my charm."

I put my feet into Momma's gold sandals and swayed my hips back and forth.

"The orchestra's divine—don't you think? I hire them for all my soirées. A soirée is a party like they have in La France. All my parties are like La France; you should come more often. What was your name, handsome stranger? Douglas? Well, how do you do, Douglas? So glad you could join us. The first time I saw you, I just knew you were part of polite society. Only the best people are in polite society, you know. Oh, you like my dress? How nice of you. You think red's my color? Everyone says so."

I sipped champagne and swayed my hips, sipped and swayed, sipped and swayed. Occasionally, I twirled. I was a very graceful twirler.

"Why, you dance divinely," said a grown-up voice.

I froze mid-twirl. Aunt Melanie was standing in the doorway. Daddy had called her after all. There I was in Momma's red dress and gold sandals holding the crystal sherbet full of sweet tea.

"A little early for champagne, don't you think, sport?" She took the glass from me. "You be really careful hanging that dress back up. Your momma spent a fortune on it for her honeymoon and never got to wear it. She wanted to go to Charleston and stay at a nice hotel, but, instead, your daddy took her camping." She turned and walked back up the hall.

My heart was pumping so hard I could hardly breathe. I scrambled out of the dress, hung it up carefully, slipped on my T-shirt, and went looking for Aunt Melanie. I found her sitting in the den, flipping through her *Cosmopolitan* and smoking. Momma didn't like smoking or *Cosmo* in the house, but I wasn't about to say something at a time like this. In fact, I couldn't think of anything to say at all. I stood in the doorway, waiting for her to speak or send me to my room without supper or something.

"*Gilligan Island*'s on. You're missing it."

I stood there for a minute, thinking I hadn't heard right. She picked up the remote and clicked on the TV without looking up from her magazine. I sat on the floor in the corner and watched Mary Ann serve the Professor some coconut cream pie.

"Where did she get the crust?" Aunt Melanie asked.

"Ma'am?"

"I mean, she'd need Crisco and flour and whatnot to make a piecrust, but all she has is coconuts. Where'd the crust come from?"

"I dunno," I said.

"And why on earth did Ginger wear a sequined gown and heels to take a three-hour tour on a boat?"

"I don't think you're supposed to take it that seriously."

"Oh. You mean it's just make-believe? It's not real, it's just play, right? Harmless play?"

"Yeah. I guess so."

"So, the actors are just pretending it's coconut cream pie? It's probably just whipped cream from backstage or something."

"I guess so."

"And when Ginger's gown is always clean and pressed even though she's been on a deserted island for years, it's just make-believe. Harmless play, right?"

"Yes, ma'am."

"And as long as Ginger puts the gown back really careful, I guess nobody needs to know."

"No, ma'am."

"But Ginger would never drink tea while playing in a fancy gown, would she? Wouldn't want to risk spilling anything on a dress that cost your momma a whole week's paycheck, okay?"

"Okay."

Aunt Melanie tousled my hair and asked me to hand her an ashtray. As I was giving it to her, I told her I'd never heard the story about Momma and Daddy going camping on their honeymoon. In fact, I'd never heard Momma mention a honeymoon at all.

"I'm not surprised she never talked about it," said Aunt Melanie. "It was such a disappointment for her. She was all packed and ready to stay at the Mills House Hotel in Charleston. She spent way too much on the red dress and said she would outshine all the Charleston ladies in it. She would have, too. But at the last minute, your daddy told her the Mills House Hotel was booked, and, instead, they were going to his brother's fishing cabin at the lake. She spent her honeymoon swatting mosquitos and cooking for him while he fished. The marriage was over before it got started good."

I SPENT THE afternoon lying on the floor watching *Gilligan* followed by *Family Affair* and *The Lucy Show*. When *Lucy* signed off, Aunt Melanie asked me if I had any homework to do.

"No, ma'am. It's only the first day. They didn't give us any homework."

"Well, then, I guess I'd better get something on for dinner. It doesn't look like your momma's gonna make it home in time. She still got any more of those pole beans in the freezer?"

She stood and held the cover of the *Cosmo* up to her chest. The model had on a ruffled blue bikini, and the bottom side of her boobies was hanging out.

"Maybe you could design me something like this? What do you think? Think I could carry it off?"

I knew she was kidding, but I blushed anyway. She laughed, tossed the magazine on the sofa, and went in the kitchen.

"I guess I'd need a little more material after all. I should probably keep my under-boobs to myself—don't you think?"

"Yes, ma'am. It's vulgar."

She picked up the latest *Vogue* and tossed it to me.

"You're too classy for vulgar *Cosmo*, so read your *Vogue* and get inspired. I'm counting on you to become the next Bill Blass so you can get me out of this town."

I followed her into the kitchen and started flipping through *Vogue*. It was the September issue and thick. Naturally, I'd been through it cover to cover a couple of times already, but you couldn't read *Vogue* too often, because you never knew when inspiration would strike. They'd put Kim Alexis on the cover since she was the fashion star *du jour*.

"I think Kim's okay," I said to Aunt Melanie. "But she always does the same sideways smile, so I don't really get the big deal. I prefer models with more versatility. Those are the kinds of models I'll have walking in my fashion shows when I make it big."

"That right?" Aunt Melanie mused. She glanced over her shoulder as she pulled stuff out of the freezer. "Who's your favorite?"

"Iman! She's so exotic. I have to have her walk for me. And I'll convince Cybill Shepherd to return to modeling.

And Twiggy! And Veruschka! They'll all come because my shows will be ultimate fashion events." I wheeled around and held my hands out. The times to come were vivid in my mind. "I'll have them on the beach in Malibu, and all of Hollywood will come. Oh my God, it'll be amazing!" I winced. "I'm sorry, I shouldn't have taken the Lord's name in vain. I meant to say, oh my gosh."

"I thought fashion shows were in New York or Paris?"

"I'm a fashion rule breaker."

"Of course. I knew that," Aunt Melanie said with a soft smile on her face.

My favorite picture in the September issue was of Diane von Fürstenberg, herself, lounging on a green sofa, holding up a little mirror to her cat. I showed it to Aunt Melanie.

"Why is she holding a mirror to her cat? What's the point?"

I stared at it again.

"I don't know. It's art. Don't question it; just let it wash over you."

Aunt Melanie shook her head.

"How did this family ever produce you?" She came over and kissed me on the forehead.

She looked at the picture of DvF. "The lady is glamour personified."

"I want a fashion empire like hers," I said.

"Keep drawing, kid. You'll be even bigger."

I went back to my room and pulled out my big sketch pad that Aunt Melanie had given me for my last birthday. She'd also given me some colored pencils she said real artists used. I flipped through some of the fashion sketches I had made and compared them to the DvF and Halston looks in the magazine.

My stuff suddenly looked too showy and glam, too seventies. It was 1980 now, so I needed to bring it down a couple of notches. The eighties were going to be all about class and simplicity, just like DvF. I started drawing. I drew a girl in a long suede skirt to the floor with a slit up the back, not the front. I made it rich, dark brown, almost mahogany. And for the top, I drew a simple, oversized silk blouse in jade. No, that's not right. Cranberry? No. Plum! Mahogany and plum. The perfect look for the eighties. I got so wrapped in my fall collection that I forgot all about getting caught wearing Momma's dress.

# Five: I Want to Screw Him

THE NEXT MORNING at school, there was a scrap of paper taped to my locker. I knew what it was even before I got close enough to read it.

*"I want to screw him."*

It was Carleen's note about Doug that she had passed to me in Good Citizenship class the day before. I had a quick flashback of Jimbo knocking my books out of my hand and Kimberly Ann watching and laughing. It had to be the piece of paper she was waving at the end of school yesterday.

I reached up to tear it down, and Jimbo's hand slammed against my locker. Jimbo was strong for a skinny boy.

"Who do you want to screw, fag? Huh?"

People were gathering around my locker. Jimbo glanced at the two dozen kids coming in for a show and glared back at me. The students leaned in, reading the note and laughing.

"Do you even know what it means?" Jimbo asked, sneering.

The other kids' voices washed over me.

"He don't know how to screw."

"He wants to screw a boy."

"Eww, gross! He's sick!"

Kimberly Ann and the Anns appeared.

"The note's about Doug Appleby, the new boy. I'm sure he'd be real interested to know about it. Mrs. Holt would, too."

People started talking.

Someone asked, "Appleby's a fag?"

"Gotta be. They're all fruits in California."

"No way. He's no sissy."

I tried to push Jimbo aside and tear off the note, but he pushed me down to the floor and put his boot on my chest.

"The note stays, faggot. And I'm gonna beat your butt at break. It's gonna be fun watching you die."

Mrs. Morgan came out, put her hands on her hips, and demanded to know what was going on.

"Nothing, Mrs. Morgan," said Kimberly Ann, helping me up. "Timmy slipped and fell in his new shoes."

I got up and saw somebody had ripped the note off the locker. Jimbo had disappeared into the crowd.

"Well, hurry up, Timmy. You're all already late," said Mrs. Morgan.

About five minutes after class started, Doug came rushing in. He'd missed the whole thing.

During class, somebody passed me another note.

*"I'm going to kill you."*

It wasn't signed, but I knew who it was from. Jimbo. I held my arms under the desk and started scratching them. I kept on scratching them and scratching them until they bled. When Mrs. Morgan finally noticed, she dropped the chalk.

"Timmy, my God, did you do that when you fell?"

I held up my bloody arms. Carleen screamed, and Kimberly Ann turned so white I thought she would faint.

"It's the heartbreak of psoriasis. I need to go to the school nurse."

Mrs. Morgan grabbed me up out of the desk by my upper arm.

"Psoriasis? Good God, boy," she said as she hurried me out of the class and straight to the nurse's office.

When we got there, Mrs. Morgan said, "Look at what this boy has done to himself."

Nurse Darleen looked up from her *National Enquirer*, her expression bored. She motioned for Mrs. Morgan to seat me on the examining table and told her she could go back to class. Mrs. Morgan pushed me to the table. She turned to me one last time, shook her head, and left.

"Well, I guess the first thing we have to do is clean all this up." Nurse Darleen put her cigarette in her mouth as she cleaned my arms with antiseptic. She looked at my arms and asked how long I'd been scratching myself like this.

"I don't know what you're talking about, Nurse Darleen. It's the heartbreak—"

"That ain't no psoriasis, and we both know it. If you're gonna lie, at least do a better job of it." She walked over to her bookcase and pulled out a large, heavy volume. She flipped the pages and then held the book right in front of my face. It was a full-color picture of the grossest infection I'd ever seen.

"You see anything like that on your arm? That's psoriasis. I think you've got a case of 'I want my momma-itis.' You looking for a ticket home?"

"I...I don't know."

She put her hand on my forehead. "You're feeling kind of hot. Why you sweating and breathing so fast? What's wrong with you, boy?" Nurse Darleen put her stethoscope in her ears and her cigarette back in her mouth to listen to my heart.

"Lord have mercy, boy, it's like a marching band in there. Your heart's beating so fast."

"Maybe I'm having a heart attack," I said.

Nurse Darleen snubbed out her cigarette and looked at me a minute.

"You ain't having no heart attack at fifteen. You're afraid of something. Ain't you?"

"No, ma'am. I've just got a heart defect and the heartbreak of psoriasis and maybe tired blood and combination skin."

She brushed the damp hair out of my face and smiled gently.

"It's okay, boy. I know it's tough for you. I'll write you a note and call your mother. You have to learn to face these things, though. It's only gonna get worse."

I couldn't think of anything worse than death at the hands of Jimbo, so I figured going home early was plenty better.

"Momma's at work, so could you call my aunt Melanie? Her number's 5738."

While I was waiting for Aunt Melanie to get there, Nurse Darleen cleaned up my arm with antiseptic and told me to go home and have some tomato soup and a Coke.

"Make sure Melanie gives you some of those Captain's Wafers. They make everything better."

When we got home, Aunt Melanie cleaned up my arm some more with Bactine and gave me tomato soup with saltines and ginger ale, which I thought was more grown-up than Coke. I started to say something about Captain's Wafers, but I didn't want her to make a special trip to the grocery store.

"Why don't you tell me what happened. Was it Jimbo again?" she asked.

"Nothing happened." But I started crying as I said it. I was so mad at myself for crying.

Aunt Melanie took me in her arms. "It's all right, baby, it's okay. You have such a hard road."

I cried and cried and cried. Jimbo had called me a faggot. I wasn't sure what one was, exactly, but whatever it was, it made everybody hate me, so I couldn't be it. God wouldn't make me into something that everybody hated, would he?

That night when Momma came home, Aunt Melanie told me to go back to my room and work on my drawings. I could hear her and Momma talking, and, suddenly, Momma ran into my room and grabbed my arm.

"Did you hurt yourself, baby? Are you okay?" She examined my arm and saw it was almost healed. "Oh, it's nothing. You have a mosquito bite or something? I bet it was just a mosquito bite. Maybe a bunch of mosquito bites. How many times do I have to tell you not to claw at mosquito bites?"

She dropped my arm and walked out. "Melanie, you overreacted again. There's nothing wrong with my little baby boy. He just got some mosquito bites is all."

As I lay in bed, I could hear their muffled talking in the kitchen. "He's not like that, so stop saying it!" Momma said in a loud voice. Soon after, Aunt Melanie left.

The next day, I begged and begged to stay home, but Momma wasn't having any of it.

"You're not missing school just because you clawed at some mosquito bites. Besides, you put enough Bactine on your arms to drown a rat. Get dressed."

"But, Momma, it's not my arms."

Momma stopped packing my lunch and turned to me, hands on her hips. "Well, what is it, then? Huh? I've got to be at the courthouse by eight, so out with it."

"I dunno. Nothing, I guess."

"Okay. I packed you a banana and a sandwich made with lean ham. We're slimming down this fall, remember?"

"Yes, ma'am."

"And be sure and get a Fresca from the canteen. Not a Sprite. You know how many calories are in a Sprite, don't you?"

"Yes, ma'am."

"And I put a special surprise in there, too. One of those SlimFast bars. They're just like chocolate candy. You like those, don't you?"

SlimFast bars tasted like sawdust, but I nodded and told her I loved them.

Momma dropped me off at school. She gave me a kiss on the mouth like always and said, "Have a nice day," as she drove off.

I was walking into the school when Jimbo and Tom, one of his idiot followers, jumped out from behind the crepe myrtles and blocked my path. They were dancing around and waving their arms like peacocks.

"Have a nice day. Have a nice day," they kept repeating in a high-pitched singsongy voice. "Have a nice day, Timmy, have a nice day. Oh, Timmy..."

I tried to walk around them, but they kept blocking my way. Before I knew what happened, Tom grabbed my lunch bag, opened it, and pulled out the SlimFast bar Momma insisted I take. He and Jimbo laughed like hyenas.

"What is this? Timmy's on a ladies' diet! Trying to get slim fast, fat ass?" Tom said.

"I bet Mrs. Morgan eats these," Jimbo chimed in.

"It's a candy bar," I said, red-faced, as I tried to grab it back. Tom jerked the bar away from me, and I dropped my books all over the sidewalk. The bell rang, and Jimbo and Tom ran into class, showing the SlimFast bar to everybody they passed. "Look what Timmy brought for lunch!"

I picked up my books, repeating out loud, "It's a candy bar, that's all. It's just a candy bar."

All day, I tried to lay low and make myself as invisible as possible. At lunch, I sat with Carleen and saw Kimberly Ann nudge Kathy Ann and Lisa Ann until they got up and came over to our table.

"How's your diet going, ma'am?" Kathy Ann smiled like a weasel. "My grandma eats those things, and she's an old lady."

Carleen stood up in a fury. "Get outta here, you stringy-haired trash. Mind your own business, or you won't grow up to be a grandma."

Mrs. Morgan, who was sitting at the other end of the table, stood and, in a very loud voice, asked what was going on. Nobody said a word because the eyes of every kid in the lunchroom were on Mrs. Morgan, standing there, holding something in her hand.

A SlimFast bar.


THE FOLLOWING DAY, I opened my locker before Good Citizenship class, and a hundred SlimFast bars fell out. Everybody in the hall laughed, and several people stomped on the bars, grinding them and making a big mess.

*I'm not going to cry.*

*I'm not going to cry.*

*I'm not going to cry.*

It all happened so fast. I couldn't stop the tears. I tried to gather up the SlimFast bars, but kids kept stomping on them, busting open the packaging and spewing chocolate and crumbs all over the place. Then, the bell rang, and we all had to go to class, but I couldn't because of all the mess to clean up.

Just then, Doug walked up with the trash can from Mrs. Morgan's classroom. Without saying a word, he helped me pick up the SlimFast bars. I was grateful but horrified that he saw how the rest of the kids treated me. There couldn't be any doubt that he knew I was the class sissy—the butt of every joke. Yet, he was helping me. The cute, sophisticated new boy from California who everyone wanted as a friend or boyfriend was risking social suicide by helping a pariah like me. I couldn't quite believe it, but maybe I had a new friend.

When we finished, Mrs. Morgan was standing in the hall, the classroom door shut behind her. "Thank you, Doug. You're very nice. I'm sure Timmy appreciates it. Go back to class and take a seat. I'll be back in a few minutes."

When Doug was gone, Mrs. Morgan told me to follow her. She took me to Mrs. Holt's office. I sat in the outer office while she talked to Mrs. Holt in private. She came out and told me to keep my seat, and then she went back to her class. After a few minutes, Mrs. Holt came out and sat next to me.

"I've called your father. He's coming to get you in a few minutes. I don't think you should complete your school day."

I started crying again. My father!

"What did you tell him?" I asked.

"I told him everything that happened. I told him you need a strong male hand."

"But I want to go back to class. I'll be good. I need to learn. There's a math test."

"It's for the best," said Mrs. Holt, looking away from me. "Your mother's got so much on her right now, trying to raise a child by herself. It's past time for your father to take charge."

She stood and looked at me, her hands on her hips.

"I hope it's not too late." She went back into her office.

I sat there, unable to stop crying. Miss Amanda, Mrs. Holt's secretary, offered me a Kleenex and a butterscotch, which helped a little.

I was on my third butterscotch when I heard the Lil' Ole Tow Truck roar to a stop in front of the school. Daddy came in and saw me sitting there, eyes red. The tears started flowing again at the sight of him. He looked at me without saying anything. Mrs. Holt ushered him into her office and shut the door. They were in there for a while. When he came out, he walked past me and told me to get up, and I followed him out to the truck. The radio was off. We rode in silence for a long time.

"I'm taking you back to work with me. Everette left me in charge of the whole gas station today, and I had to lock the place up because of your little stunt. I hope I don't get fired."

# Six: The Lake of Fire

AS DADDY AND I arrived at the Amoco, he pointed at a little old lady in a Lincoln Continental waiting for someone to pump her gas.

"God knows how long the old broad's been waiting."

He told me to sit down in the station and wait for him. When he finished pumping and the lady had driven off, he came back inside, wiping his hands on grimy towels.

"Don't just sit there like a bump on a log. Get off your ass and help me."

"But you told me to sit here."

"Quit your damn whining. All you ever do is whine. I hate a whiner. If you're gonna miss school, you're not gonna spend it sitting on your ass. You're gonna make yourself useful. Come on."

He motioned me into the service bay where an old Nova was up on the lift.

"Hand me a tool when I ask for it, and don't fuck it up."

I had never heard Daddy say the F word before.

"Don't look so damned shocked," he said. "A boy's supposed to learn to cuss. It's natural. Your momma's turning you into something unnatural. Now, hand me the quarter-inch ratchet."

I had no idea what a quarter-inch ratchet was, so I handed him my best guess.

"Shit, boy, that ain't no ratchet. Get me the ratchet. Quarter inch."

I made another try, but I guessed it wasn't right either.

"Dammit, can't you hear? Don't you know what a ratchet is?"

He reached around me and picked up a tool and shook it in my face.

"This is a ratchet. A boy ought to know what a ratchet is. What kind of boy are you? What's the matter with you?"

"I don't know!" I yelled. "I don't know, I don't know, I don't know!" I kept hearing myself yell and couldn't believe I was yelling at my Daddy, but I couldn't stop.

"I don't know what a ratchet is! I've never even heard of a ratchet! I'm doing the best I can!" I stomped my feet and kept yelling. "I'm doing the best I can! I'm doing the best I can! They weren't my SlimFast bars, Daddy! Momma made me eat them! You both think I'm fat! *I hate those damn SlimFast bars!*"

I pushed the big tool chest, and it fell over. There was a gigantic crashing sound, and tools went everywhere. Daddy and I stood there looking at the chaos. His mouth was open. I couldn't believe what I had done. I couldn't believe I'd yelled at my own daddy. We looked at each other, and he had the strangest look on his face. He'd never looked at me like that. It was like he didn't know who I was.

Quietly, I said, "I didn't want the SlimFast bar."

Without saying anything, he squatted to pick up the tools. I squatted too, and he put his hand up. "Don't," he said in a low voice. "I'll clean up. You go around back and play or something. I'll call your aunt Melanie to come get you."

He started picking up the tools, and I stood, looking at him.

"Go on around back," he said quietly, without looking at me. "Here, wait a minute."

He dug in his pocket and handed me a quarter. "Buy yourself a Coke. You need it. You need something."

I put the quarter in the machine, opened the little door, and pulled out a bottle. I took the Coke around back where Everette kept a bunch of wrecked cars. They were scattered about in an empty field backing up to the woods. I was completely alone and liked it. When I was alone, nobody could get mad at me for not knowing what a dang wrench was.

Amid the junked cars, there was an old, wrecked Chrysler I liked to look at. It was dented and rusty, but I could tell it had been really glamorous once. If only someone had taken care of it.

"Hey, man, tough day?" a voice said.

I turned and saw Doug walking toward me. His hair caught a slight breeze.

"What are you doing here?" I asked, suddenly out of breath. "Why aren't you in school?"

"I skipped at break."

"Skipped? You mean played hooky? You'll get in big trouble."

"So what? I did it all the time back home in LA."

"But this is Patriot Christian Academy. You have to follow the rules."

He stopped and leaned against the Chrysler. "Screw the rules. Let's go grab lunch at the pool hall."

"No, I'd better stay here. I think my aunt Melanie is coming for me."

Doug looked at me for a minute and then started walking around the car. "Man, this was some nice car in its day. A '61, I'm sure of it. Check out the canted headlights."

"What does canted mean?"

"At an angle, see?"

I walked around to the front and looked at the headlights, angling away from each other. "They're funny looking."

"Yeah, crazy. They don't make them like that anymore. Nothing else looked like it, though. You gotta admire anything unique."

We studied the headlights together for a bit.

"Heard a loud crash in there. You okay?" Doug nodded toward the garage.

"Oh, yeah. I'm okay. I made a big mess. I knocked over Daddy's tool chest. It was an accident."

"Like hell it was," he said and smiled at me. "My mom and dad used to scream and crash things all the time before they finally broke up." He turned and leaned against the bumper.

"Are your parents divorced?"

"I think it'll be final soon."

"Where's your daddy?"

"He stayed in LA. He's got an apartment in West Hollywood."

"When are you gonna see him? You want to see him?"

"I dunno. Yeah. Yeah, I do want to see him. Don't know when it'll happen, though. He writes me and calls every Sunday night."

"Are you and your daddy close?"

"We used to do lots of stuff together. My parents would take me to the beach every weekend. There's this place on the beach. The whole, wide beach and anybody can go there because it's a state park. Pretty cool."

"Wow."

"Then, all of a sudden, they started yelling at each other every night. I'd go to my room, and I'd hear them yelling and stuff crashing. Finally, one day, Dad moved out, and Mom and I got in the Datsun and started driving. She said she was taking me where she came from. A week later, we crossed the state line into South Carolina, and here I am."

"Here with me," I said.

"And a '61 Chrysler."

"How'd you know I was here?"

"I saw that crazy tow truck through the window in math class. I'd seen it before. I thought it must be your father."

"Math class," I said, suddenly remembering I should have been in school. "How was the test?"

"We didn't have it. Mrs. Means said we'll have it tomorrow when you can be there. No sweat."

I was relieved. I'd studied and was ready and didn't want to get behind. We leaned against the Chrysler for a few minutes more, feeling the hot sun beat down on us. It felt good. I wanted to bake in it.

"Do you miss your daddy?" I asked.

"Yeah, I miss him."

"Do you love your daddy?"

"Sure I do. Do you love yours?"

"Of course I do. It's a sin not to love your daddy."

"Then there must be a lot of sinners in this world."

"Oh, there are."

I watched him run his hands through his hair. I caught a quick glimpse of his armpit hair through his ribbed sleeve.

"I never really knew Momma and Daddy as a married couple," I said. "They got divorced when I was little. He's always been around town, but..."

"But he's not around for you," said Doug.

"I guess," I said in a low voice.

"Did your parents get married because you were coming?"

"No! I'm sure they loved each other. Momma said she was in college and decided she couldn't be apart from him, so she dropped out after a few months, and they got married."

"Okay. I'm sure you're right."

We paused and looked out toward the woods for a while. My head was spinning. I was really talking with the new boy—he'd come to find me! I wanted him to be my new friend and had no idea how to make it happen, but now, he was making it happen. I looked over at him. In the sun, his auburn hair seemed to have golden highlights. He saw me looking at him and smiled. His eyes were bright. I knew then I would never forget this moment.

"So what's up with the girl you always hang out with—what's her name? Darleen?"

"Carleen," I said.

"Yeah, Carleen. She seems cool."

"She sure is. We've been friends since kindergarten. She's real nice." Then, I remembered how Carleen said Doug was a cute fox and she was going to get him to flirt with her. "She's got a boyfriend. His name's Juan. He's older, and they're totally in love. He's real strong. I think he's a bodybuilder or something. Or maybe a professional boxer. I don't really like him, though, because he's so possessive of Carleen. I mean, if a guy even looked at her, Juan would probably punch him out."

"Wow. Maybe Carleen needs to break up with him."

"Oh no! They're in love, and they'll probably get married right after graduation in a couple of years. He's only possessive because he loves her so much. He's possessive in a good way."

"Okay, whatever. I'm just surprised that there's a guy named Juan in this town. I'm kind of impressed, actually."

I had no idea why that impressed him. "Juan's not local. And he's older."

"How about that Kimberly Ann chick? You know her well? She seems to think she runs things around here."

"I guess she does. Her daddy's a doctor, and they live in that big house that looks like Tara and sits way back from the road on the way out to Patriot Christian. She's real active at First Baptist. In fact, Kimberly Ann's gonna try to save your soul."

"She's what?"

"Gonna try to save your soul. Everybody figures since you're from California, you probably aren't saved, and she's kinda in charge of soul-saving at Patriot Christian."

"You don't say?"

"I do say. So, is it?"

"Is it what?"

"Is your soul saved for Jesus? Do you have a personal relationship with Jesus Christ?"

Doug thought about it for a minute. "What does that even mean?"

"It's kinda hard to explain if you didn't grow up Baptist. I'll let Kimberly Ann fill you in. She's real good at telling people how they should think."

Doug laughed.

"What's so funny?" I asked.

"At my last school, the kids were interested in surfing and pinball and TV and stuff. Here, in the first week, kids want to save my soul. Whatever that means."

"Saving your soul is very important. It's the most important thing,"

"You tell me how to save it, then," said Doug.

"Oh no. Kimberly Ann really does it best, so it'd be better for you to wait for her."

Doug laughed again. "Whatever you say."

We leaned against the old car in silence for a while.

"Today was really messed up," I said.

"I know."

"Those weren't my SlimFast bars."

"I know."

We paused for a few minutes. The rapid-fire patter of a woodpecker resounded deep in the woods. Just then, Aunt Melanie came walking around the Amoco.

"Hey, little man, I came to take you home," she said.

She eyed Doug and walked up to the Chrysler and stuck out her hand. "Hello. I'm Melanie Ashburn. I'm Timmy's aunt. What's your name?"

Doug took her hand and shook it. "I'm Doug Appleby."

"You don't say." She shot me a sidelong glance. "Skipping school, are we?"

Doug shrugged.

"Don't worry," she said. "I won't tell your mother, but I am going to take you back. If we hurry, I can have you back by fifth period. Just tell Mrs. Holt you got sick and went out into the woods to throw up."

"You think she'll buy it?" asked Doug.

"Of course not," said Aunt Melanie. "She'll think you were out there smoking cigarettes, but she won't expel you if she doesn't think you left the school grounds. Believe me, I've known Edna Holt for a long time. One of these days, I'll tell you about the time I corrupted her little brother. Let's go, you two."

Doug grabbed my arm and whispered in my ear, "Your aunt's cool."

After Aunt Melanie dropped Doug off, I said, "I don't think Doug's saved."

"Why do you say that?"

"Well, I told him Kimberly Ann would try to save him, and he said he didn't know what I meant. Then he laughed."

Aunt Melanie laughed a little, herself.

"Don't laugh, Aunt Melanie. Saving your soul is important. It's the only way to keep from falling in the Lake of Fire."

Aunt Melanie looked at me. "I'm sure his soul is fine. I don't think any of us are gonna come across the Lake of Fire anytime soon, so relax."

We drove in silence for a few minutes, and she said, "He's a nice boy, isn't he?"

"Yes, ma'am. He's real nice, and I think he's smart too."

"I think he's a good kid to have as a friend. Don't you?"

"Yes, ma'am."

# Seven: Great White Shark

MOMMA WAS MORTIFIED when she got home. I knew it because she kept saying how mortified she was. She was on the phone to Mrs. Holt before I could stop her.

"I can't believe you sent my boy home when it was those other boys who caused all the trouble. After all the money I pay in tuition to that school. I just want my boy to have a good, quality education, and what happens? He's tortured by a bunch of white trash boys... What?

"Why, I said white trash, and I meant white trash. The Abernathy boy's grandmother took in laundry, and his grandfather trapped squirrels. Squirrels! They ate them! And here he is torturing my son. How could you allow such a thing and call yourself a Christian woman? If my granddaddy the judge was still around, he'd straighten things out. Huh?"

Momma stiffened and pursed her lips. "I'll calm down when Jimbo and Tom are expelled from your so-called Christian Academy, that's when I'll calm down... Excuse me? Well, I should hope you talked to his parents... They said what? My son...flamboyant? Why I never! How dare you! Why, my son is as masculine as any man in this town. He is very talented and has flair and may not go out for sports much, but I raised him right. Detention? That's not nearly enough for those two trashy boys. You must guarantee that you can protect my son from those...those hellions."

Momma arched her back as if slapped. "I will not calm down! My son will be back in school tomorrow, and I expect him to get full credit for today. He did absolutely nothing wrong. You are lucky to have such a talented boy in your school." She hung up the phone and stared at it. I quickly went to my room.

Several moments later, Momma came to find me. I was sitting on the floor and making sketches. She sat next to me, stroked my hair, and sighed. "What'cha workin' on, honey?"

"Just my designs," I said. "Momma? Are you all right?"

Momma gave me a side shoulder hug. "Oh, of course I am, sugar. I was just having a little come-to-Jesus with Mrs. Holt. You'll be back at school tomorrow, and there will be no record of what happened today. I made Mrs. Holt understand that she punished the wrong student. Now, tell me about your drawings."

THE NEXT MORNING at school, I saw a yellow Datsun with California plates pull into the parking lot. I'd never seen California plates before in person, but I recognized them from the picture in the *World Book*. They were purple with yellow letters. I thought they were cool. I stopped by a crepe myrtle and pretended to tie my shoelaces as I watched Doug get out of the car.

His momma was real pretty. She had blonde hair that she pulled back with a barrette, and she was wearing a purple tank top. She watched him as he crossed the parking lot and walked toward the building. I watched him too. He wore khakis, of course, since we weren't allowed to wear jeans at Patriot Christian Academy, but his were cut different. They weren't flared like everybody else's. His were straight legged and wrinkled. They hugged his behind.

And his T-shirt— It was black and said Patti Smith in jaggedy letters across the front, and across the back, it said *Radio Ethiopia.* It was crazy! Who was Patti Smith? Did Doug go to Ethiopia? I'd read about Ethiopia in the *World Book*, but I'd never known anybody who went there. I could see other kids looking at it.

Lisa Ann and Kathy Ann walked straight up to him and blocked his path. "Cute blouse, big boy. You borrow it from your sister?" Lisa Ann smirked triumphantly. Kathy Ann giggled at Lisa Ann's witticism.

Doug stopped and looked at the two of them. I stood and tried to stay hidden in the branches of the crepe myrtle. The Anns' triumph turned into defiance as they stood their ground, but they started to look uncomfortable as he kept staring.

Finally, he spoke. "My sister's dead. She drowned in the ocean, so, no, I didn't borrow this from my sister." He stared at Lisa Ann for a minute more, then turned and walked into the school.

The entire day, everybody, especially the girls, talked about Doug's personal tragedy.

"Oh my God, Lisa Ann asked him if he wore his dead sister's clothes!"

"Lisa Ann is such a big mouth. You should never talk about people you don't know."

"I would never do such a thing as talk about other people I don't know. It's not Christian."

"No wonder his momma moved back to South Carolina."

"No wonder his parents got divorced."

"I heard he had a girlfriend in California."

"I heard she was real pretty and blonde."

"I heard his girlfriend's name was Summer and they hung out at the beach together all the time."

"I heard his girlfriend Summer died in the same drowning accident as his sister!"

"I heard his sister's name was Patti and that's why he has the T-shirt. It's like a memorial T-shirt."

"I heard his sister Patti's father wasn't Doug's father and that's why her name was Smith and Doug's is Appleby. They were only half-brother and sister, not that it matters in the eyes of the Lord."

"I heard his sister Patti Smith was attacked by a shark!"

"That's not all. I heard his sister Patti Smith and his girlfriend Summer were attacked by a shark and eaten! Great white sharks eat people, you know. Especially in California."

"I heard he was surfing with his sister Patti Smith and his girlfriend Summer when they were attacked by a shark and he barely survived!"

"I heard he fought off the shark and was almost killed trying to save his sister Patti Smith and his girlfriend Summer!"

By lunch period, most of the girls in tenth grade were in tears talking about Doug's near-death experience with a great white shark and the tragic death of young Patti Smith and Summer.

Carleen and I sat at the end of the teacher's table, and I watched Doug sit alone at the end of the table with the JV football players. They all ate in silence today. When Carleen said it was time to go to the library, I said not yet.

Kimberly Ann got up from her table and walked over to Doug. She sat and took his hand. She was holding his hand! The whole school was staring. She bowed her head in prayer while holding his hand. He watched her and didn't shut his eyes. When she finished, she stood and, with all eyes on her, walked back to her table.

The other girls pounced.

"Oh my God, what did he say?"

"How does he cope?"

"Does he have a new girlfriend?"

Kimberly Ann held up her hand and commanded silence from her table—the entire room, actually, except for Doug who didn't look up from his lunch. Then, Kimberly Ann spoke in the loudest whisper I'd ever heard.

"He thanked me for my ministry. He said he doesn't have a girlfriend because he isn't ready to move on. I insisted he come with me to Young Ambassadors this weekend and he said—" She paused dramatically, tears welling. "—he said he doesn't believe there's a God." Ten girls screamed simultaneously, and the bell rang.

All the Jesus drama seemed to make everyone forget about the SlimFast bars...at least for the moment. Even Jimbo seemed disinterested in me.

Thank God.

Time for fourth period.

# Eight: Doug's Smile Makes Me Dizzy

I FILED INTO fourth-period English class with the crowd of students, and Doug took his seat next to mine.

I glanced over at him: he was looking down and writing. I felt so bad for him. I had no idea he had suffered so. Everybody in class stared at him so much that Mrs. Rogers had to stop whatever she was talking about and remind everyone we were supposed to be looking at her. I stole one last glance at Doug, and he turned slightly and met my eye. He gave me a half smile. I felt a little dizzy.

As soon as the bell rang at the end of the day, Carleen and I walked outside. Carleen grabbed my arm and steered me around the corner.

"Can you believe it? Doug's sister Patti Smith was eaten by a shark? And his girlfriend Summer? We should do something."

"Like what?"

"Go to him. Comfort him. I don't know, something. I know! I'll tell my momma about it, and she'll make his momma a squash casserole."

"And my momma can do deviled eggs. Gosh, I feel so bad for him."

Carleen glanced up and quit speaking. Kimberly Ann walked past us with several of her Anns, talking animatedly with Kathy Ann.

"Of course," Kimberly Ann said. "I can't be his girlfriend if he's not a Christian. I'll just have to convert him, is all. It's my Christian duty."

Before I knew what was happening, Carleen dashed down the hall and caught up with Kimberly Ann and her crowd. She grabbed Kimberly Ann by the arm and swung her around. Carleen held onto Kimberly Ann's wrist. "You can't convert somebody who doesn't believe in God. What are you converting him from? You convert Jews to Baptists; you don't convert atheists because they don't believe in God at all. Don't you know anything?"

Kimberly Ann stood there, eyes wide in shock. After a beat, she shook her arm free. "Did you say something to me? Did you touch me?"

Carleen continued, emboldened. "You always think you know the right answers, but you don't even know what convert means."

"She does so know what convert means," said Kathy Ann. "It means to save someone for the Lord. What's wrong with you?"

Carleen crossed her arms over her chest. "Maybe he doesn't want to be saved. Maybe he doesn't want any part of your goody-goody church. Maybe he's right, and there is no God." Every kid in the hallway sucked in their breath. You don't get a lot of blasphemy at Patriot Christian Academy.

"I'm telling Mrs. Morgan."

"I'm telling Mrs. Holt."

"I'm telling your mother."

At that very moment, Carleen's momma pulled into the parking lot, and Carleen made a dash for it. She hopped in the car with her mother. As the Dart drove off, she waved and smiled at me like a crazy person.

"Come on, girls," said Kimberly Ann to her entourage. "I've got to go wash off those white trash cooties." She noticed I was standing there and took my arm. "Does your mother know you hang out with that trashy slut? If she does, I bet she doesn't like it. Carleen's not from nice people, and you are—at least on your mother's side."

"You shouldn't call Carleen a trashy slut. She's not like that at all."

"Oh, yes she is." Kimberly Ann looked pleased with herself. "You mean you don't know?" She looked around at the other girls, who started giggling. "Just ask any boy on the JV football team or any field hand at her granddaddy's farm. I'm surprised she hasn't done it with you."

"I'm not," said Kathy Ann. "He wouldn't know how." They all laughed as they walked away.

As I waited for Momma, I saw Doug sitting in his mother's car. He'd watched the whole thing. He had the windows down, so he had to have heard. He caught my eye and nodded. Then they drove off.

I stood there staring until I heard a horn honk. Aunt Melanie was picking me up. Apparently, Momma had to work late at court again.

"You sure are quiet," said Aunt Melanie as we drove home. "Is everything all right?"

"Huh? Oh yeah, sure. Everything's fine. I've just got a lot of homework to do is all." That wasn't it, of course. How could I tell Aunt Melanie what I'd just heard about Carleen? It couldn't be true. Sure, she bragged to me about "doing it" with that guy Juan, but the football team? The field hands? Those Anns had to be lying and spreading rumors.

I decided I should do Carleen a favor and tell her about all these terrible lies being spread about her. But before I told her, I needed to make sure she knew that acting the fool with Kimberly Ann was a bad idea, and those girls were going to ruin her reputation.

That night, Daddy came over to sit with me. He brought burgers from the pool hall and sat in front of the TV drinking beer. As soon as I finished my burger and washed my plate and silverware and put them away, I asked him if I could talk on the phone. "I don't care," he said and turned up the volume on *Circus of the Stars*.

I got on the extension in Momma's room, stretched the cord into my bedroom, and shut the door. Carleen picked up on the first ring.

"Carleen, have you lost your mind? Have you gone crazy?"

She laughed. "I told you we were gonna rule the school this year, and we are. I'm starting with Kimberly Ann. I'm tired of her thinking she's the Virgin Mary or something. She's a bitch, and she ain't no virgin. She's going down."

"Carleen! You shouldn't use such language. Ask for forgiveness, quick."

"I will not. I meant it."

"Precious Lord Jesus, please forgive Carleen. She knows not what she does. Amen. I just saved your soul. You're welcome."

"So what?"

"So, your reputation's what."

"Huh?"

"Carleen, do you know what Kimberly Ann and the Anns are saying about you?"

"What do I care what they say about me?"

"Because what they're saying is awful and false and just plain mean. You need to be sitting down for this— Are you sitting down?"

"I'm lying down in the bed. Hit me with it."

"Okay, here goes. Kimberly Ann has been gossiping that you're 'doing it' with every boy on the JV football team and even..." I paused a moment to catch my breath. "Even with field hands at your granddaddy's farm."

There was a long pause.

"Carleen? You still there?"

"It wasn't every boy on the football team."

I felt like the air had been knocked out of me.

"Carleen, you don't mean it's true, do you?"

"Not completely true. There were only two guys at the farm."

"Why didn't you tell me? I thought we shared everything."

"I knew you wouldn't understand. I knew you'd react like this."

"Like what?"

"All shocked like I've done something wrong."

"I wish you'd told me."

"Why?"

"Because we're best friends."

"That's why I didn't tell you, because I figured you wouldn't want to be my friend anymore."

"Of course, I want to be your friend."

"I'm glad. Hey! You should try it."

"Try what?"

"Sex! It's so much fun!"

"It may be, but I'm saving myself for marriage. That's what Mr. Rick at First Baptist said we should do. He said it's what Jesus wants. He's even organizing a white ribbon ceremony this fall."

"What the hell is a white ribbon ceremony?"

"It has nothing to do with hell, thank you very much. It's about staying out of there, in fact. We vow to stay pure for Jesus until our wedding night and tie a white ribbon around our wrists to signify our vows."

"Oh, brother."

"You should come. It'd be all right. I know your family goes to the Holiness Church, but I could talk to Mr. Rick, and he'd let you come to our youth group. You'd love it."

"It's a little late—don't you think?"

"It's never too late for a personal relationship with Christ."

"I mean, I'm not a virgin anymore."

"It's okay. You could start over."

"I don't think it works that way, but anyway, I don't want to. I like sex. It makes me feel good."

"Carleen, exactly how many boys have you done it with?"

"Just Juan and the other guy from the farm. Ennis, I think? Anyway, after Juan left to go back to Texas, Ennis came up to me in the barn at Grandaddy's farm one day and told me I was pretty. He said he wanted to kiss me, and I let him. Then, we did it in the hayloft. I got hay in places I can't tell you about." She laughed. I thought I might throw up. "Then, there was Dean from the football team. He came up to me in the dime store one day while I was looking at records. I think he's Ennis's cousin or something. He told me I was prettier than Olivia Newton-John."

"So, you had intercourse with him?"

"Yeah, in the back of his daddy's pickup."

I knew who Dean was. He had curly strawberry-blond hair and deep-blue eyes. I quickly put him out of my mind.

"Carleen, I think you're having a nervous breakdown. People have them, you know. Marlena had one on *Days of Our Lives* last summer, and it was real realistic. I think you have the same symptoms."

"I wish I could have a nervous breakdown. Then I could get out of school."

"Carleen, why are you doing this?"

"All the girls do it. You don't think Kimberly Ann is an angel, do you?"

"Kimberly Ann's got a boyfriend, the senator's son. She's not running around after every boy who smiles at her."

"I'm not, either. They're running after me. Cute boys think I'm pretty. And Kimberly Ann broke up with the senator's son at the end of the summer. You never did keep up with the latest gossip."

"Carleen, you've got to ask Jesus to forgive you."

"Give me a break. You actually still believe in Jesus? For real?"

"Of course! And so do you. What's gotten into you?"

"I just don't believe in Jesus, is all. I decided this summer. The Bible's just all fairy tales when you think about it. Doug doesn't believe in Jesus. I bet Doug's sister didn't either, and she's dead."

"Of course, she did. She's with her heavenly father. Instead of seeing the face of the killer shark, she saw the shining face of God, and don't change the subject."

"Bull. People in California don't believe in God. Nobody out there goes to church."

"How do you know?"

"You told me. You're the one who's suddenly reading about California all the time. You've practically memorized the *World Book* chapter on California and Los

Angeles. Have you ever read one word about anybody in California going to church?"

"Yes, I have. The city of San Francisco was founded as a Catholic church. They called it a mission. The monks went there to save the Indians."

"Yeah, but it was like five hundred years ago."

"No, it wasn't. It was 204 years ago. San Francisco was founded in 1776. Don't you know that?"

"How would I know that?"

"There was a *Bicentennial Minute* about it with Vicki Carr."

"Only you would remember that. Anyway, I bet Doug's sister never went to church, and I bet Doug hasn't ever gone to church."

"Well, Kimberly Ann goes to church. She goes to First Baptist, and I bet she'll start sending the church bus to Doug's house. And she's telling everybody you're fooling around with football players and field hands, and she's right! She will ruin you in this town, and you just made it worse by telling her off in front of all her friends."

"She deserved it. It's about time somebody talked back to her."

"That is not the point."

"Then what *is* the point?"

"The point is, you're a nice girl, and you're not acting like it. Nice girls don't spread their legs for every boy who tells them they're pretty."

"That's not what I'm doing! Juan writes me letters, and Dean really likes me. He told me so. See? This is why I didn't tell you. I knew you'd get all Jesus-y on me and tell me I was going to hell. Let me tell you one thing, I'm going after Doug next. He could use some corrupting."

"What do you mean?"

"He's so cute. I'd love to get in his pants."

"Stop it, Carleen. Stop it right this minute."

"Jealous?"

"No! Why would I be jealous?"

"You think he's cute, too. Admit it. You want to get in his pants as bad as I do."

"I do not!"

"You want to run your fingers through his hair."

"I do not!"

"You practically admitted it."

"I did not!" I stood and started pacing around the room. This was really too much. Carleen crossed the line. I was scared. "I like girls, and you know it. I'm saving myself for marriage because I'm a Christian. Besides, Doug's not like that. He's a good boy."

"Ha! He's a boy, and all boys are like that. Except you."

"He is so a good boy, like me. I know he is."

"I guess we'll see when I put the moves on him tomorrow. We'll be screwing behind the bleachers by lunchtime."

"Carleen! You don't mean it. You're putting your immortal soul in danger."

"I do so mean it! You're just too immature to understand that I grew up this summer, and you didn't."

She slammed the phone down. I sat there holding the extension trying to figure out what just happened. All I wanted was for Carleen to confess her sins and get right with God. What was wrong with that? I did it out of love. Didn't she understand? Why'd she get so mad? How did she go from a nice girl who went to church every Sunday, even if it was a Holy Roller church, to a girl who has intercourse with more than one boy and says she's not a

Christian anymore? Why did she have to go after Doug? Doug would resist. He wouldn't give in. I knew it.

I hung up the phone and lay back on the bed. I thought of Carleen and Dean, the football guy, making out. I didn't want to think those thoughts, but I couldn't stop them from filling my mind. I imagined them in the pickup truck, Dean lying on top of Carleen, kissing her and even using his tongue. Suddenly, Dean became Doug, and Carleen was running her hands up under his T-shirt, feeling his bare skin. Somehow, Carleen became me, and I could feel Doug's skin. It was smooth and firm and warm. Our lips pressed together. His lips were soft. Our tongues intertwined. I became aware of my tallywacker pressing into my pants like it was straining to get out. I rolled over onto my stomach and pressed down on the chenille bedspread. Shivers ran up and down my spine.

I rolled over and sat up like a shot, out of breath. I wasn't totally sure what was going on, but I knew I shouldn't have been thinking about two boys in that way, even if I was one of them. Especially if I was one of them. I felt like I'd crossed a sinful line. Could this mean I was really a faggot like Jimbo said? I dropped to my knees and asked Jesus to forgive me and cleanse me of satanic thoughts.

"Please, Lord Jesus, all I want is to be a normal boy who likes girls like the other boys like girls. I don't understand why I don't. I want to, but I just don't get it. I always get it wrong. Lord Jesus, I didn't ask for this, and I don't want it. Please make it go away. Please make me like the other boys. In Jesus's name we pray, amen."

# Nine: Slut!

FRIDAY MORNING, I woke up feeling like I'd been punched in the stomach. Carleen and I had had our first fight, and she was going to try to get Doug to do it with her. Both thoughts made want to upchuck. I thought about telling Momma I was sick, but I realized Doug would need me to help him stand strong.

All morning, Carleen didn't say a word to me. Instead, she was all Chatty Cathy with Doug. Between classes, she touched his arm and giggled at whatever he said. At lunch, Carleen went into the cafeteria ahead of me, and I had a bad feeling I might have to eat lunch by myself. I bought my Mountain Dew and looked around the big room. Of course, Carleen was sitting next to Doug. I stood there for a minute wondering what to do. Then Doug saw me and waved me over to his table. Carleen glared at me as I sat down.

"Hey," said Doug. "I thought you'd want to sit here since you and Carleen usually eat lunch together."

"Thanks," I said. "Carleen and I have been best friends since kindergarten." I looked at her and smiled. She took a bite of her sandwich.

"Not really," said Carleen, her mouth full of Miracle Whip. Doug caught my eye.

"Carleen's just trying to be funny. We're really best friends forever."

"I'm not trying to be funny." She turned to Doug. "Timmy's still a kid. I like mature men. Like you." She lightly touched his hand as she said it. Doug quickly put his hand in his lap.

"Hey, listen, guys," said Doug. "I just remembered I've got this thing. I've got to, uh, make a call. Got to call my mom. See you later." He got up and sprinted out of the cafeteria.

"Great move, Carleen. So seductive. You're a regular Raquel Welch."

"He just didn't want to sit here with a sissy boy like you."

Anger flew all over me at the sound of the word *sissy*. Mean boys had been calling me that since seventh grade, and I couldn't believe I was hearing it from Carleen.

"Better a sissy than a slut!"

I said the word slut way too loud, and the boys from the JV football team at the other end of the table turned. Dean was one of them. He laughed and said something to the other guys. They all laughed.

I looked back at Carleen, and she'd gone completely white. In a low voice, she said, "I hate you, Timmy Thompson, and I'll hate you for the rest of my life." She got up and left the cafeteria.

I followed her to the library, and caught up to her at a stack of books waiting to be shelved.

"I'm so sorry, Carleen. That was mean. It was a mean, dirty word. You're not a slut."

She turned to me, and her eyes were full of tears.

"I did it with those boys because they like me. They think I'm pretty and so does Doug. I'm finally popular with boys, and you can't handle it."

"They're right, Carleen. You are pretty."

"How would you know," she said, fishing in her purse for a tissue. "You think Kate Jackson is pretty."

I laughed and so did she. Pretty soon, we were laughing like a couple of hyenas, and Mrs. Ouzts shushed us.

"You can't stay mad at me, Carleen. Promise me you won't. I take back the mean thing I said."

"And I take back the mean thing I said. You're not a sissy. I was just mad. But stop trying to make me feel bad about having sex, okay?"

"Okay. And no more calling me immature because I want to save myself for marriage."

"Okay."

I was flooded with relief. I had my best friend back. For now. But I had a feeling deep down that something had changed between us. Maybe she really was more mature than I was. Maybe sex made a person grow up faster. Things sure were a lot easier when we were just a couple of kids—before sex got in the way.

# Ten: PE Dread

THE BELL RANG for sixth period, and everyone trooped to the gym. This was the day I'd dreaded—the first day of PE. The girls got to stay in the air-conditioning, but the boys all had to go to the ball field in the heat. But first, we had to go to the locker room to change. This scared me even more than having to catch a ball. As we went in, Coach Duggins handed us each our gym outfits: gold T-shirts with Patriot Christian across the chest and really short gray shorts. I hung back at the end of the line, so I was the last to enter the locker room. It smelled of antiseptic and sweat. The other guys were already stripping, and some were totally naked. Nobody seemed to really notice each other's nakedness, and I knew I couldn't allow myself to look. I didn't want anybody to think I actually wanted to see a naked guy. I also didn't want anybody to see my flabby naked body.

I chose a locker as far away from Doug as possible and began to slowly undress. I turned when I heard Jimbo's voice, and he was butt naked, wandering around telling guys how incredible he was at baseball. He didn't seem to be in a hurry to get dressed, even though some of the other boys were already in their shorts. It was like he enjoyed being naked in front of all of the boys.

"Hey, new guy, Appleby, want to be on my team? I know Duggins'll make me a team captain. He knows how good I am," said Jimbo, still naked.

Doug turned in my direction, and he was also completely naked. His tallywacker was surrounded by thick, curly hair, and it was bigger than mine. It was bigger than Jimbo's too. It was a man's member, or what I imagined a man's member would look like. It was perfect and beautiful. It was long and thick, and the head had pinkish skin that looked incredibly soft. I longed to touch it, to caress it. To caress Doug. He reached up to pull his shirt out of his locker, and I saw that he had a lot of armpit hair, too. It was thick and lush. I wondered what it smelled like. Not stinky and gross like Jimbo's, but earthy and masculine and safe. I wanted to breathe him in.

Doug caught my eye, and I looked away. I was seized by fear. What was I thinking? What was I doing? If Doug saw me looking, then the other boys saw me looking, too. I wasn't supposed to look. I knew better. I was stupid, stupid, stupid. Busying myself with changing, I was going to pull off my underpants when I realized I was swelling down there. I quickly sat on the bench, in horror, trying to think of something to distract me and make me soft. Kimberly Ann. I focused hard on a mental image of her in church, piously giving testimony about how much she loved Jesus. I immediately went soft.

"What do you say, Appleby, you any good?"

"Never really played baseball before. I was into surfing back home. Played some soccer."

"Soccer! That's for sissies. I bet Timmy here just loves it, don't 'cha, Timmy?"

My words got caught in my throat, but luckily, Coach Duggins stuck his head in the room and barked at us to move it.

"Jesus, Thompson, how long does it take?"

WE RAN OUT onto the baked clay and lined up. I was on one end of the line, and Doug was on the other. It must have been a hundred degrees, and I was sweating everywhere. I hated sweat. Coach Duggins stood in front of us and looked us over. He had a new bushy moustache he had grown over the summer, kind of like Tom Selleck's. He also had on one of those golf shirts with the ribbed short sleeves like Doug's, and his biceps were really big. He had a deep tan like he had spent the summer at the beach. I was standing there thinking about all this when, for the second time that day, I realized I was being yelled at.

"Timmy Thompson!" yelled Coach Duggins. "What are you standing there for? Didn't you hear me tell everybody to give me three laps around the field? Are you deaf, boy?"

I started running to catch up with the other boys who were already halfway around the football field. The sweat was pouring now. I seemed to sweat more than any other boy at Patriot Christian.

Coach Duggins shouted out from behind us. "Get the lead out, Thompson. You ate too many Little Debbies over the summer. You need to slim down." He wasn't ever in the Army, but he probably wished he'd been.

I already had a stitch in my side when Jimbo lapped me.

"Move it, lard butt," he said. Most of the other boys were right behind him, catcalling.

"Fatass."

"Queerbait."

"Sissy."

Every boy who lapped me had to get in his two cents. I was about halfway through my first lap when Coach

Duggins said, "All right, Thompson, that's enough. We don't have all day."

I ran over to the other boys and tried to catch my breath. I stood next to Tom Walker.

"You sure do sweat," Tom said. "Pee yew."

"Yeah, fatty, how can you stand it?" someone behind me said. I didn't turn around to acknowledge it. I chose to rise above.

"All right," said Coach Duggins. "Knock it off. Time to pair up for baseball. Jimbo Abernathy, you pick a team, and new guy, Appleby, you pick."

Jimbo and Doug stood in front of us and started choosing their teams. I knew I'd be the last one standing. I always wished they'd run out of spots before they got to me and I could just go to the library and read a book, but it never happened.

For his third choice, Doug pointed directly at me and said, "I'll take him."

I stood there blinking in the sun, until Coach Duggins said, "Can't you hear, Thompson? Move it! Jesus!"

I dashed forward to my new team, so giddy with excitement I tripped over my shoelaces and landed flat on my face in the dirt. I rolled over, and all the kids looking down at me started screaming. Coach Duggins leaned over me and told me I was bleeding. He took a Kleenex out of his pocket and rammed it up under my nose, grabbed my hand, and pulled me up.

"Jesus, boy, you're bleeding like a stuck pig. Your momma will kill me. You gotta get to the school nurse. Appleby, you chose him; you take him. Tommy Walker, you take over as team captain. Okay, you two, MOVE!"

Doug took me by the arm and started leading me back into the school. I was sweaty, bloody, my shoes were untied, and my shirttail was out, but I didn't even notice because I was alone with Doug again.

*He chose me! He actually chose me! Me!*

We got to the nurse's office, and her assistant, Evelyn, was sitting behind a counter working a crossword puzzle. She looked up at us over her reading glasses and said Nurse Darleen had stepped out for just a sec, and we should have a seat. She handed me one of those little Kleenex packets women keep in their purses and took my old one between her fingertips. Doug and I sat on the plastic chairs.

"I'll call your mother," she said.

"Yes, ma'am."

"Are you okay?" asked Doug.

"It's just a nosebleed. I get them all the time. I'm sure I'll be fine. I'm sorry you had to leave the game."

"I'm not. Shit. I didn't want to be out there in the hot sun playing ball with those rednecks."

I started to tell him to watch it or he'd get in trouble because profanity was not allowed at Patriot Christian, but I figured it was the way sophisticated kids talked in California, and I didn't want to be unsophisticated. That was my chance to show him I was cool and not a redneck, so I didn't say anything about the bad word and pretended like it was no big deal.

"Oh," I said. Then, I changed the subject. "I'm really sorry about your sister."

He looked at me and laughed. What was so funny? Just then, the nurse came in, smelling like cigarettes.

"Watch it, here comes Nurse Ratched," Doug whispered.

"No, it's Nurse Darleen," I corrected. Doug laughed again, but I still didn't know why.

"I didn't know you boys were here," Nurse Darleen said, smoothing down her pink smock top. She didn't wear a real nurse's uniform. "Evelyn, you should have called me." Evelyn didn't look up from her crossword.

Nurse Darleen waved us into the examining room. "Come on in, boys, come on in. That's right, you too, new boy. What's your name?"

"Doug Appleby."

"Doug Appleby, that's right. Your momma's one of the Herlongs, isn't she? She was Annette, right? Arlene and Howard's daughter? The one who up and moved to Los Angeles? That right?"

"That's right. We're back."

"Well, I can see that," said Nurse Darleen with a big smile. I sat up on the examining table, but she was still standing in the doorway facing Doug.

"You tell your momma we're looking for her down at the Gilgal Baptist. All the Herlongs go to Gilgal. You tell her she's welcome anytime, and you too. You're a Herlong too—you know it? I've got cousins who married Herlongs, so I guess that makes me a Herlong too, don't it?" She put a hand on Doug's shoulder. "Now, you tell your momma that we don't care that she ran off with some boy to California now that she's back home where she belongs. We're not judgmental at Gilgal."

"I'll tell her. Um, Nurse Darleen? I think Tim's nose is bleeding again."

She swung around in my direction.

"My Lord, I almost forgot about you, Timmy, sitting here all quiet and all. Let's take a look." She took my face in her hands and pointed it up to the light.

"Oh, it's just a nosebleed, Timmy Thompson." She turned back to Doug and said, "He gets them all the time."

She looked down at me, squeezed my shoulder, and said, "I think it's about to stop. You'll be just fine. You managed to get yourself a little skinned up, though, so let me clean you up a bit." She turned to the counter with all her supplies. "You tell your momma I said hey, all right, Timmy? How's things at First Baptist?"

Just then, Momma burst in. "Where's my baby? Oh my Lord, Timmy, are you all right? Thank God Evelyn called me. Darleen, how is he?"

"He's just fine, JoAnne. It's just another nosebleed. He fell on the ball field and got a little skinned up is all."

Momma grabbed me and gave me a big hug. She released me and faced Nurse Darleen.

"The coach is too hard on those boys. Making them roughhouse on the bare ground in this heat. I'm going to have a talk with the headmaster."

Momma suddenly noticed there was another kid in the room.

"And who's this fine young man? Who's your little friend, Timmy? You got yourself another little friend?" She turned to Darleen. "Timmy has more friends than he knows what to do with, but there's always room for more."

"That's Doug Appleby, Annette Herlong's boy," said Nurse Darleen. "You remember Annette, don't you?" Her voice had a slight edge when she said "Annette." Momma and Nurse Darleen exchanged quick looks.

"He brought me up from the ball field," I said.

"Well, of course, I remember Annette Herlong." Momma turned to Doug and added, "The prettiest girl in Edgewood High School. My Lord, she was popular with the boys. And look at you. You are the image of your pretty momma."

Doug just stood there. I guessed he didn't know what to say, being from California and all.

"Now, you tell your momma JoAnne Ashburn Thompson said hello, okay? She'll remember me. I was an Ashburn. You tell her, okay?"

"Yes, ma'am."

"Well, I'm glad to see your momma taught you manners even if she did raise you in California. You're such a nice boy; why don't you come have supper with us tonight? You and Timmy could play till suppertime, and I could take you home afterwards. It would give me a chance to visit with your momma, and I'd just love that. You can call your momma from right here, can't he, Darleen?"

My heart raced. I wasn't ready for this. I needed a bath and I needed to change clothes and God only knew what I would wear. My best slimming black shirt was dirty, and I hated how I looked in everything else. *He can't come tonight, he can't come, oh my God, what if he can't come?*

"I've got homework, and Mom always makes me do it first. I'm not supposed to go over to other kids' houses on school nights," said Doug.

My heart sank. I was disappointed and relieved at the same time. I needed time to prepare for Doug's first visit.

"Y'all have homework already? It's only the first week," said Momma. "It's practically still summer. Well, okay, but only if you promise not to make yourself a stranger. You stop by our house any time. I know Timmy would love to see you, isn't that right, Timmy? We live in the yellow brick one-story not too far from the Bi-Rite. I'm sure you've seen it."

My mouth was completely dry, and I just sat there while Nurse Darleen put a Band-Aid on my shin. By now, the school day was over, so Doug went out front to wait on his mother.

Momma helped me out to the car and held the door for me. When she started to reach across me to buckle my seat belt, I told her I could do it myself. "Of course you can, honey. You're such a big brave boy."

As soon as she got behind the wheel, she started asking me about Doug.

"I had no idea Annette Herlong's boy was in school with you. Why didn't you tell me? He sure is a good-looking boy—don't you think? Oh, what am I saying, you wouldn't know about that, would you? I mean, if he was a pretty girl, you'd know it, wouldn't you? You're getting so big and strong and brave, I bet the girls are all over you, aren't they? I bet Kimberly Ann Mingees would just love it if you asked her for a date. Why don't you?"

"Mom. I don't like Kimberly Ann Mingees."

"Oh, of course you do. She's from the nicest family. You know they just built one of those new houses out by the country club. Why, her mother was just a few years behind me in high school. You should call her. Give her a thrill."

"Mommaaaaa."

"What?"

We drove in silence for a while. Then, I finally said, "Doug's sister drowned in the Pacific Ocean. Did you know that?"

"Sister? Annette Herlong had two children? And one died? I've never heard that."

"It's true. She was surfing with Doug's girlfriend, Summer, and a shark attacked them."

"I just can't believe I've never heard it. Her cousin Linda does my hair every Saturday, and she's never said a word about a dead child. It's the kind of thing people talk about."

When we got home, Aunt Melanie was just pulling up in her orange Vega. She was "between jobs" again and looked after me a lot when Momma had to work late. Momma practically leaped out of the car and ran to her to tell her my news about Doug's dead sister. Aunt Melanie stood there on the lawn, her hands on her hips.

"I don't believe it," she said.

"It's absolutely true!" I said. "Nobody would make up something like that."

"You'd be surprised what people would make up."

"Well," Momma said, "Tim says everybody at Patriot Christian is talking about it. If it's not true, I guess we'll hear about it soon enough. Oh gosh, I've got to get back to work, so I can't stand here and gab about it all day. Thank you so much for helping out again, Melanie. Now, Timmy's gonna be fine; he's just a little shook up is all."

"You know I'm always happy to help you. Timmy and I'll have fun like we always do," said Aunt Melanie. "Don't worry about anything."

"Well, I do worry about poor Annette Herlong losing her only daughter, if she had one, I guess." She kept standing there in the yard, running her hands through her hair. "I mean, if she really lost her daughter to a shark attack, then I have to do something. I'll have to stop by the Bi-Rite on the way home to get some more mustard and pap-a-rika so I can make some of my 'Sold My Soul to the Deviled Eggs' and take them over to her. I'll just give her a quick call to make sure it's convenient."

"Don't rush off to buy paprika just yet," said Melanie. "I tell you, it didn't happen. That boy of hers is making it up for some reason."

"He is not!" I said, following her in. "He's a nice boy and smart too. He took me to see Nurse Darleen after I fell. He wouldn't lie. I know him."

"It could explain the divorce and the sudden move," said Momma. "Goodness gracious, look at the time. I know the judge is gonna bawl me out for staying away so long. I gotta go." With that, Momma dashed back to the car and drove off in a cloud of exhaust.

"Come on in," said Aunt Melanie. "I think I might be able to rustle up some SpaghettiOs."

"It's true, Aunt Melanie. I know it is. He even wore a T-shirt with his sister's name on it. It was a memorial T-shirt."

"Really?" said Aunt Melanie. "What was her name?"

"Patti Smith. She and Doug had different daddies. That explains the different last names."

"Patti Smith, huh?" She shook her head. "Don't move."

Aunt Melanie went out to her Vega, brought back a cassette tape, and handed it to me. It said *Patti Smith Band* and *Radio Ethiopia*.

"Patti Smith is a rock singer," said Aunt Melanie. "He got a T-shirt at one of her concerts. He doesn't have a sister. He never had a sister. He made it up to shut up some busybody. Can't say I blame him."

I was stunned and confused. This couldn't be true. "Maybe his mother named her after her favorite singer, or something," I said, searching for an answer. Any answer.

"You're hopeless, young man," said Aunt Melanie, shaking her head. "This boy Doug can do no wrong in your eyes, can he?"

"It's not that. It's just..."

"Um huh. Come on, let's go in."

Later on, after dinner, I was in my room doing my homework and I heard Melanie make a call.

"Uh-hum. That's what he said. Eaten by a shark... I know, I know. It's crazy as can be. Who knows why kids say what they say... Oh, don't give him a hard time. He's new to this town and to his school. Give him a break... Shoot, he's no crazier than anyone else walking the streets of this town. I say if he makes up big stories, he'll fit right in... Okay, bye-bye."

She hung up and walked down the hall to my room. "I was just on the phone with your friend Doug's aunt Linda. She said Annette Herlong never had a daughter. She only had one child, and it's Doug."

"I just can't believe he would lie," I said.

"Oh, it's not a big deal. Everybody lies now and then. Now, don't go telling everybody at school about this, and don't go get on the phone to Carleen. He'll be found out soon enough. It's not your job to tell on him."

After she left, I sat there in my room, stunned at the news. How could he make up something like that? How could he let everyone in the school think he'd suffered such a personal tragedy when he hadn't? How would I cope with this knowledge he'd lied? If we were going to be best friends, which I was planning on since we sat next to each other in every class, he'd have to learn that lying is a sin. I'd have to save him. Once I saved him, we'd become best friends.

Momma came home that night with eggs and paprika despite what Aunt Melanie said. She'd hardly gotten home before she started boiling water for the eggs.

"Momma, I don't think the story about Doug's sister is true. Did you talk to Aunt Melanie? She called Doug's momma's cousin Linda."

Momma looked up from her boiling water, her hair starting to frizz out. "Yes, Melanie and I talked when I got home. I don't know why a boy would tell such a lie. It'll get back to his mother and hurt her so. I think it's all the more reason for us to pay them a visit. It's high time. Why, I went to high school with Annette Herlong, and she's lived here for over a month, and I have yet to even give her a call. Your MeeMaw would roll over in her grave if she knew I was being so rude. I called Annette, and she said they'd be home all morning. Reach in the Frigidaire and hand me the mustard and mayo, will you?"

# Eleven: Sold My Soul to the Deviled Eggs

THE NEXT MORNING was Saturday, and Momma was up early ironing my new khakis and my best blue button-down shirt. She arranged the "Sold My Soul to the Deviled Eggs" on one of her deviled egg platters and garnished them with a sprig of parsley. She let me add the last-minute sprinkling of paprika. For color.

She put on a floral print dress from Belk's end-of-season sale last fall. It wasn't the most fashion-forward thing she had, but it was flattering. I held the deviled eggs in my lap as we drove to Doug's house. I was so nervous I had to really concentrate to keep from dropping any of the eggs.

The house Doug and his momma were renting was a cute little red brick ranch with a huge magnolia tree in the front. I gingerly carried the eggs to the door, and Momma rang the bell. Doug's momma opened the door wearing gym shorts and a tight tank top. Her blonde hair was pulled back into a ponytail with several damp wisps surrounding her face.

"Hey, Annette," said Momma. "It's me, JoAnne Ashburn from high school. I've been so remiss in not paying a call on you that I'm just flat-out ashamed of myself. So, I said to little Timmy, here, I said, 'Timmy, we're just gonna rectify it and pay a visit to Annette

Herlong.' I'm so glad you let us barge in on your Saturday." She stood there smiling at Doug's momma.

For a couple of beats, Doug's momma stared at the platter, then blinked and summoned a smile. "Why, JoAnne, it's been forever." She looked down at me.

"And you brought eggs. I wouldn't know how to make something like that." She held the door open for us.

"What a cute outfit, Annette," said Momma, touching her on the arm. "Were you just doing some Jazzercise? I thought about buying one of those Jane Fondas last Christmas after all the holiday baking, but I just couldn't do it, what with her being a traitor and all. Oh my goodness! What an absolutely adorable living room! I just love what you've done with it. Why, it's so simple and easy care. It's just ideal. Don't you think so, son?"

I looked around at the sparse room. It was the polar opposite of our antique-filled living room. There was a sofa against the far wall with some sort of colorful Mexican-looking blanket thrown across it. There was a rocking chair and a smallish TV on a rickety TV stand. It had aluminum foil on the rabbit ears. There was a nondescript wooden coffee table with art magazines strewn across it. Over the sofa was a large painting with brush strokes that seemed to be random, but when I looked at it a minute, I realized it was supposed to be a man. A naked man. With a big you-know-what.

"What interesting artwork," said Momma.

"Thank you," said Doug's momma. "I do love abstract expressionism—don't you?"

Momma tittered a bit but didn't respond.

"It's by an emerging West Coast artist," said Doug's momma, studying the painting. "He was a dear friend of my ex-husband's. Still is. Very dear. I guess you could say he got the husband, and I got the painting." She laughed and Momma joined in, but she seemed confused. I sure was.

"Where are my manners," said Momma. "I'd like you to meet my son, Timmy. Timmy, say hello to Doug's mother, Mrs...."

"I go by Herlong. I never took my husband's name. Made it easier when we split up. Pleased to meet you, Timmy." She shook my hand just like a grown-up. "I've heard a lot about you from Doug."

I shook her hand, my mind reeling. Really? Doug had been talking about me? I wondered what he'd been saying. How much did he talk about me? Was it good stuff, or did he tell her I got a bloody nose during PE?

"I just got back from a run," said Doug's momma. "I lost track of time, and I'm a sweaty mess, but I could make some herbal tea if you'd like, JoAnne."

"A run? Where were you running to? Oh, you mean you went jogging. I've heard jogging is all the rage in some parts of the country. I can't imagine running anywhere unless I was being chased by a bear or something; can you, Timmy? Oh my goodness, aren't fads a funny thing? That must be how you've kept your cute figure. I swear you haven't gained an ounce since graduation. You were the prettiest girl in the class, in the whole school, even."

Doug came into the room. He was wearing gym shorts and the same Patti Smith T-shirt he wore the other day to school.

"Look who's here," said Doug's momma. "Timmy and his mother just dropped in for a visit and brought these lovely eggs, isn't that nice?" She picked up Momma's egg platter and pushed it into Doug's hands. "Why don't you take Timmy and the eggs and go back to your room. You two can have a snack and do boy stuff while JoAnne and I get reacquainted."

Doug led me back to his room. It was like a real hippie palace. He'd strung some beads across the door just like Rhoda's little apartment on *Mary Tyler Moore*. Inside, there was a bed, a desk and chair, and a really nice-looking stereo system with lots of records. I ran my hand along the spines of the records, touching what he had touched, trying to absorb his choices.

Doug put the platter down on the desk and ate an egg. "Pretty good. What do you call these?"

"They're deviled eggs, of course. Momma calls them her Sold My Soul to the Deviled Eggs. Haven't you ever had any?"

"No, man. Mom doesn't make stuff like this. It tastes like it has mayonnaise in it."

"Of course, it has mayonnaise in it. How else would you make deviled eggs? Mayonnaise, mustard, hard-boiled eggs, salt and pepper, and paprika. For color."

"Mom never buys mayonnaise, and we don't have any salt in the house, so I'm sure she'll never make any of these."

"Momma makes them all the time, whenever anybody's sick or she has to take a covered dish to a church supper or when somebody new moves to town, like you and your momma. What does your momma fix for sick people and church suppers?"

"I guess it hasn't ever come up. How's your nose? You recover from your spill?"

"Yeah, thanks. I don't usually fall and stuff, you know."

"Don't sweat it. It was hot and miserable out there. It was like freaking Death Valley. I can't believe they made us run around in the heat. Mom was pissed that I sweated in my school clothes."

"Yeah, I was pissed too," I said, hoping Doug would notice how I could toss off a bad word like he could. That's how sophisticated I was. "But what else are they going to do? We have to have PE."

"They could have let us use the gym with the girls when the weather's real hot. What did they think we were going to do to them?"

"Momma says boys should never be allowed to see girls sweat. She says it ruins the allure. Besides, she says ladies don't sweat. They glow."

Doug laughed. "They glow, huh? Whatever. I guess I've got a lot to learn about the South."

"I could teach you. I could be your tour guide to the South." I shut up because maybe I was being too forward.

"Sure, you can be my teacher." Doug smiled and laughed a little, and I felt a warm glow inside.

"Hey, want to listen to some music?" Doug asked.

"Sure."

"What kind of music do you like?"

I thought about it for a minute. "I like Barry Manilow? And ABBA?"

"I don't have any of that. How about Patti Smith?" Aunt Melanie was right. She *was* a singer.

"Okay, sure. I like her music a lot," I lied.

Doug pulled an album out of his stack. "I just got her latest."

On the cover was a picture of a skinny lady holding up her arms. She had hairy armpits. It was really gross, but I didn't say anything. He put the record on. "This is my favorite song on it."

A deep voice came out, raspy, but still feminine. She was pounding, *"Because the night belongs to lovers..."* It sure wasn't anything like the Olivia Newton-John records Momma sometimes listened to.

I picked up the album. The next song was called "Ghost Dance." It was slower than "Because the Night," but her voice was still pounding, like it was coming after me. Then, there was this song with a bad word in it. The title had that word Daddy used when he talked about Negroes. She screamed it like she was out of control. Doug turned it up real loud, but his momma never complained or anything. She was screaming the bad word that Momma always told me not to use.

We sat there on the floor of his bedroom, just listening to the unbelievable music. Doug was staring into space, and I was watching him stare. The last song was called "Godspeed," and I couldn't say she was a really good singer. I mean, she didn't really hit all the notes like Toni Tennille or Vicki Lawrence, but she sounded like she was ripping her heart open. I'd never heard anything like it.

I suddenly had an urge to put my arms around Doug and hug him tight. It was almost overwhelming. It was all I could do to stop myself from reaching out to him. Thinking about hugging Doug frightened me. I knew boys weren't supposed to feel like that, so why did I? If it was wrong, why did it feel good to be with him?

I realized I was staring at him, thinking these thoughts, when he looked back at me. He looked right into my eyes. It was like he knew what I was thinking. I didn't move. I didn't dare.

Just then, I heard Momma's voice. "Come on, baby, it's time to go. You two can get together some other time and listen to records again. Maybe some different records next time."

The moment was broken, and Doug got up and turned off the record player. "I guess you gotta go. It was fun having you over. You're the first friend I've had over since we moved here." He called me his friend. Best friends! The coolest guy in school was my best friend!

"Maybe you could come over to my house sometime," I heard myself saying. He gave me a hug. He felt warm.

"Sure," he said. "That'd be great. You could play some Manilow for me."

As we were about to walk out the door, Momma seemed to remember something. She turned to Doug's momma. "I hope you're enjoying your church home at Gilgal Baptist. I know all the Herlongs go to Gilgal. I'm sure it's a comfort to be back."

"Oh gosh, Gilgal," said Doug's momma. "Yes, I grew up in that church, but I'm afraid we haven't made it out there yet."

Momma looked stricken. She put her hand to her breast. "Your poor mother must be mortified. Oh my. I guess it's a good thing your grandmother, dear old Miz Eva, isn't around to see this. Everybody used to say the preacher wouldn't unlock the door to Gilgal till Miz Eva said it was time."

Doug's momma stood a little straighter. "Yes, my family has a history at the church, but I make my own decisions, thank you."

She began shutting the door, but Momma used her pump to block it. "I know just the thing. We'll take you with us to First Baptist. Won't that be fun? You want to branch out and find a new church home and establish yourself as your own person, isn't that right? Well, I can certainly understand. We'll be by about nine thirty tomorrow so we can get a good parking place before the ten o'clock services, all righty?"

"I really don't think so," said Doug's momma.

"Why, of course you want to," said Momma. "I can't imagine why you wouldn't. Why, Pastor Earl Don is doing a whole sermon series on Life Lessons from the Bible. Doesn't that sound inventive? I'm just loving it; aren't you, Timmy? See how he loves it? Anyway, we'll be here at nine thirty sharp."

"JoAnne. I said no. Thank you."

Momma stood there looking confused. Then she spoke again. "Well, we'll just take Doug, then. Won't it be fun, Timmy? Wouldn't you like to go to church with us, Doug? You'll meet all the kids there, even the ones who go to the public school. They have Royal Ambassadors and Sunbeams for Jesus—all kinds of youth activities. Why, the youth minister, Mr. Rick, is the sweetest young man. He'd just love you; I know it. What do you say?"

She looked expectantly from me to Doug to Doug's momma. I got excited at the thought of Doug walking into church with me. Everybody would see we were best friends. I looked at Doug and tried to telepathically communicate to him that he needed to say yes.

"It's okay, Mom," said Doug. "I'd like to go." Doug's momma looked at him like he'd just sprouted a third ear.

"Well, it's all decided then," said Momma. "We'll be here at nine thirty. Sorry you can't join us, Annette, but we'll take real good care of him. Bye-bye now!" And we were off.


ON THE RIDE home, I felt so weird. I knew thinking about hugging Doug was a bad thought that I wasn't supposed to be having, but it was so nice. He was my new best friend. It all gave me a funny feeling in the pit of my stomach and an overwhelming desire to tell Momma. I usually told Momma everything. She loved me and would know what to do.

It took until we were pulling into the driveway for me to get up the nerve to mention it. She turned off the ignition, and it was now or never, so I spoke.

"Momma? Can I tell you something?"

"Of course, baby. You know you can tell me anything. Go ahead," she said, smiling.

"I had this feeling today like, I don't know, um." I cleared my throat. "Like Doug said he was my best friend; isn't that great?"

"That's great, honey," said Momma.

"And I wanted to put my arms around Doug and hug him. Is that weird? I couldn't stop thinking about it. I just wanted to put my arms around him."

Momma dropped her smile and stared out the windshield. She put her keys in her purse and started to get out of the car.

"I'm sorry." I wasn't sure why I was apologizing.

Momma froze, partially out of the car. She replied without looking at me, "You stop being silly. You just got excited because he said he's your friend. Everybody has weird thoughts sometimes; you're no different. Just ignore them, and they'll go away, okay? Just ignore them."

That was the end of the conversation. She seemed so unhappy with the question that I decided to never mention anything like that to her again.


WHEN MOMMA AND I went inside, I told her I wanted to ride my bike uptown to the ten-cent store to see if they had the Patti Smith album.

"Who is she? Is she like Patti Page?" asked Momma as she was riffling through the freezer for something to start for dinner.

"Not exactly," I said.

Momma dropped a frozen pound of ground beef in the sink to thaw and turned to me with her hand on her hip. "You don't mean the awful mess Doug was playing for you, do you? It was just junk. I can't believe Annette didn't go right down the hall and turn that trash off. Surely, you don't like that, do you?"

"Well, yes, kinda," I said, leaning against the counter.

"What about all the other music I've bought you—good music?" asked Momma. "What about the Cher album I got you last Christmas? Have you forgotten about Cher?"

"No, ma'am," I said. "Of course I haven't forgotten about Cher."

"And what about the Bette Midler album you got with your birthday money? I love the Divine Miss M. What about the album Aunt Melanie got you last Christmas—What was it called? Alba? Abner?"

"ABBA, and I still like it. I can like different things, Momma."

"I wish you'd bring out the Helen Reddy album again. I really like 'Delta Dawn.' I'm kind of a 'Delta Dawn' myself—don't you think?" said Momma, laughing. "A woman of mystery?"

She started snapping her fingers, swaying her hips, and singing. "*Delta Dawn, what's that flower you have on? Could it be a faded rose from days gone byyy?*" She took my hands and started twirling me across the terrazzo floor. We sang together.

"*And did I hear you say he was a-meetin' ya here today to take you to his mansion in the sky-eye.*"

We kept dancing as Momma sang solo. *"She's forty-one and her daddy still calls 'er baby."*

Then I sang, *"All the folks 'round Brownsville say she's crazy."*

Then Momma, *"'Cause she walks downtown with her suitcase in her hand."*

Then me, in the deepest voice I could manage, *"Lookin' for a mysterious dark-haired man."*

We were both laughing so hard we were crying. Momma pulled me to her and gave me a big hug and held it. "Aw, honey," she said as she held me. "You go on and get your album even if it is awful music. I guess I just don't want you to grow up. I want you to stay my precious little baby boy forever and ever. I want you to be safe and happy. All I want for you is a nice, safe, happy, normal life. Just a normal life." She was crying for real now.

"I love you, Momma," I said in a little voice.

She squeezed me harder. "I love you too, baby boy." She held me for a few more moments, then let out her breath and pulled away.

She started to dab her eyes with a paper towel as I dashed back to my room to put on my shorts and Keds.

"Wait a minute," she called out. "Grab my purse and bring it to me." She gave me a ten-dollar bill. "Save your allowance money. You take this and go buy whatever you want at the dime store."

I didn't know what to say. Momma almost never gave me money over my allowance, mainly because court reporters didn't make a lot. I would be real careful about what I bought with this money.

# Twelve: I am Woman

THE TEN-CENT store was only four blocks away, so it didn't take me long to get there. I parked my bike by the door and walked inside.

The whole place smelled like stale popcorn and bubble gum. I walked to the record aisle and was a little surprised they had *Patti Smith Easter*. They didn't always have all the latest hits at the ten-cent store. In fact, they had a bunch of copies. I guessed Patti Smith wasn't a big seller around here. It was $7.98, which left two dollars from the ten Momma gave me. I had to use it on something special, so I riffled through the singles bins and found two Helen Reddy singles for a dollar each. One was "I Am Woman," and the other was "Angie Baby." Momma would love them.

The checker at the ten-cent store was Jimbo Abernathy's second cousin Debbie, the same Debbie who liked to bum cigarettes and beer from Carleen's momma. She was older than me and had graduated from the public high school three years ago. I guessed she was pursuing a career in retail now. I put the records on the counter and saw a tiny girl sitting under the cash register, pulling the hair out of a Barbie. The girl looked up at me and waved. I waved back.

"Are you babysitting, Debbie?" I asked.

Debbie looked down at the girl and gave her a swat. "LaTrelle, what did I tell you about bothering the customers?" The girl started to cry.

"She wasn't bothering me." I felt bad that the girl got hit because of something I said. "Whose child is she?"

"She's mine. Who'd you think she belonged to?"

"Oh, I don't know. I guess I didn't realize you were married."

Debbie rolled her eyes. "I ain't. You don't have to get married to have a baby, you know, or don't they teach biology at that fancy school of yours?"

I blushed, embarrassed at the turn in the conversation. "Patriot Christian isn't fancy." I purposely missed the point, trying to get the conversation away from Debbie's sex life.

Debbie ignored me and picked up the record. "If you're buying this Patti Smith album for your aunt Melanie, she's already got it. I sold her the cassette last week."

"It's not for her," I said.

"Then who's it for? I know your momma doesn't want this."

"It's for me. I like it," I said.

Debbie looked from me to the album and back again. "*You* like it?" She shook her head and mashed the buttons on the cash register. "Who likes Helen Reddy and Patti Smith? Jimbo said you was strange." She took my money, and I left without saying anything else.

I wasn't going to let Jimbo Abernathy's trashy cousin make me feel bad. Who the heck was she? Some nobody clerk at the ten-cent store. I bet she dated lots of trashy boys and maybe even had some trashy babies. I laughed to myself as I biked home with my new album. Maybe that's what Patti Smith should call her new band—The Trashy Babies. I decided this was the new, self-confident me. I was best friends with the coolest guy in school. I knew all about the coolest new music. This was the start of a new me rising above this Podunk little town.

Momma was real happy with the Helen Reddy singles I gave her. She teared up a little.

"Baby, I gave you that money to spend on you—to get something to make you happy, not to buy something for me."

"Buying these for you made me happy, Momma."

Her tears started again. She hugged me and told me how much she loved me and promised to make me spaghetti just like I like it for dinner. Then, I went to my room and put on Patti Smith. That dried her tears real fast. It took about two minutes for her to come in and tell me to turn it down. I did, and I shut my door and sat real close to the speakers. Even so, when "Rock N Roll N-Word" came on, she came back to my room and put her foot down.

"You can't listen to that song. It's vile," she said. "I will not have that trash blaring in my house. I know I said you could have the album, but you'll just have to skip over that song."

That was okay because it wasn't my favorite song anyway. I really loved "Because the Night," and I listened to it over and over again. I daydreamed about me and Doug going into the night together. I wasn't sure what we were supposed to do "into the night," but it made me feel good imagining us walking into the woods behind the school after midnight with no one to see us or bother us. We would lie on the ground under the trees with Doug holding me in his arms. I felt safe in those daydreams. I knew I shouldn't be thinking things like that about a boy, so I decided I wouldn't tell anybody. They were just for me.

That night after supper, I got Carleen on the phone. I had to tell her all about my day with Doug. I told her that Doug was my new best friend and then corrected myself and said he was my new best guy friend.

I told Carleen she would always be my best *best* friend, boy or girl. I got super excited and told her all three of us could start hanging out, listening to music and doing stuff, but she didn't seem too interested. In fact, she didn't seem like she wanted to talk about Doug at all.

"What's the matter?" I asked. "I thought you liked Doug. You flirted with him. I thought you really liked him."

"He's okay," Carleen said.

"He's more than okay. He's the coolest guy I've ever met. Nobody around here is nearly as cool."

"Why don't you marry him if you love him so much?"

"I never said I love him! Besides, boys can't marry boys, and I wouldn't want to marry one even if I could."

"Boys can so marry boys. There's this place in Florida where they do it."

"You're making it up." I didn't know whether to believe her. How could there be someplace in Florida where boys could marry boys?

"I am not making it up. Remember my twin second cousins twice removed, Charlene and Marlene? Well, Marlene went off to junior college to get a degree in X-rays, and she came back a lesbian." She paused to let the dramatic news sink in.

"I'm not real sure what a lesbian is," I said.

"You're such a space cadet! A lesbian is a homosexual woman. It's a woman who likes girls, or licks girls, as my cousin Charlie says." Carleen laughed at her joke.

I didn't quite get it but was still grossed out. "By 'like' do you mean love? Like they want to be girlfriend and girlfriend?"

"Of course, it's what I mean," said Carleen.

"But not love like men and women are in love, right? It's what Youth Minister Rick told us. He said it's a mental illness for a boy to like a boy or a girl to like a girl in that way."

"Momma says the same thing about Marlene, but I don't know. I think lesbians wish they were men."

I thought about it for a minute. Was that it? Was a homosexual really just a boy who wanted to be a girl and a girl who wanted to be a boy? I didn't want to be a girl. I liked being a boy just fine, so maybe I wasn't a homosexual after all. Maybe I was normal. I felt relieved.

"Carleen? What do they do? How do girls, you know, do it?" I only vaguely knew how boys and girls did it; I had no idea how two girls could do it. It seemed impossible. I figured whatever I heard would be disgusting and probably involve licking, but I couldn't stop myself from asking.

"Oh, I know this," Carleen said confidently. "Cousin Charlie explained it all to me. He said they use dildos. They have these belts they wrap around their waists, and they have a special hole right in front where they put the dildo. That way a woman can walk around swinging it like a man. That's what Charlie said."

I was completely confused. "They use what? I thought a dildo was like a dummy. A dodo."

"No, lame brain. Don't you know anything?" She sighed with exasperation. "A dildo is a fake penis. A fake dick! Lesbians wear fake dicks!"

I was so horrified I almost dropped the phone. Where did Carleen learn all this stuff? Did some women really like to walk around with fake dicks hanging from them? How far did they hang? How did they fit them into their panties? I had so many questions, but I did not want to ask any more.

"Are you still there?" asked Carleen.

"Okay, so Marlene went to junior college and came back a lesbian. What does that have to do with Florida?"

"Well. When she came back with her degree in X-rays, she got a job at the medical school over in Augusta. She lived with her momma and commuted for a while, but then she moved into an apartment in Augusta with this woman named Della. Della is a doctor and played softball for the Georgia Bulldogs. Anyway, Marlene's momma told my momma, and Momma told me that Marlene and Della went to Florida and got married. They exchanged rings and everything. There's this place down there where they can do it."

"Where in Florida is it?"

"It's a secret. You just have to know. It's not like you can look it up in the phone book."

"I've only been to Florida once. It was when Momma and Aunt Melanie and I went to Pensacola. I didn't see any signs for any kind of homosexual marriage place."

"They don't advertise it. They have to keep it secret. You have to be one to know about it. It's like a secret club. All the homosexuals know each other, and they spread the word." Just then, I could hear Carleen's mother in the background calling her to dinner, and we hung up.

My mind raced. Was there really a place where homosexual men could marry other homosexual men?

Then, they could come back to South Carolina and live among us! Everybody would think they were just roommates, but they would really be real-life married men! I couldn't stop thinking about it.

Momma wondered why I was so quiet at dinner, but of course I couldn't tell her. I'd upset her enough for one day. I just said I had a lot of homework to do, so after dinner I went back to my room. I even skipped *Battlestar Galactica*, which I never missed because I really liked Captain Apollo. It would be impossible to concentrate on it tonight since my brain was so full of images of homosexuals getting married in Florida.

I didn't have any more homework to do, so I tried to distract myself by working on my designs. I found myself sketching wedding dresses and men's tuxedos. What would two homosexual men wear to a wedding in Florida? Would one of them wear a wedding dress? Would he be the wife? What did it mean to be the wife? Did one guy in a homosexual couple have to wear women's clothes?

I decided it probably wasn't true, and they both wore tuxedos, but really nice ones. I drew a picture of two men in formal wear, and then I tore it up into tiny pieces and threw it away. I put the scraps in two different trash cans because I didn't want anyone to put it back together and get the idea that I was a homosexual who wanted to go to Florida and get married to a man. It would be a sin. Pastor Earl Don talked about that kind of sin a lot, so I knew it was a real bad sin.

I lay on my bed and tried to think about something else. Images of Doug in formal wear floated in my head as I drifted off to sleep. And I had the most vivid dream. It was unforgettable.

I was on the beach in Miami, standing in the edge of the surf. The waves were pounding and crashing almost like there was a hurricane, but the sun was shining. I had on a white dinner jacket, black tie, and black pants rolled up to my calves. I was barefoot. Then, Claudia Turner, the most beautiful former Miss South Carolina ever, appeared and started singing "Once Upon a Time," just like she did at Miss America when she was First Runner-Up. It was such a pretty song. So romantic. A dozen beautiful ladies in tasteful, one-shoulder Grecian gowns from Halston's 1976 collection accompanied her on harps.

I became aware that Doug was walking across the sand, toward me. He was in a tuxedo shirt but no jacket. His pants were rolled up like mine, and his tie was undone, as were several buttons on his shirt. His shirt billowed in the ocean breeze, and his hair was windswept. He walked up to me and took my hands. Our eyes locked. Bert Parks appeared with a Bible in his hands to perform the ceremony. "I now pronounce you man and man," said Bert Parks. "You may kiss your husband."

Just before our lips met, I sat up in bed, covered in sweat. It was the second time I'd crossed the line imagining me kissing Doug. There was a swelling in my pj's, and I was scared. I got out of bed and on my knees.

"Precious Lord Jesus, this is Timmy again. I thought you were going to help me? I really need you to cleanse me of these sinful thoughts. You know I just want to be a normal boy, but I can't do it alone. Please help me. Now would be a good time. In Jesus's name we pray, amen."

# Thirteen: The Sin of Sodom

MOMMA WAS TRUE to her word and pulled up in front of Doug's house at exactly nine thirty Sunday morning. Before we could get out of the car, Doug came out in a blue button-down shirt, khakis, a blue blazer, and a burgundy tie. I'd never seen him dress in such grown-up clothes before, and I thought he looked real good.

He got into the car and said, "Hello, Mrs. Thompson." He sat next to me, and I tried not to stare at him. Momma asked him questions, and he told us his mother borrowed the outfit from her cousin the night before because they didn't really have church clothes. His mother even put some sort of stuff on his hair to slick it down. It made me think of a cover model on that men's magazine they had at the drugstore, *GQ*. I wondered if I could find some stuff like that to put on my hair.

We arrived at church in time for Momma to take her usual parking place. Our church looked like a lot of First Baptists—red brick with big white columns. Mrs. Morgan called it Greek Revival in Good Citizenship class when she was talking about the significant buildings of South Carolina.

When I walked into church with Momma and Doug, all eyes were on us. Everybody likes a newcomer, and I'm proud to say we got the catch of the year. I spotted Kimberly Ann sitting with her parents. She just about stared a hole through me. Jimbo was there too, sitting away from his parents with some boys from school. He was fidgeting with his tie, but he saw us; I guarantee it.

We sat, and Doug leaned over to me and whispered, "Shouldn't there be some crosses or statues or something?"

"Of course not," I whispered back. "Baptists don't worship graven images." The only thing hanging on the wall of the sanctuary at First Baptist was a big, old-fashioned clock with a hanging pendulum, swinging back and forth, ticking and tocking. It was on the back wall opposite the pulpit within eyesight of the preacher.

The organist started playing, the choir stood, and we all began singing a good old Baptist blood medley—"Nothing But the Blood, Saved by the Blood of the Crucified One," and of course, "There is a Fountain Filled with Blood." Doug had a funny expression on his face, and he didn't exactly sing out. I noticed the youth minister, Mr. Rick, wasn't there. That was strange. Maybe he was on vacation or something.

It was obvious Doug had never been to church. He didn't have any idea what to do. He didn't know the hymns or anything. I was glad I was there to show him the way. When it came time for the sermon, our pastor stood and stepped to the pulpit.

Pastor Earl Don Busbee had been called to First Baptist seven years ago, and everybody just loved him. He wore a white three-piece suit, with matching loafers and belt. I was surprised that a man of his stature didn't know better than not to wear white after Labor Day, but it was his signature look. He also buttoned every button on his vest even though *GQ* said a gentleman always leaves the bottom button unfastened. I made a mental note to tell him if I ever had the chance. It might relieve a little pressure on his stomach.

His message was on the sin of Sodom, or as he called it, "A Lot of Trouble." Everybody laughed except Doug, who didn't get it. Anyway, Pastor Earl Don's sermon went on and on, longer than usual. He really got wrapped up in it. The clock was ticking and tocking, and the pendulum was swinging, but he didn't seem to notice it. He started talking about stuff he didn't usually talk about—embarrassing stuff. Sex stuff. He talked about sexual promiscuity and homosexuality, which he said always followed promiscuity. It started to make me real uncomfortable. He talked about the wickedness of Sodom:

"*The cry* of the abomination of the Sodomites was *great before the face of the Lord*!

"There is no more horrible sin than the *Sin of Sodom.*

"Beware! *Do not mock the Lord!*"

At that point, Pastor Earl Don took out his handkerchief and wiped his brow.

"Lot's wife wanted one last look, and why? Because of lust! Her heart was filled with *lust*! And the Lord in his righteousness turned her into a *pillar of salt*!"

He wiped the back of his neck.

"*Do not mock the Lord*! Beware the sin of *Sodom*!

"Beware the sin of *sexual perversion! Awesome is the wrath of God!*"

As Pastor Earl Don went on and on, I sank into my pew. Pastor Earl Don's words were like a stake in my heart. It was like he, and not Jesus, had heard my prayers about being a normal boy.

I turned and looked at Doug beside me. He was staring straight ahead. I couldn't tell if he was paying attention or not. I thought of last night's dream and was filled with desire and fear. I was certain there was something inside me that was bad and might turn me into a pillar of salt if I wasn't careful. It occurred to me that I should stay away from Doug since he was in all my sinful dreams lately, but I didn't want to. I didn't think I could. It wasn't his fault I had these thoughts, and besides, he was the first boy ever who was my real friend. He was the first boy who liked me and wanted to hang out with me. I would just have to keep praying harder and figure out a way to be Doug's friend and live a Christian life.

When Pastor Earl Don was finished, he was just about to sweat through his three-piece suit. He wiped the front and back of his neck and stuffed his wet handkerchief back in his pocket. That grossed me out. I looked back at the clock. It was already eleven, and we hadn't even gotten to the altar call! First Baptist services never ran over! I looked out the window and saw the Methodists starting to leave. They were definitely going to beat the Baptists to the Sunday buffet at the country club.

As the ushers hurried with the collection plates, Pastor Earl Don quickly ran through some announcements including the next meeting of the Ladies' Missionary Society and the need for chaperones at the upcoming youth lock-in. Then he paused, cleared his throat, and said that Mr. Rick had submitted his resignation effective immediately and had left the church and the town. What a shock! Everybody liked him so much. Pastor Earl Don didn't explain why and said the search for a replacement would begin as soon as possible. I hated to hear it because the youth group had been so great since Mr. Rick had come last year. I figured he must have found a great new opportunity someplace else and had to grab it fast.

The altar call began when Miss Hortense led the choir in "Just as I Am." They sang for a while, and I thought maybe nobody would come down for an altar call that Sunday since we were running late and there were probably ten or twelve pot roasts in danger of burning.

But, you'll never guess who came down at the prime moment. Kimberly Ann Mingees. What was she doing? She had already rededicated herself to Christ at least five times since she got saved and baptized not even two years ago. But, come down she did, and Pastor Earl Don gave her a big hug.

The choir finished the hymn, and he spoke: "I am so inspired by the dedication to Christ displayed by our very own Kimberly Ann Mingees. She is rededicating herself to Christ today and has something to say. Go ahead, Kimberly Ann."

He handed her the mike, and she took it like a pro. "Thank you, Pastor Earl Don. I am rededicating myself to Christ today because I have a new friend who I fear is in danger of falling into the Lake of Fire because he doesn't know Jesus."

There was a gasp across the congregation. I thought I heard Doug grunt.

Kimberly Ann continued, "He doesn't know Jesus, and yet he goes to Patriot Christian Academy." More gasps. "So, I am rededicating myself to Christ today so I can lead this lost lamb to salvation. I am the vessel of Jesus. Praise!" Everybody in the congregation joined her in "Praise!"

After church, when everybody was visiting on the lawn out front, Kimberly Ann made a beeline to me and Momma and Doug.

"Hello, Mrs. Thompson. So nice to see you bringing visitors to the church."

"Why thank you, Kimberly Ann," said Momma. "Don't you look pretty as usual. What a pretty dress."

By now, Kimberly Ann's parents had walked up. Her daddy, Thomas Mingees, was a doctor and, I had to admit, handsome. Aunt Melanie always said Dr. Mingees was a good-looking man. He had broad shoulders and narrow hips, and I heard he had a bench press in his garage. I looked at his firm chest and decided it must be true. Kimberly Ann's mother, Doris Mingees, always wore expensive clothes, and she had a cute and trendy Dorothy Hamill hair cut. She was blonde like Kimberly. I heard she went all the way to Columbia to have her hair done.

"JoAnne Ashburn, how are you?" asked Dr. Mingees, using Momma's maiden name for some reason. He took her hand. "You look lovely as always."

"Yes, doesn't she," said Mrs. Mingees in a tight voice. "What a pretty dress. Didn't I see it in Belk's window last year?"

"Why, I bet you did," said Momma. "I got it at the end-of-season sale. They have such great sales at Belk's. I didn't realize you shopped there."

"I don't," said Mrs. Mingees firmly, with a look on her face like something smelled bad.

"That certainly is a pretty dress you're wearing," said Momma. "I feel sure I saw the pattern at the fabric shop. Is it Simplicity? Did you make it yourself?"

Mrs. Mingees fixed momma with an icy stare. "I buy all of my clothes at Tapp's in Columbia. We've been trading there for years. They know my taste."

"All this talk of shopping is over my head," said Dr. Mingees. "Why don't you introduce me to these two fine young men? This can't be your son, Timmy, can it? He's so grown-up." Dr. Mingees took my hand in such a firm grip it hurt. I tried my best to grip hard back.

"And this is Doug Appleby who I told you about," said Kimberly Ann.

"Well, of course, Annette's boy," said Dr. Thompson. "Another fine young man." They shook hands.

"JoAnne, I didn't realize you and Annette were such close friends," said Mrs. Mingees.

"Annette and I were in the same grade all the way through school, so when I heard she had moved back to town, I just had to go pay a call. Timmy and I dropped by yesterday with some of my Sold My Soul to the Deviled Eggs. They live in the cutest house. I just love what Annette's done with it. All sorts of Mexican things. It's downright exotic."

"Now that you two have moved from fashion to home decorating, I think I need to leave you to it and go have a word with Pastor Earl Don," said Dr. Mingees. "JoAnne, I come over to the courthouse at least once a week to have lunch with Judge Hampton. Why don't you join us someday?"

"I'd love to," said Momma.

"Great," said Dr. Mingees. "You all have a blessed Sunday."

He started to leave, and Mrs. Mingees grabbed his hand in a vice grip. "I'll go along with you, honey. I don't need to talk fashion with JoAnne. Come along, Kimberly Ann."

"I'll be there soon, Mom," said Kimberly Ann. "I want to have a word with Doug."

Momma saw somebody else she knew and wandered off to chat, leaving the three of us alone.

Kimberly Ann took Doug's hand, right in front of everybody. "Douglas."

"Douglas? You can call me Doug."

"Oh no, this is a serious conversation, and I believe I should use your Christian name."

"Let me guess. I'm the sinner you were talking about up there when you were—what do you call it?—redecorating your life?"

"Rededicating my life, and, yes. It's true." Kimberly Ann flipped her hair behind her shoulders and looked Doug in the eye. "I've lifted your mortal soul up to the Lord in prayer every night since we met. I've heard His voice, and I know He put me here on Earth to save you so you can have a personal relationship with Jesus Christ."

"If you're hearing voices, you might want to see a doctor about it," said Doug, pulling his hand away. I laughed, and Kimberly Ann glared at me.

"Why are you here?" she said to me. "Can't you see Douglas and I are having a private conversation?"

"He's here because he's my friend," said Doug. "I don't like people who are rude to my friends. I didn't ask you to come over here and save my soul. My soul is doing just fine on its own."

Kimberly Ann was shocked. She looked from Doug to me and then checked to see if anyone else was within earshot. She took a deep breath. "That's just Satan talking. I know it. I know you lied about your sister. I know you never had a sister in the first place. Your aunt Linda's told everybody at the salon about your lies. God only knows why you would fib so, but I declare here and now that I forgive you, and, more importantly, God forgives you. I would like to formally invite you to come with me to Royal Ambassadors. They meet every Sunday evening in the fellowship hall here at First Baptist. Daddy always takes me, and we can pick you up. That way, you could ride in Daddy's new Cadillac. Wouldn't that be fun? I want you to experience the joy of knowing Jesus and leaving your sinful lifestyle."

"Not interested," said Doug. "You don't know anything about my lifestyle, and if you think the road to heaven was made for Cadillacs, then you're the one whose soul needs work."

Kimberly Ann turned white as a sheet. "Why... why...why, how dare you."

"Besides, Tim and I have plans."

"Plans? With Timmy? You're turning me down for Timmy Thompson? Did I hear you right?" Kimberly Ann's eyes went wide.

"You heard me," said Doug. "I'm not your pet project, and I'm not looking to get saved from anything."

Her jaw practically dropped to the ground. She stalked off in the direction of her parents without another word. I was stunned.

"Why don't you come over and listen to records tonight?" said Doug. "I said we had plans, and I wouldn't want to get caught lying to a good Christian like Kimberly Ann."

I looked beyond Doug and saw Kimberly Ann with the Anns, talking and pointing back toward us. This couldn't be good.

"Doug, I don't think anybody's ever told off Kimberly Ann like that ever."

"Then it was about time. She had it coming."

"Yeah, but..."

"But what? Are you coming over tonight or not?"

"Sure, I'd love to." I was trying to act cool, but I really wanted to squeal with delight. "But it's a school night, so Momma might not let me."

"Here she comes. I'll ask her."

"No, wait till we get to the country club and she gets something to eat."

Momma walked up and smiled at us. "Did you boys have a nice chat with Kimberly Ann? Isn't she a pretty girl? And so clever, don't you think? Don't get too many ideas, Mr. Douglas, because I think she's got eyes for Timmy here. Don't you think so, Timmy?" Doug stifled a laugh with a cough.

"Momma, I thought Kimberly Ann was dating a senator's son," I said.

"Oh no, it was just a summer fling. Dr. Mingees has assured me they weren't serious at all."

"Well, it makes it perfect, doesn't it, Tim?" said Doug as he put his hand on my shoulder. I laughed, delighted at our little secret that we kept from Momma.

# Fourteen: The Winner Takes It All

AFTER CHURCH, MOMMA took Doug and me to the Sunday buffet at the Crestview Country Club. We weren't members, of course, but my granddaddy had been one of the founders, so Momma had an open invitation from Floyd, the club manager, to come for the Sunday buffet anytime she wanted. She'd never taken him up on his offer before, but that Sunday was special because Doug was with us.

As we were being seated, I looked around for the Mingees family and was relieved they weren't there. But just as we were getting in line at the buffet, in walked Dr. and Mrs. Mingees and Kimberly Ann. I wanted to hide, but Momma waved and called out, "Hey!"

Dr. Mingees made a beeline with the others trailing him. "Well, isn't this my lucky day, running into pretty JoAnne Ashburn twice in one day."

"Why, JoAnne, what a surprise to see you here," said Mrs. Mingees. "I thought guests had to be escorted."

Dr. Mingees scowled at his wife.

"What? I'm just saying I'm on the membership committee, and I would know if JoAnne had applied for membership, that's all."

"Oh, I hope I'm not intruding," said Momma. "Floyd said we could come for Sunday dinner any time, and I don't think I've been here since my daddy passed."

"You're welcome anytime," said Dr. Mingees. "Your daddy founded this place, and I, for one, would enjoy seeing your pretty face anytime. If anyone ever asks, you just tell them you're my guest." He looked at Doug. "Good to see you again, young man. You be sure and get a big helping of macaroni and cheese. You can't get anything like that in California."

"That's for sure," said Doug. "Oh, and hey, great Cadillac."

Kimberly Ann glared at both of us like daggers were going to fly out of her eyes.

"Thank you, young man. I'd be happy to give you a ride sometime, just let me know."

"That would be heavenly," said Doug.

Dr. Mingees looked confused for a moment and then smiled. Kimberly Ann steamed. Doug was so brave! It was exciting to be around him!

As the Mingees were about to leave, Momma said, "Kimberly Ann, you sure do look pretty today. I just love your dress."

"Thank you, ma'am; it's from Tapp's."

"Yes, dear, I'm sure it is. Timmy, honey, don't you think Kimberly Ann looks pretty today?"

Kimberly Ann narrowed her eyes at me, as if daring me to speak. No words came.

"She looks like a regular angel," said Doug.

"Come, dear," said Mrs. Mingees as she grabbed her daughter by the arm. "Let's sit outside on the terrace today. It's so crowded in here. Anybody can get in Crestview these days." And they were gone.

"What was all that about?" Doug asked.

Momma looked up at Doug. "Whatever are you talking about?"

"Kimberly Ann's mother was a real bitch."

"Douglas!" Momma looked shocked but smiled just a touch. "What would your mother think?"

"She'd agree."

"Well, just this once, I'll let you get away with it, but you need to keep a civil tongue in your mouth, young man. This is the Lord's day, after all."

At the buffet, I grabbed an extra piece of fried chicken and piled another spoonful of macaroni and cheese on my plate. I expected Momma to say something, but she just smiled and encouraged Doug to put more on his plate. All he had was green beans, black-eyed peas, spinach, and rice.

"Goodness gracious, Doug, you're a growing boy. You need to eat more than beans and peas. Besides, Dr. Mingees was right, Crestview's Sunday macaroni and cheese is the best. There's an old colored lady named Ethleen who makes it. She does it all at home, and you can only get it on Sundays. I don't know how she makes so much in her little kitchen, but there always seems to be plenty. It's like the miracle of the loaves and fishes; I swear it is. My daddy hired her on as a cook when he first opened this club all those years ago. She retired a few years back, but everybody insisted she keep making her macaroni and cheese, so she does."

We took our plates to a table near the terrace doors, and Momma stirred her tea and looked toward the Mingees's table. Doris Mingees was turned around in her chair, running her mouth to the woman at the next table.

"Doris and I have been dear friends for years," said Momma. "We've known each other since forever. I suppose she has her moods, but, really, she's just a delight, and did you see how pretty little Kimberly Ann is smitten with our Timmy?"

She beamed at the both of us. Doug kicked me under the table. He took a bite of the macaroni and cheese. His face lit up. "Hey, this really is good."

"What'd I tell you? We'll make a Southern boy out of you yet," said Momma.

Doug laughed. "If anybody can do it, you can, Mrs. Thompson."

"Why, Doug, you flatterer. Aren't you just the cutest thing."

"Hey, Momma," I said, seizing the moment. "Is it all right if I go over to Doug's and listen to records tonight?"

"Well, I guess so—even though it's a school night—if Doug's mother thinks so. Did she invite you, Timmy?"

"Well..."

"It's fine, Mrs. Thompson," said Doug. "Mom told me to invite him. He can come for dinner, too."

"We're eating dinner right now, honey," said Momma. "The evening meal is called 'supper' in the South. That's especially true on Sunday when we eat a big meal in the middle of the day and a smaller meal later on." She smiled at Doug indulgently and then turned to me. "Timmy dear, it's all right with me if that's what you want to do and Doug's mother invites you. But you know you'll be missing breakfast for dinner like we do every Sunday. I was going to do pancakes and sausage tonight."

I swallowed hard. I loved breakfast for dinner night, but there was no way I was going to miss an opportunity to be alone with Doug. Plus, Doug had told Kimberly Ann I was coming over, so I had to.

"I know, Momma. I'm sorry to miss it. Thank you for letting me go. Maybe you can ask Aunt Melanie to come over for pancakes with you."

"Don't worry about me; you just go have fun. Now eat up, you two."

"I don't want to eat too much, Mrs. Thompson, because Mom's making my favorite tonight," Doug said.

"Your favorite? What's that, dear?"

"Tofu and asparagus stir-fry."

Momma's fork hit her plate with a clank.

"What fu?" asked Momma.

"Tofu. You know, soybean curd."

"Oh, Doug, you card. You're pulling my leg. Isn't he funny, Timmy? Soybean curd. Whoever heard of such a thing? It sounds like something they feed pigs in Japan." She laughed at her humor.

"I'm not pulling your leg, Mrs. Thompson. Tofu is made from coagulated soy milk, and then it's used in a million different ways. It's kind of a basic for vegetarians."

"Honey, you can't tell me your mother is serving you coagulated anything."

"You're a vegetarian?" I asked.

"Of course he's not," said Momma, looking doubtfully at his meatless plate. "He's a good Christian boy."

"I'm not really a vegetarian," said Doug. "I'm close, though. Mom and I don't have meat every night, and when we do, it's usually fish."

"Well then, I insist you go back to the buffet, young man, and get yourself a nice big piece of fried chicken and maybe some steamship round."

"No, thank you. I'm fine with what I have."

"Now, Doug Appleby, you do as you're told. A boy needs meat. Go on, now. March."

Doug actually did it. I don't think he'd ever experienced Momma in her march mode before.

LATER AT HOME, Momma told me I didn't really have to go to Doug's if I didn't want to. "I think that boy's telling tall tales again, but just in case this tofu stuff is real, you don't have to eat coagulated bean curd just to be polite. God will understand."

"Of course I want to go, Momma. We're gonna listen to records. Please let me."

"I didn't say you couldn't go. Of course you can."

"Besides, I really think Doug was joking at dinner today. Nobody really eats gross stuff like that."

"Of course not. But maybe I should make you a sandwich first."

I agreed, just to be on the safe side. One ham sandwich later, Momma dropped me off at Doug's. Doug's momma let me in and waved at Momma as she drove off.

"Dinner will be ready in a few, so you boys get washed up. We're having a tofu and asparagus stir-fry, Doug's favorite."

Ugh, it was really happening. I was going to face a plate of coagulated bean curd. For a second, I wondered if I could catch Momma and go home for pancakes, but then Doug smiled at me and nudged my arm. "Don't worry— you'll like it. Mom's a great cook. Besides, it's super good for you. Come on, let's wash our hands."

I relaxed and realized she'd said stir-*fried*. If it was fried, it couldn't be all bad.

It turned out that "stir-fry" didn't mean fried like anything I'd ever had before. I was pretty sure there was no Crisco involved at all. I watched as Doug's momma dropped chopped asparagus into this large, round pan that kind of looked like a big bowl.

"It's called a wok," she said. "Have you never seen one before?"

"No, ma'am."

"It's the most common cooking implement in the world. A billion people in China use one every day. See how the shape allows the heat to be evenly distributed? It's a brilliant way to cook."

It was cooked really fast, and we sat down to plates heaped with sticky rice. She served us each a mixture of asparagus and onions and peppers and stuff that must have been tofu on top of the rice. I had learned to like, or at least appreciate, asparagus since Aunt Melanie told me they were elegant and Jackie Kennedy Onassis's favorite. The tofu was weird, though. Kinda squishy and soft, like really thick Jell-O. I ate it because it was the polite thing to do, and, besides, I was hungry. Doug's Momma passed me a bottle of soy sauce and said I might like it. I ended up using a lot of it. It was the best part of the dish. I told Doug's momma I enjoyed it, just like Momma taught me.

"Where did you find tofu in Edgewood, Mrs. Herlong? I've never seen it at the Bi-Rite."

"I have a friend in LA who packs it in dry ice and ships it to me. Costs a fortune, but what can you do? I can't imagine cooking without it. It's so versatile. It's the only way I know to get it until I can find a proper Chinese market in this part of the country."

"Good luck with that," said Doug, and they both laughed. I felt a little insulted.

"How was church today, boys?" asked Doug's momma.

"It was fine," I said.

"It was crazy," said Doug. "The preacher talked all about the sin of Sodom. He got all worked up and started sweating. I thought he was going to pop his cork."

Doug's momma rolled her eyes. "I heard what happened to the youth minister, so I guess I'm not surprised that was the topic of the sermon today."

"What happened to him?" I asked.

She paused and played with a piece of asparagus on her plate.

"He was fired."

"Fired? But why?"

"It doesn't matter. Whatever the reason, he's gone."

"Mom, you're hiding something," said Doug.

"Finish your dinner."

"Mom. Total honesty, remember? It's a two-way street? We talked about this on the long drive cross country."

I'd never heard anybody talk to his mother in such a grown-up way. It seemed weird. My mother would have thought I'd lost my mind if I suddenly started talking to her like an adult.

"You're right, son. Okay, here goes. The youth minister was fired for...for..." She looked up at the ceiling and took a deep breath. "Your mother will kill me for saying this, Timmy, but I don't believe in shielding children from reality." She looked straight at me. "The youth minister was a homosexual man. A gay. That's why he was fired."

I stared back at her, my heart thumping in my chest.

"He was, is, a white homosexual man who was seeing a black homosexual man—in secret, of course—but someone saw them together and tattled to the preacher. The preacher called him in for a meeting, and, to his credit, he told the truth. He said it was all true, and he was in love. With a man."

"How do you know all this?" asked Doug.

"Cousin Linda cut my hair this afternoon. She knows everything that goes on in this town."

"So he really told the preacher he was in love with a man? A black man?" Doug asked.

"The preacher's secretary was listening at the keyhole. She and Linda are thick as thieves. He was fired on the spot and advised to get out of town immediately. I understand he and his lover were seen packing up the car and heading toward I-20 before sunset."

"Where'd they go?" asked Doug.

"Far away from here if they're smart. I don't know. Maybe Atlanta. I've heard it's become quite the hub of gay life."

"So, they were sinners," I said, trying to process it all. I mean, I knew we were all sinners, but he was a youth minister engaging in homosexual acts, so it was kind of an extra serious sin.

"I did not say they were sinners," said Doug's momma.

"But Youth Minister Rick told the youth group a bunch of times that homosexual acts are a sin, and we should never even think about doing them." As I said this, I realized I'd been thinking about committing homosexual acts with Doug pretty much all the time. I wasn't really sure what homosexual acts were, so my fantasies were kind of vague, but they were still powerful.

"If they were guilty of anything, it was love, and love is not a sin. I don't pretend to understand homosexuality, and it can surely be a shock to discover someone close to you is gay." She and Doug exchanged looks. "But it still comes down to love, and love can never be a sin, or at least that's how I see it."

"But it's why God destroyed Sodom," I said. "Men were lying with men."

"That is not true," said Doug's momma, forcefully. "The story of Sodom has been distorted and misused in the name of hate and ignorance. Your mother won't like me saying this either, but you should never listen to that ridiculous Pastor Earl Don. Do you know what the sin of Sodom really was?"

I shook my head, completely confused.

"It was rudeness and lack of hospitality. That's it. The small-minded people of Sodom treated the angels rudely and with violence. It wasn't about gay sex at all."

"How do you know all that?" asked Doug.

"Don't forget that I grew up around here, going to Sunday school at Gilgal Baptist. I've read the Bible cover to cover. Don't look so surprised, son. Just because I don't believe anymore doesn't mean I forgot everything I ever learned about the Bible."

I was struggling to make sense of everything. "But Pastor Earl Don has preached on Sodom before. A lot, actually. It's one of his favorite topics. He wouldn't mislead us, would he?"

"I don't know what's in his heart. I'll tell you what, Timmy. You read the story of Sodom yourself, and do it with a completely open mind. Then, decide what it means to you. Don't let people tell you what to think, even pastors in the pulpit." She pushed back from the table. "Thus endeth the lesson for today. Now you boys go back to Doug's room and listen to records. I need to clean up this kitchen."

"Come on," said Doug. "Your mother will be here to pick you up at eight."

When we got to his room, Doug pulled out the latest ABBA album, with the cellophane still on it.

"I saw this at the store the other day and thought you'd like it."

"And how! I've been wanting to hear it. But I didn't think you liked that kind of music."

"I don't usually, but I figure if you like it there must be something to it."

I felt thrilled that a boy who was so perfect cared about my music taste. The album was called *Voulez-Vous*, which was French and the name of one of the songs. I could tell Doug didn't like it. It was kinda dumb, but I liked the beat so much I didn't care.

Suddenly, Doug jumped up, grabbed my hand, and pulled me up. "Dance with me."

I was horrified. Boys didn't dance with boys, and I told him so.

"Bullshit. Let's dance." He pulled me to him and led me in a jitterbug/shag hybrid that made no sense, but nothing really made sense in that moment. He twirled me out and pulled me to him, and I felt my body against his, our hearts beating in unison. Then, he twirled me back out again. It was the most thrilling moment of my life, until the next moment.

The song ended, and Doug plopped onto the bed, pulling me down with him. We lay there next to each other. He never let go of my hand. I didn't move. I could hardly breathe. His hand felt warm and strong. He gently stroked his thumb back and forth, and warmth rushed over my body. The next song started. It was "I Have a Dream," and I thought mine was coming true, lying there with my new best friend. It felt good to have a boy as a friend. I'd never had one before. I felt like we could talk about anything, and I could trust him completely. I felt like I could even talk to him about the one really big issue in my life—the sin of Sodom.

"Do you think your momma's right and the sin of Sodom is just rudeness?"

"I guess. What difference does it make?"

"It makes a ton of difference. If sodomy's not a sin, then Mr. Rick shouldn't have been fired. I can't believe our pastor would preach something that's not true."

"He was grossed out by the thought of his youth minister being into men and doing it with a black guy. Of course he fired him."

"He had to feel like the Bible compelled him."

Doug rolled his eyes. "The Bible gave him an excuse, just like Mom said."

"Pastor Earl Don has been the minister at First Baptist for years. Everybody loves him. When my grandmommy died, he was so good to us. He's Bible based. I just can't believe he'd take action that wasn't biblically correct."

"Think about it, Tim. He was sitting across his desk from a gay man who'd been with a black man. He broke every rule in this town. The preacher had to fire him; he just needed to find a reason for it in the Bible. Hey! I'll fire him for the sin of Sodom and he'll go away and we can all forget it ever happened."

"I don't know. Hey, where's your Bible? Let's read about Sodom ourselves and figure it out."

"I don't have a Bible." Doug chuckled. "Don't have a gun, either."

"What does that mean? Whatever. Why don't you go get your mother's then?"

"We don't have a Bible in the house. You'll have to wait till you get home to read one."

The song ended, and Doug jumped up and restarted it. "That song's pretty good—don't you think? It's about something." He sat right next to me. "It's really emotional—do you feel it?" He took my hand and put it on his chest.

"I feel it." I didn't want to move my hand. Ever.

We sat on the bed and listened to the rest of the album with Doug telling me what he thought about the songs and me agreeing. How could I not agree with someone so smart and full of insight? When he looked at me with those Sprite-bottle eyes, I was ready to believe anything he said.

I wondered if Doug and his momma could really be right about Pastor Earl Don. If the sin of Sodom didn't have anything to do with men lying with men, then what did that mean for me? When I sat through those sermons on Sodom, I always knew deep down the pastor was preaching directly to me. Of course, I'd never lain with a man, and until tonight, I'd felt sure it was a serious sin to even think about it. Could it really be possible the pastor was wrong and what I was feeling wasn't sinful? I looked at Doug and wanted to believe it with all my heart.

MOMMA PICKED ME up right at eight, just like she said she would.

"You seem quiet tonight, honey," she said as we were driving home. "Everything all right?"

"Sure, Momma. I'm just tired, I guess." I wasn't tired at all. I couldn't wait to get home and find my Bible.

"I've got some cake for you when we get home. You didn't fill up on awful tofu, did you?"

"Actually, it wasn't that bad. I put lots of soy sauce on it, so it was nice and salty. Think I'll just go to bed."

Momma put her hand on my forehead. "You don't have a fever. Are you sure you're feeling all right? You're passing on cake. Did you and Doug have a fight or something?"

"Oh no, nothing like that. We had a great time listening to records. I always have a great time with Doug. I'm just tired. I'm really not hungry."

I took my King James Bible to bed and opened it up to Genesis 18 and 19 and read the whole story twice. I'd never actually read it before. I knew I should read the Bible cover to cover, and I'd tried several times, but the King James Version was so hard to understand. There were other versions, but the King James was the one we read in church, so it was the official one. I always got bored about the time I got to the begats and put it aside.

It turned out the Sodom story was really weird and confusing. These two angels came to earth to visit Sodom and Gomorrah. They took the appearance of men, and Lot, one of the few righteous men in town, invited them to his house to spend the night. So far, so good. Then, the men of the town all went to Lot's house and demanded the two strangers be brought out to them so that they might "know" them. What the heck? Why were they so upset, and what was the big deal about wanting to "know" them? What did they want to know?

I kept reading.

Lot pleaded with the men of the town not to act "wickedly," so I guessed he knew they wanted to do bad things to the angels. Did that mean bad sex things? Must have been, otherwise, why would Pastor Earl Don get so upset about it?

Then it got seriously gross. Lot refused to let the angels out, and, instead, he offered up his two virgin daughters to the crowd. Why would he do that? It seemed way worse than the crowd wanting to "know" the angels.

I sat back against my pillows and thought about it. What was so bad that it would make Lot offer to turn over his daughters? Maybe the crowd wanted to force bad sex things on the angels? But that would be rape, not just sex. Of course, rape was wrong. Could a man be raped by other men? Whoa. I'd never thought about that before.

I needed to keep reading. I flipped over to Ezekiel 16. Verses 49 and 50 were real eye openers:

*Behold, this was the guilt of your sister Sodom: she and her daughters had arrogance, abundant food, and careless ease, but she did not help the poor and needy. Thus, they were haughty and committed abominations before me. Therefore, I removed them.*

I lay down and considered what I'd just read. Maybe Doug's momma was right, or at least partly right. The story was about rudeness and inhospitality, sure, but it was about a lot more. Mainly, it was about violence. The people of Sodom and Gomorrah didn't help the needy, which was bad, but a ton of people were guilty of that. They wanted to rape those poor angels. That was a way bigger sin than not helping poor people. Was the sin of Sodom really rape and violence? That seemed serious enough for God to destroy the city.

But what did any of it have to do with me and Doug? When I dreamed about him, it was all so sweet and nice. When I spent time with him, he made me feel warm inside. None of it seemed to have anything to do with the awful, violent men of Sodom. I just wanted Doug to kiss me and hold me. Would God have destroyed Sodom and Gomorrah if the crowd of men told Lot to send out the angels so they could kiss and hold them? I didn't think so.

Maybe Doug's momma was right when she said homosexuality was really about love, and love was never a sin. Maybe Mr. Rick and the black guy were in love? If so, I hoped they'd made it to Atlanta where there were probably other guys like them. Maybe they could even go to Florida and get married like Carleen's cousin.

Plus, Lot wasn't so righteous. Offering up his virgin daughters? That seemed like a super serious sin. And then God turned his wife into a pillar of salt, whatever that was. The story was nuts. What did she do to deserve that? I knelt to pray before turning off the light.

"Dear Lord Jesus, thank you for the tofu dinner, and especially for the soy sauce so I could get it down. And thank you for Doug's momma and for the story of Sodom and Gomorrah. I just read it for the first time, but I guess you know that. I don't think it means what Pastor Earl Don keeps telling us it means. I'm not trying to be prideful by thinking I know more than the preacher, but in this case, I just don't see how he gets all the homosexual stuff out of the story of Sodom. I just think it's a stretch. Do you think this means that what I feel inside when I see Doug isn't really bad? Maybe it's not bad at all? You gave me these feelings, so how could they be bad? Right? Did you send Doug's momma to me as a messenger to get me to read the story myself? If so, thanks. And thanks for Doug. He's really sweet, and I really like him. So, anyway, bless Momma and Aunt Melanie and Carleen and Doug's momma and, most especially, bless Doug. Oh yeah, and Daddy. Amen."

I got in bed and turned off the light. I thought about telling Momma about my new ideas about Sodom but decided against it. I didn't think she'd understand.

# Fifteen: I Have Flair

AS I ARRIVED at school the following morning, I was shocked to see Kimberly Ann running toward me. "Wait up! I need to tell you something." She stopped me at the lockers. "Are you excited about the lock-in?"

"Gosh, Kimberly Ann, I've never been before, and I hadn't really planned on it this year."

"But you have to go! It's the biggest event of the year at First Baptist. How can you miss it?"

Christmas or Easter were probably bigger deals at the church than the annual Halloween youth lock-in, but I caught her drift. The thought of being locked into the church social hall all night long with Kimberly Ann, the Anns, Jimbo, and every kid who laughed at the SlimFast bars made my stomach hurt. Besides, the whole point was to keep you up all night! It always sounded awful to me, and Momma never made me go.

"I'm in charge of the planning committee, and this year's lock-in will be the best ever. We're going to have games, lots of important biblical lessons; plus, my parents are donating Chick-fil-A! They're bringing it all the way from Columbia! I know you love Chick-fil-A."

"Who doesn't?" I said. Maybe it wouldn't be that awful to go. I almost never got a chance to eat Chick-fil-A.

"And, we'll get the chance to meet the acting youth minister. Her name is Rachel, I think."

"Aunt Melanie told me they were only looking at females for the new youth minister."

"But wait till you hear the best part. We're taking over the entire Sunday school building for a hell house!"

"What's a hell house?"

"It's like a haunted house, but more biblical. We take away all the ghosts and vampires and stuff because it's all just Satan trying to tempt us. With a hell house, we learn about the wages of sin."

"Will it be like going to hell?"

"It'll be worse. It'll be hell on earth. The theme is the seven deadly sins."

"What are the seven deadly sins?"

"Oh, you know, sloth, gluttony, stuff like that greed, I think."

"What exactly is sloth?"

"Come to the hell house and find out. Oh, come on, say you will."

"Why do you want me to come so bad?"

"Because we're friends; you know that, silly." She put her hand on my forearm as she said it. "We've known each other all our lives, after all. We've always gone to church together. I just don't want you to miss out on a really good time. Besides, you're so creative, maybe you could help on the planning committee."

"You think I'm creative? Gosh, thanks. Momma tells me I have flair."

"You absolutely have flair. You have more flair than any boy in this school. All the other boys know how to do is hunt and fish and punch each other on the arms. You're the only boy I'd want on the planning committee."

I started to think maybe Momma was right about Kimberly Ann and she really was a good Christian girl. Deep down.

"Well, I guess I could be on the planning committee, and if I'm going to do it, then I'll have to go to the lock-in."

"Yay! And bring your new friend Doug along, too. I'm sure he never experienced anything like a lock-in back in California. He'll love it."

"I can ask, but he's not very churchy."

"If you're going, he's sure to go. You're good friends, right? You took him to church and the country club, after all. If anybody can talk him into it, you can."

"I thought you'd be mad at him after the way he talked to you after church."

She lowered her eyes. "Doug is a lost soul who needs to be brought to Christ, I'm sure you'll agree. I'm not mad at anyone. It was all Satan talking, not Doug." She sighed. "Doug's soul is a challenge. It's my fall project. That's why it's so important for you to bring him to the lock-in. Hey, it's time for class. I'm so glad you said yes!" She was off in a flash.

Later that day at the library as Carleen and I were reshelving books, I told her about it.

"Hey, Carleen, what do you think about going to the Halloween lock-in?"

"Why would I want to be locked in all night at First Baptist with everybody I hate? Besides, I don't even go to that church."

"Anybody can go. You don't have to be a member of First Baptist. I guess you have to be a Christian, but that's the only requirement."

"Great! Then I don't have to go. I already told you I don't believe in Jesus anymore."

"Carleen, you really shouldn't say that so loud. It could get you expelled."

"Ha! I should be so lucky."

"Anyway, I know you don't really mean it. You've got to come to the lock-in. I'm on the planning committee. Kimberly Ann asked me today."

"Kimberly Ann asked you? Really? What's her deal?"

"She said I'm creative."

"She wants something."

"Maybe she just recognizes my talent. Did you ever think of that? She said I'm the only boy in school with flair."

"That's one way to put it."

"One way to put what?"

"Nothing."

It wasn't nothing, and it hurt, but I didn't say so. "I'm going to ask Doug. I bet he's never been to anything like it."

"Of course you're asking Doug, and of course he'll say yes." She rolled her eyes.

"What does that mean?"

"Your new best friend. You're always together. I'm surprised you even bother to come to the library with me anymore."

"Carleen, I told you you're still my best friend and always will be."

"Sure. Whatever." She shelved a few books in silence and then suddenly turned to me, her face close to mine. "When was the last time you invited me to church with you and your mother? Huh? Never. When did you invite me to that hoity-toity country club, huh? Never. Cute Doug with the auburn hair you love so much shows up in town and you're totally obsessed with him. You're doing things with him that you've never done with me."

"But we aren't even members of the country club." I realized this answer was dumb even as it was coming out of my mouth.

"But you took Doug there, didn't you." This wasn't a question. "Your mother wouldn't have let you invite me because she thinks I'm white trash."

I didn't have a response because Momma really did kind of think that.

"I knew it. You can't even deny it." Her face was getting red. "The only reason we've ever been friends is because nobody else would talk to the sissy boy or the fat girl."

"Carleen, I don't know why you're being this way. Don't call me a sissy. I'm not a sissy."

"Yes, you are! That's why you're always up Doug's butt."

"Up his what? Gross!"

"Oh, really? I thought boys like you liked it."

"Like what?"

"Like getting it up the butt."

"Carleen, you're being disgusting. And what do you mean by 'boys like me'?"

Carleen rolled her eyes again. "You know exactly what I mean. I'm done with beating around the bush, listening to you tell me how much you like Kate Jackson and you don't notice cute boys. Well, you sure noticed Doug. And you're always with him. You're in love with him—admit it. You want him to screw you up the butt."

"I do not!" I meant it. It sounded disgusting.

"You do so, and you know it, I know it, Kimberly Ann sure knows it. She said you've got flair, remember? She was just being nice. Flair means fag."

I dropped the books I was reshelving, and they hit the floor with a loud thump. Mrs. Ouzts shushed me from across the room. I looked at Carleen, and she looked away. She knew she'd gone too far. I couldn't believe she could be so mean. We'd been best friends since kindergarten.

"Carleen," I whispered. The bell rang. She grabbed her purse and ran out of the library without looking at me.

# Sixteen: Freedom '8o

DOUG MUST HAVE noticed how upset I was the rest of the day because he came up to me after sixth period.

"Hey, buddy, let's go home and change and go bike riding this afternoon."

"Bike riding? But it's a school night, and we have homework. Mrs. Means really loaded us up with algebra. I'll never get through it."

"Sure you will, but first, you need to get out and get some exercise. What do you say?"

"I don't know. I'm not feeling very good." I really just wanted to go to my room, close the door, curl up on the bed, and cry. I didn't want to get emotional in front of Doug.

He grabbed my arm and pulled me over to the crepe myrtles. "Look, I don't know what happened between you and Carleen today, but you obviously had a fight and maybe you want to talk about it or maybe you don't, but what else are you going to do? Sit at home alone, eat Pop-Tarts, then feel guilty about it? Come on; I thought we'd ride out to that Slave Lake everybody talks about. You can tell me all about it. You know you're dying to tell me about local history and what an amazing town Edgewood is."

I laughed for the first time since lunch. "I'll have to ask Momma."

Doug motioned to Momma's Catalina pulling up to the curb. "Speak of the devil, as you people like to say."

He sprinted up to the car, and Momma rolled down the window. "Well, hello there, Doug. Don't you look handsome today." He really did, with the afternoon sun catching the blond highlights in his auburn hair.

"Thanks, Mrs. Thompson. Hey, I was wondering if Timmy and I could go bike riding today. It's a great day—don't you think? He could show me Slave Lake."

"Listen to you with your 'you all,'" said Momma. "Pretty soon, you'll be saying *y'all* like a proper South Carolinian."

He laughed and flashed his perfect white teeth. "It's because Timmy's such a good influence on me. He's teaching me to be a good Southerner."

"Well then, I guess I have to say yes to your bike ride so you can continue your lessons." Momma giggled, and Doug smiled at both of us.

"Thanks, Momma," I said, getting into the car. "Doug, I just need a few minutes to change clothes, and I'll meet you at the corner, okay?"

"Sounds good, buddy."

Doug was already waiting on me by the time I got to the corner. It had taken me longer than I thought it would to figure out what to wear. I finally settled on a pair of plaid shorts from last summer and a T-shirt from last year's church revival. On the front, it said Moved by the Spirit and on the back, First Baptist, '79. It was dark blue and fit loose, so I thought it would work.

We biked to the town limit, which was about five blocks. I figured Doug could go faster than I could, but he stayed right beside me the whole time. I was trying not to sweat and breathe hard, but the hills got me. At the town limit, there was a narrow paved road, which was really just wide enough for one car. It was called Slave Street and cut through some pine woods. After about a quarter mile, the woods gave way and a little lake suddenly appeared. It was Slave Lake. I'd never seen it so pretty. It sparkled in the autumn sun. There was a little breeze that actually had a slight chill to it. It was almost October, but it usually stayed hot around here until Halloween. I welcomed the chill and hoped we'd have an early fall. I looked good in fall colors.

We stopped our bikes. "This is it," I said.

"It's really beautiful. Why do they call it Slave Lake?"

"Because this used to be part of an old plantation called Oak Grove. The slaves built a dam to create this lake to provide water for the plantation. There were slave quarters on the other side of the lake. That's where the name came from."

"Slave quarters. Damn. For real? Are there any remains of them?"

"Maybe. Everything burned down during the war. Kimberly Ann is descended from the plantation owners. She says her family owned more slaves than any family in the upcountry."

"She's descended from slave owners and brags about it? Sounds about right."

"She always says the Yankees burned down the grand plantation house, but they never came through here. They burned Columbia, but we're a hundred miles away in the wrong direction. I think maybe the freed slaves did it."

"It would serve them right. You people sure love to talk about the Civil War. It's like it just happened last week."

"If you'd ever heard my grandmother talk about it, you'd think it was still going on."

We both got off our bikes and walked to the water's edge. Doug picked up a rock and threw it. It skipped across the surface of the lake. I'd never seen anyone actually do that before. It was really impressive. I was sure I was too uncoordinated to do something like that, but Doug could do anything.

"Hey, how'd you do that?"

"It's not so hard. My dad taught me."

"That must have been nice. My dad never taught me anything."

"I could teach you."

"Oh, no, don't bother. I'm sure I couldn't." I didn't want Doug to see me throw like a girl.

"Sure, you can. It's not hard." He picked up another rock—one that was smooth from the water—and showed it to me.

"You find a rock like this one with a flat side to it. Then you just give it a toss like so." He threw it so that it headed over the water on a straight, flat path. When it hit the water, it bounced three times. "You try it."

He helped me find a stone. I planted my feet and did a few practice throws before I threw it for real. It barely made it past the water's edge and plopped right beneath the surface.

"I told you I couldn't do it." I really wanted to stop throwing rocks. I was embarrassed for Doug to see how big a sissy I really was.

"You can do it. You just need a little practice." He handed me another stone, but that time, he stood behind me, reached around, and took my hand. His breath was on my neck, and his chest was pressed against my back. "Throw with this motion." He guided my hand back and forth a few times. "See how it feels?" I'd stopped breathing, and there was no way I could form words to respond.

"Now, throw," he said into my ear.

I did, and it actually worked! It skipped! "I did it! I really did it!"

I jumped up and down, and before I had a chance to think about what I was doing, I grabbed Doug in a big hug. He hugged back. He kept hugging. He pressed the hug tighter. My heart started pounding. He moved his hand up my back and caressed the back of my head.

Suddenly, I heard Carleen's voice in my head. *You're in love with him.* Holy crap, she was right. I was in love with a boy, this boy, but I couldn't be. It wasn't right. It wasn't Christian. God wouldn't do this to me. I pushed him away.

"What's the matter?" Doug asked.

"Nothing. I'm just tired of throwing rocks is all." I started to walk away. Doug grabbed my arm and stopped me.

"You thinking about that fight you had with Carleen?"

"I guess so."

"Let's have a seat on the grass, and you can tell me about it."

We sat staring out at the water for a few minutes. Doug wasn't rushing me as I tried to figure out what to say. Finally, I just started talking.

"I think she's jealous of us."

"Of us?"

"Yeah. She says ever since you came here, I spend so much time with you that I don't have any time for her. She was mad that I invited you to church and the country club when I've never invited her to either. I tried to tell her we're not even members of the country club and it was a one-time special thing, but she was still mad."

"How long have you two been friends?"

"Forever. Since kindergarten. It's always just been the two of us. We never really had other friends."

"When you put it that way, it makes sense that she'd be jealous. Suddenly, there's this new boy who's hanging out with you."

"I wasn't trying to make her jealous."

"Of course not. Hey, I like Carleen. I think she's a cool girl. Maybe we should invite her to do some stuff with us."

"I guess so." I didn't like the idea. I loved being alone with Doug, and Carleen liked him and wanted to be his girlfriend.

"You could invite her to this lock-in thing, and all three of us could go together."

"You'd really go to the lock-in?"

"I won't lie and tell you I like the idea, but I'd go if it would help things between you and Carleen."

"That's really nice of you, but I'm not sure inviting Carleen is such a good idea."

"Why not?"

"She called me some names that I'm really upset about. I'm not sure I can just call her up and say 'Hey, let's go to the lock-in' like everything's hunky-dory between us."

"It must be serious if you're pulling out the big guns like 'hunky-dory.' Might want to watch your language, buddy."

I giggled despite myself. "Stop it, you're so mean." I blushed because I was suddenly super aware that I was acting like a girl. "She called me names, and I'm damn mad. How about that?"

"Better." He smiled. I loved his smile.

"She said I was a sissy and worse." He dropped his smile but didn't say anything. He held my eyes. "I hate the word sissy. The other boys have always called me sissy when they really wanted to be mean."

"What was worse?"

"She called me a... Well, you see, Kimberly Ann had told me I had flair, which Momma also told me."

"You do. It's a compliment."

"I guess so. Anyway, I told Carleen that Kimberly Ann said I had flair, and Carleen said that flair means fag. She said Kimberly Ann was really calling me a fag, and Carleen thinks I'm one, too."

"Wow. That's really low. I hate that word."

"Then, she said I was up your butt all the time, and I wanted to— Oh gosh, I can't say it." I blushed deeply at the thought of it. He put his hand on my shoulder.

"You don't have to say any more. I get the gist of it." He started rubbing my back, and, without warning, I burst into tears. He pulled me to him, and I cried into his T-shirt. He held me and let me cry. When I was cried out, we sat in silence for a few minutes.

"I've seen the way the other kids treat you. It's just like how I was treated at my last school in California."

"Are you serious? I can't imagine anybody treating you that way. You're so cool and together."

"I'm neither one of those things."

"What happened? I mean, you don't have to talk about it if you don't want to."

Doug stared off at the lake. "His name was Matt, and I thought I was in love. We hung out together all the time. We went surfing together, had sleepovers, all the usual stuff. One night, at a sleepover, he pressed against me and he was hard."

"Oh, wow. What happened?"

"He reached around and stroked me and made me hard, too. Then, we stroked each other and made each other come."

I didn't know what to say because I'd never gone that far with anyone.

"I'd never messed around with a guy before, and Matt and I started messing around a lot."

I felt a little jealous, but I didn't say anything.

"Then, other kids at school started pointing at us and laughing. The word spread that we were boyfriends. Somebody scratched FAG on Matt's locker. He really freaked out and stopped having anything to do with me. It was terrible. I missed him and just wanted to be around him, but he wouldn't let me come close."

I started to tear up again.

"So, one day, I cornered him after school when nobody else was around and suggested we go to the beach and just hang out. We'd always loved the beach. I said we could talk it out, just the two of us. He agreed. We met Saturday at this great big rock where we were hidden from anybody else. I took his hand and pulled him in close. I could tell he wanted me to. He was so gentle. Then, I tried to kiss him, and he resisted and pushed me away. That was when the other boys appeared."

"Other boys?"

"A bunch of bullies from school. They said 'Caught you, fag. You were right, Matt, he's a real fudge packer.'"

"Matt was one of them?"

"Yeah, it was a setup. Matt was trying to convince them that he was straight and not a homo, and he served me up to save his skin. They all jumped me and beat the crap out of me."

"Even Matt?"

"Especially Matt. He landed the hardest blow, right in my gut."

"That's horrible."

"When I got home and Mom saw how bloody and bruised I was, she made the final decision to move here."

"I had no idea you had gone through all that."

"So, when I got here, I decided I'd be cool and aloof so nobody could get close to me and hurt me again. Then you walked into the gym. Once I saw you, I knew I'd let my guard down and let you in."

He lay down beside me. I looked at him. His green eyes were so beautiful. Then he kissed me. Right on the lips. I couldn't believe it was happening to me. I didn't even shut my eyes.

When the kiss was over, I was sure I looked shocked, because I was. I'd just had my first kiss, and it was with a boy. Not just any boy, but Doug, the cutest, smartest, and most amazing boy I'd ever met. It was perfect.

"I guess we're just a couple of sissies," he whispered.

"You really noticed me the first day in the gym?"

"How could I miss you? You wouldn't stop staring at me."

"I was not staring at you!"

"Were too. You got called out by the teacher twice."

I stared up at the sky for a few moments.

"But it's a sin."

"What's a sin?"

"This. You and me. Kissing. Feeling."

"Says who?"

"Says the Bible and Pastor Earl Don and everybody."

"Did our kiss really feel so sinful?"

"It really didn't."

"How'd it make you feel?"

"It made me feel good. Real good. Amazingly good."

"It made me feel good, too. Tell me this: if it was such a sin, why'd God make us this way?"

"You think God made us this way?"

"Sure she did."

He smiled at me so adorably that I decided to let the "she" comment pass.

"How do you know?"

"Think about it. Could you ever change? Could you ever be any other way? Could you imagine ever wanting to get it on with Kimberly Ann?"

"Ew, gross, no."

"Haven't you felt different from the other boys every day of your life?"

"Yes. I mean, no. I mean, yes, I've always felt different."

"Then you were born this way, and God made you this way. Do you think you're a big old heavenly mistake?"

"Well, sometimes."

"Stop! You're not a mistake. God made you this way on purpose."

I thought about it for a minute. "I thought you didn't believe in God."

"I don't, but you do. Work with me."

I laughed. "I think you're cute." I'd never said anything like that to a boy in my life. It felt amazing to say it. Suddenly, I felt free.

"I think you're cute, too," Doug said.

"Who, me?"

"There's nobody else around here."

"I'm not cute. I'm fat, I don't have veiny biceps, and my hair's way too short."

"You're not fat at all, especially not compared to the lard-butts waddling around this town." I giggled again. "You've got gorgeous brown eyes and those long lashes! Just beautiful."

I batted my eyes a couple of times. Sue me.

"Plus, you've got hot legs. Check out those calves. They're huge!"

It was true. I had nice legs.

"I think they're genetic. Daddy has big calves, too."

"I bet you'd have beautiful brown hair if you'd let it grow a little."

"Daddy won't let that happen. He thinks it's sissified."

"Perfect! We're sissified! Sissy pride!"

"Sissy pride!" I said, pumping my fist in the air.

He lay back on the grass beside me and held my hand. The sky had never looked so beautiful. I didn't ever want to leave that spot.

"Tim, I think you should forgive Carleen."

"Why? She was so mean to me."

"She's hurt because she's never had to share you before. You two have been friends too long to let a few bad words end everything."

"I guess you're right. But she should ask for *my* forgiveness."

"She should, but you could go ahead and forgive her anyway. Then, you could invite her to the lock-in. Actually, maybe you two should go together, and I'll take a pass."

"Yeah, right, you're not getting out of it so easily."

"Okay, okay, I said I'd go, and I will. Tell her the three of us will go together. It'll be great."

"Okay, I'll do it."

We lay on the grass hand in hand for a while. "I can't believe I actually told someone that I'm a hom...ah...a sissy. I'm not sure what the right word is."

"The word is gay. We're gay. Everybody in California uses it."

"Gay like happy? That's exactly how I feel. Gay. We're gay. I'm gay. Gay, gay, gay."

"Don't wear it out."

I laughed. "I'm just getting used to it."

"You know, we probably shouldn't talk about the gay thing to other people. I mean, I think my mother's cool about it, but I don't think anybody else in this town is."

"I agree." Suddenly, gay didn't seem so happy as I thought about how Momma or Kimberly Ann or especially Jimbo would react if they knew.

"We should probably start heading home. It's getting to be dinnertime, excuse me, suppertime, and our mothers will be wondering where we are."

"Okay." I looked at him, hoping he'd kiss me one more time.

"But first, I want to kiss you again," he said. We kissed while lying on the grass.

WHEN I GOT home, Momma told me to wash up for dinner. I went into the bathroom, shut the door, and looked at myself in the mirror. I was surprised to find I looked the same. I sure didn't feel the same. I felt a lot more grown-up than I had that morning. I'd been kissed! For real! I smiled at my reflection. It was a new day.

# Seventeen: Carleen's Crew

THE NEXT DAY, I was ready to talk to Carleen. I was going to have a long talk with her at lunch and later in the library. I would tell her I was sorry I had let Doug come between us, and I understood she was hurt. I would tell her I forgave her for the mean things she had said. I thought she would be as upset as I was by our breakup, and I imagined her hugging me and tearfully promising never to call me names again. We would vow to remain best friends forever.

Not exactly.

She gave me the cold shoulder all morning, which didn't surprise me. What did surprise me was lunch. Doug and I walked into the cafeteria together. and I was totally shocked to see Carleen already seated with none other than the former Anns, Jaime and Patti. They were sitting at a table with three other girls who had never really been a part of any group, and all of them were laughing like crazy at something Carleen had said.

Doug leaned toward me. "When did this happen?"

Jaime and Patti and the others looked in our direction and started whispering and giggling among themselves.

"Come on," said Doug, taking my arm and leading me right to their table. "Go speak to her." He nudged me forward.

"Hey, Carleen," I said.

Carleen put down her Mountain Dew and looked straight ahead, not at me.

"Jaime, did someone say something?" she said.

"I thought I heard some hot air," said Jaime to a round of giggles.

"Patti, what do you think?"

"I smell bad breath. Ew," said Patti. They all laughed at Patti's gross attempt at humor.

"Carleen, can we talk?" I asked. "Maybe at the library after lunch?"

Carleen turned to look at me for the first time. "Oh, Timmy. I didn't see you standing there. I told Mrs. Ouzts this morning that I quit. From now on, I'll be spending break with Carleen's Crew, right, girls?"

The other girls all nodded in agreement. "Yeah, we're Carleen's Crew," said Jaime.

"Carleen," said Doug, "This is really important. Tim is trying to make up with you."

"The only makeup *she* wants is Bonnie Bell Dr. Pepper lip gloss." Carleen pulled a tube out of her purse and held it up. "Here you go, precious, want some?" The other girls died laughing. I felt like she had stabbed me through the heart.

Just then, Kimberly Ann walked up. "Come on, Timmy and Doug, sit with us. We need to talk about planning the lock-in anyway." She took my arm. "You were always too good for this trash. I don't know why you lowered yourself all those years, but you don't have to anymore."

"Enjoy the stuck-up table," said Jaime.

"Yeah. The stuck-ups," said Patti, apparently struggling for something original to say.

And with that, Doug and I found ourselves eating lunch with Kimberly Ann and the Anns, the most popular kids in school. I didn't really like any of them, but they all suddenly seemed to like me.

"We might as well call a meeting of the planning committee for the lock-in," said Kimberly Ann. "We're all here. Doug, you can be an honorary member of the committee." She flipped her hair and giggled while she said it. She was the only person I'd ever known who could giggle and speak at the same time.

"I'm just here to eat lunch," said Doug, peeling a banana.

"Oh, don't be a spoilsport. You can help Timmy with decorations. That's what we decided you should do, Timmy—decorations. You've got so much flair and all."

At the word "flair," anger swept over me.

"What do you mean?" I demanded.

Kimberly Ann looked sincerely surprised. "Nothing. You're creative, is all. That's why we want you for the planning committee."

Doug touched my shoulder. "It's okay, buddy."

"What else could I have meant?" said Kimberly Ann.

"Nothing, I guess," I said.

She reached across the table and took my hand. "I know you've been through a lot, now that Carleen has shown you how common and trashy we've always known she was. But it's all right now. You're with friends." She smiled at me like an angel.

"I guess so."

"Of course, so. For goodness sake, Timmy, our mothers were in school together and even pledged the same sorority. We're the same kind of people. Nice people from nice families. It's time you hung out with the right sort."

I thought about it for a moment. "Momma always said you were a nice girl."

"Isn't that sweet. Your mother's just a sweetheart, isn't she, girls?"

"Just a sweetheart," said Kathy Ann.

"Just darling," said Lisa Ann.

"And she's so pretty," said Kimberly Ann. "Obviously, good looks run in the family. Don't you think so, Doug?"

Doug looked up from his fruit. "Sure. Tim's mom's a real looker."

"Now that it's all settled, let's plan ourselves a lock-in!" The Anns cheered, and we spent the rest of lunch and break planning the event.

At the end of the school day, Doug and I were walking out, and I was feeling pretty good.

"I think I was wrong about Kimberly Ann. She really is a nice girl."

"Gag me, Tim."

"What? She was so nice to us today."

Doug rolled his eyes. "She's still the same girl she always was. She's got some reason for kissing up to us. I don't know what it is yet, but believe me, there's something in it for her."

"Maybe. Or maybe she's really the good Christian girl Momma always said she was."

"Tim, listen. Kimberly Ann was never nice to you before today. And now that Carleen has her rival girl gang, the 'Leens verses the Anns, or whatever, suddenly butter wouldn't melt in her mouth."

I laughed. "Buttah wouldn't melt in her mouth? Where'd you learn to talk Southern all of a sudden?"

He smiled that smile that always melted my heart. "I guess you're a good influence on me."

I went weak in the knees. "I wish we could kiss," I whispered.

"Me too." I heard his mother tap the horn. He winked at me and got in the car. They both waved as they drove off.

"There goes your boyfriend," said Jimbo, flashing a limp wrist and wiggling his butt as he walked to the school bus. Some other boys laughed at me, but I hardly noticed. I was in love. There was no other word for it. I was in love with Doug Appleby.

# Eighteen: Into the Woods

THE LOCK-IN was Saturday night, so I had to spend all day Saturday helping Kimberly Ann and the rest of the planning committee set up. Doug agreed to come along at Kimberly Ann's request for his "muscle power." I was glad to have him, especially because there seemed to be endless tables and chairs to put out. He was a lot stronger than I was, but I kept up.

We strung miles of twisted black and orange crepe paper across the ceiling. We'd each been assigned three pumpkins to carve so that jack-o-lanterns would light the way into the building. A whole bunch of kids and some parents were upstairs setting up the hell house in the Sunday school rooms. The idea was to feature one deadly sin per Sunday school classroom. I was too busy setting up downstairs to go up there. I didn't like scary stuff, anyway.

Our new acting youth minister, Rachel, and Pastor Earl Don arrived a couple of hours before the kids were due to be there, along with the chaperones, including Mrs. Mingees. She announced that her husband would be coming later with the Chick-fil-A.

Shortly before start time, Kimberly Ann declared the place fully decorated and ordered us to put on our costumes. "I will be the Virgin Mary," she declared. Doug chuckled, and she glared at him.

Doug and I were the only boys on the planning committee, so we ducked into the boy's room to change alone. Doug had helped me plan my David costume, which just consisted of a tunic Aunt Melanie had sewn for me, a pair of sandals, and a slingshot. Everybody would get it from the slingshot. He never told me who he was going as, though. He told me he'd decided on someone, but I didn't know anything else.

As excited as I was to see what biblical character he'd come up with, I was even more excited when he started taking off his clothes. I'd seen him naked before in the locker room, but this time, I didn't have to look away.

"Take a picture—it'll last longer," he said. I laughed.

"I locked the door so nobody'll walk in on us."

I suddenly realized I had to take my clothes off in front of him. I was overcome by shyness. I wasn't fit like he was and didn't want him to be disappointed in me. I started to go into one of the stalls to take off my shirt.

"What are you doing?" he asked.

"I'm just changing. I'm shy."

He moved toward me and took my hand. "You weren't so shy when we were making out by the lake."

I blushed. He unbuttoned my shirt and slipped it off. I was intensely aware of every ripple, pimple, and imperfection. He just smiled at me and kissed me softy on the lips. He ran his hand lightly down my chest. My heart was racing, and I threw my arms around his neck and kissed him with all my might. He kissed back.

Then, he pushed me away lightly. "We can't go out there to your church function with a couple of woodies, you know." I laughed and looked down at my raging erection through my pants. Then at his. "I would love to do something about that," he said. "But the other kids might start wondering what we're doing in here so long."

I agreed, but I could have stayed in the bathroom fooling around with Doug forever.

He helped me into my David outfit. Then he showed me his. It was a lot like mine. Mine had a gold collar that Aunt Melanie said symbolized David's royal heritage. Otherwise, they were the same.

"I'm Jonathan," he said. "Your aunt Melanie made it for me, but I made her promise to keep it a secret."

"Jonathan? David's best friend?"

"They were more than best friends. They were gay lovers."

It excited me to hear him use the word "lovers."

"I've never heard that."

"It's true. I called my dad in California. He's joined this church in LA that's all gays."

"Why would your dad join a gay church?"

"Think about it a minute."

I did. "Holy moly, you don't mean..."

"I'll explain it all to you later. For right now, you'll have to believe me that Jonathan and David were boyfriends. Dad says the minister out there talks about it all the time."

"Whoa. Are you sure?" Actual gay boyfriends in the Bible sounded like a crazy idea.

"Look it up and read it yourself, just like you did with Sodom and Gomorrah. It's in First Samuel, I think. Is that a book in the Bible?"

"Yes, very good."

"And that's not all. Dad said there were gay lady lovers in the Bible, also. Ruth and Naomi. That's another one you should look up."

"Gay ladies? Are you sure this is the Bible we're talking about?"

"Read it and see what you think."

Before Doug and his momma, no one had ever told me I could read the Bible and decide for myself what it meant. It seemed almost sacrilegious. It was also exciting.

"Hey, wait a minute. You're not going to go out there and give your presentation on Jonathan and say he was a gay and in love with David, are you? You can't do that."

"Don't worry, I won't. I don't have a death wish. I'll just say he and David were friends. It's not like anyone's going to be listening."

"Kimberly Ann will be, and so will Pastor Earl Don and Youth Minister Rachel."

Just then, there was a banging on the door. It was Lisa Ann. "What are you two doing in there so long? It's almost time to open the doors."

We walked out, and Kimberly Ann stopped me short. She was dressed to kill in golden robes and a headdress with golden threads woven in it. Beneath it, her blonde hair had been hot-rollered into a mass of long, soft curls. Above it floated a golden halo. She even had on gold high-heeled sandals. It all looked custom-made and expensive, but it didn't look like a woman having a baby in a stable.

"Isn't Kimberly Ann beautiful?" asked Mrs. Mingees.

"Yes, ma'am," I said. "I thought she was going as Mary?"

"She is. Can't you see it?"

"I thought Mary was supposed to be a poor woman from a backwater town who had to have a baby in a stable," said Doug.

"Nice to see you've been reading your Bible," said Mrs. Mingees. "But Kimberly Ann chose to come as the exalted queen of heaven, the Blessed Virgin."

"Cool, she's Queen Mary, and Tim here is King David. The royals are in charge of the lock-in," said Doug.

Mrs. Mingees just sniffed and busied herself fussing with Kimberly Ann's hair.

Pastor Earl Don and Youth Minister Rachel officially opened the doors. All the kids came pouring in, not just from First Baptist but also from other Baptist churches in town. There were a lot of bathrobes and sandals, some fake beards, and few people who got really creative. Dean from the JV football team came as Adam with little shorts covered in leaves and nothing else. I couldn't help noticing his nipples were cold. Pastor Earl Don frowned.

"I can't believe Pastor ED's going to let him in like that," whispered Doug.

"Dean's grandmother owns half the timberland in the county. She's richer than God. Dean could have walked in here naked, and the pastor wouldn't have said a word."

"Me either. He's pretty cute."

I elbowed him in the ribs. "Stop it!" But he was right. Half-naked Dean was definitely cute.

"What are you two giggling about like a couple of girls?" Kimberly Ann took Doug by the arm, cupping her hand around his bare bicep. I wanted to push her hand away because that was *my* bicep, but I kept quiet. "We need to get everyone organized for the biblical parade."

Pastor Earl Don stepped up to the podium at the far end of the room. "Are you all ready to be locked in?"

"Yeah!" everybody yelled.

"Once locked, no one can leave. I order the doors locked!"

Across the room, Youth Minister Rachel was about to shut the doors when they banged open, and Carleen, Jaime, and Patti waltzed in. The three of them stood there in front of all of us, Carleen flanked by her crew, all posed with their hands on their hips like they were a girl group waiting for applause.

"Did we miss anything?" asked Carleen.

Kimberly Ann rushed up to them, her gold lamé rustling.

"Well, if it isn't Mrs. Liberace," said Carleen. Doug laughed, and I elbowed him again.

"What are you doing here?" Kimberly Ann hissed. "I don't remember inviting the Holiness Church."

"My family goes right here to First Baptist," said Patti. "Carleen's my guest."

"And all the other Baptist churches were invited, and we go to Gilgal," said Jaime.

"Of course, you do." Kimberly Ann dripped with condescension at the mention of the tiny country church.

"They're all welcome," said Youth Minister Rachel. "And what great costumes. Who are you?"

"I'm Bathsheba, and these are my handmaidens," said Carleen to dropped jaws around the room.

"Who's Bathsheba?" asked Doug.

"Only the adulterous lover of King David," I said.

"Maybe she's the one who turned him gay," said Doug. I pressed both hands over my mouth to keep from laughing out loud.

"Well, I'm sure you'll have a very instructive lesson for us when your turn comes," said Rachel. "Now, everyone line up for the biblical parade."

Everyone paraded around the perimeter of the room in their costumes while a boom box pumped out contemporary Christian music. Carleen's Crew didn't so much parade as strut. All three were wagging their hips, and Jaime and Patti were carrying Carleen's super long purple train. What were they up to?

First up with her presentation was, of course, Kimberly Ann. She stepped to the podium in her golden finery, and, across the room, her mother dimmed the lights and turned on a projector. As paintings of Mary appeared on the wall behind her, Kimberly Ann extolled the great virtues of the virgin mother who gave birth to the Christ child. I caught Carleen's eye, and we both rolled them at once. Then she looked away. For a minute, we forgot we were supposed to hate each other.

When Kimberly Ann finished, she waited for applause, which came from Kathy Ann, Lisa Ann, and Mrs. Mingees.

"I didn't know we were supposed to bring slides," said Dean.

Next up were Kathy Ann and Lisa Ann together. They introduced themselves as Ruth and Naomi. I could have died. Doug and I both burst out laughing. Mrs. Mingees quickly shushed us. Kathy Ann and Lisa Ann started speaking, and they were really good. They talked of the famine that led Naomi to the land of Moab where her son married Ruth. They talked of the death of their husbands and sons and how hard it was to be two women alone in the ancient world. Ruth and Naomi vowed to stay together in the face of their hardships because of their commitment to each other. Then, Kathy Ann read from the Book of Ruth, First Chapter:

*"Do not press me to leave you or to turn back from following you! Where you go, I will go; where you lodge, I will lodge; your people shall be my people, and your God my God. Where you die, I will die—there will I be buried. May the Lord do thus and so to me, and more as well, if even death parts me from you!"*

The room fell silent. I leaned in to whisper to Doug, "That sounds like a marriage vow."

"Do those two play on the softball team?" Doug asked.

"Yes. Why?"

"Because I think we aren't the only freaks at Patriot Christian."

I looked again at Kathy Ann and Lisa Ann. It took me a few minutes before it hit me.

"You don't think—"

"Next up is Timmy Thompson," said Pastor Earl Don.

I approached the podium and gave my speech about David and Goliath. It was really just a recitation of the facts of the story of slaying the giant. I wasn't going to talk about why this story appealed to me, but, inspired by the Anns and the presence of Doug, I gathered my courage and decided to ad-lib.

"The story of David and Goliath is the story of a boy who nobody took seriously. He was different, and nobody thought he was worth anything. But just because somebody's different doesn't mean he's not worth anything. In fact, David did what nobody else could do; he slayed the giant. None of the big, strong popular men could do it, but David could. How? By being smart. David was smarter than any of those popular guys because he had to be. When you're different, you have to be smarter and better than anyone else." I looked out at the crowd. Most of the kids weren't really paying attention, but Kimberly Ann hand Doug were. So was Pastor Earl Don who had a slightly confused look on his face.

"And if you're smarter than all the popular kids, you can grow up to become the greatest king your country has ever known." I stopped and took a step back. Doug applauded loudly while all the other kids stared at him.

"Thank you, Timmy," said Pastor Earl Don. "That was an interesting version of the story of David and Goliath. I don't want any of the popular boys and girls to think you can't be as good as David just because you're popular. Why, there's no reason why you can't be popular and smart at the same time. There's no need to think you have to be"—he used air quotes with the next word—"'different' in order to make it in this world. Just look at our Kimberly Ann here. She's popular and smart. Instead of being different and trying so hard, you could try not being different, then it's not so hard to be a success, see, kids? Let's see now, next up is our new boy, Doug Appleby. Come on up, Doug."

Doug took the podium. "I'm new at all this Bible stuff, but one character really caught my attention. I'm Jonathan, the closest and most devoted friend to King David." Several kids snickered. "Jonathan was the son of King Saul who was threatened by the rise of David. In fact, Jonathan warned David that his own father, King Saul, wanted to have David killed." Doug looked straight into my eyes. "In the First Book of Samuel, it says:

*"The soul of Jonathan was bound to the soul of David, and Jonathan loved him as his own soul. Saul took him that day and would not let him return to his father's house. Then Jonathan made a covenant with David, because he loved him as his own soul. Jonathan stripped himself of the robe that he was wearing, and gave it to David, and his armor, and even his sword and his bow and his belt."*

That also sounded like a marriage vow. It sounded like a marriage vow directed at me. I felt a little dizzy. I'd never heard anything so beautiful.

Doug continued, "The story of Jonathan and David reminds me a lot of the story of Ruth and Naomi. A whole lot." He looked at Kathy Ann and Lisa Ann, who looked back. "When Jonathan died, David was deeply grieved. This is from the first chapter of Second Samuel. It's written as a poem:

*"Saul and Jonathan, beloved and lovely!*

*In life and in death they were not divided;*

*they were swifter than eagles,*

*they were stronger than lions.*

*How the mighty have fallen in the midst of battle!*

*Jonathan lies slain upon your high places.*

*I am distressed for you my brother Jonathan;*

*Greatly beloved were you to me;*

*your love to me was wonderful, passing the love of women."*

Everyone stood in silence as Doug stepped away from the podium and returned to my side. I wanted to take his hand but didn't dare.

"Well, wasn't that interesting, boys and girls?" said Pastor Earl Don. "Maybe next, we can have a more conventional story. Let's see who's next. Carleen Hightower, our guest from the Holiness Church. Maybe you can give your denomination's take on a Bible story."

Carleen and her crew pranced up to the podium and struck a pose, right knee cocked, and hands on hips.

"I am Bathsheba, the queen of King David. His *real* love." She leered at Doug as she said it. "While she was innocently bathing on the roof, David saw her and was overcome by desire." Carleen began running her hands over her breasts and hips. Most of the boys started laughing, and Pastor Earl Don shushed them. "But David done her wrong. She was already married to another, yet David SEDUCED her!"

As if on cue, Patti leaned down and pressed a button on a boom box that was stashed under the podium. It was the opening strains of "Heat Wave" by Martha Reeves and the Vandellas. Patti and Jaime immediately started swaying and *ohh-ohh*ing and *doo-wopp*ing.

"Bathsheba felt it too. It was like..."

She paused for effect.

"A heat wave."

And she started singing.

Loud.

Off-key.

Patti and Jaime were *doo-wopp*ing and swaying in perfect unison.

> *Whenever I'm with him*
>
> *Something inside*
>
> *Starts to burning*
>
> *And I'm filled with desire*
>
> *Could it be the devil in me*
>
> *Or is this the way love's supposed to be?*
>
> *It's like a heat wave*
>
> *Burning in my heart*
>
> *I can't keep from crying*
>
> *It's tearing me apart*

At the words "heat wave," Patti and Jaime ran their hands across their brows as Carleen did a combination butt wiggle and dip.

*Whenever he calls my name*

*Soft, low, sweet, and plain*

*Right then, right there...*

*I feel, yeah, yeah*

*Well I feel that burning flame*

At "burning flame," Carleen stuck out her tongue and licked her finger like it was, well, like it was a Popsicle. Pastor Earl Don and Rachel both stormed the podium and shut down the boom box.

Doug started applauding and yelled out "Yeah!" I looked at him, and he shrugged. "I know they've been mean to you, but at least they're not boring."

Pastor Earl Don had a different idea. "Young ladies, you have fallen far short of the spirit of this lock-in. This was not a Bible story, but a bunch of lewdness. I will not tolerate it. Your parents are being called at this moment, and you three will be expelled from the lock-in. Patti, I am particularly disappointed in you as a member of this church."

"Come on, girls," said Carleen as the three of them pranced and swayed their way to the door. Just before exiting, they turned and, in unison, bowed and waved. The crowd went crazy with applause and cheers. There was lots of catcalling from the guys. Pastor Earl Don rushed to the stage.

"Okay, kids, show's over. That's enough of that. I'd like to announce that Dr. Mingees has just driven up with Chick-fil-A for everyone!" Everybody cheered as Dr.

Mingees came in with a big box filled with fried chicken sandwiches, coleslaw, and waffle fries.

"Yay! Chick-fil-A! Have you ever had it?" I turned to Doug.

"I've never even heard of it."

"It's only the most delicious fast food ever created by God. Come on."

I filled up two plates with sandwiches, slaw, and waffle fries. We each got a big cup of fizzy punch from the punch bowl that had a frozen Jell-O rings floating in it.

"Hey guys, come sit with us," said Kimberly Ann, patting a seat next to her and the Anns.

Doug started to sit next to Kathy Ann, but Kimberly Ann grabbed his arm and pulled him down into the seat next to her.

"Don't you just love Chick-fil-A?" she asked. "The closest one is all the way in Columbia, and Mother and I always stop by when we're on one of our shopping trips."

Doug pulled out his sandwich and took off the top bun. "Why are there pickles on a piece of fried chicken?"

Kimberly Ann reached over and took his two pickle slices with her fingers. Gross. She popped them in her mouth.

"Mmmm, delicious."

"Maybe I'll just eat the slaw," said Doug.

"Nonsense, you have to at least try it," said Kimberly Ann.

"Yeah, try it." I was already half through mine.

He took a bite and chewed slowly. He swallowed. He sat in silence, contemplating his sandwich.

"Well?" Kimberly Ann and I said at the same time.

"It's awesome."

We all applauded as Doug took a second bite.

"Little by little, we're turning you into a Southern boy," I said.

"Little by little, I'm getting diabetes," said Doug. I laughed.

"So," Doug said. "Naomi and Ruth. Interesting choice."

"So," Kathy Ann said. "David and Jonathan. Interesting choice."

"See you at the softball games."

"See you at the Liza Minnelli concert."

"There's a Liza Minnelli concert?" I said. "I love her." Doug and the Anns all laughed.

Kimberly Ann, frustrated that the conversation wasn't about her, interrupted. She put her hand on Doug's arm. "Douglas, I am so pleased you've taken such an interest in reading the Bible. Jonathan is such an original choice. Of course, I would expect you to come up with an original, smart choice."

"You know what Tim said about people who are different having to be smart."

"Oh, Doug, you're not different. Not like Timmy, anyway. Why, I predict that pretty soon, you'll be the most popular guy in school."

"I'm not trying to be popular."

"And yet you're sitting here with the three most popular girls." She giggled and flipped her blonde hair.

"And Timmy."

"Yes, and Timmy."

I took a sip of my punch and exchanged glances with the Anns.

"Douglas, I've been praying for you. You know I have."

Doug rolled his eyes. "Listen, Kim..."

"I've been praying for you to see the light. I want you to know the joy of a personal relationship with Jesus."

"I'm okay, really."

She stood. "No, you're not."

The room went silent, and everyone turned to look at our table.

Kimberly Ann put her hands on her hips. "I was going to do this later, but God has guided me to this moment. Douglas Appleby, I declare here in the house of God that your soul belongs to Jesus Christ!"

"Amen," said the Anns.

"Don't do this, Kim," said Doug.

"You are a lost soul, Douglas Appleby. A lost soul that was brought to me, and by the grace of God, I accept the responsibility of saving this lost soul."

"Don't make a spectacle of yourself, Kim," said Doug.

"Kimberly Ann, maybe we could talk to Doug about Jesus quietly and at another time," I said.

"Quiet, Timmy Thompson! Stop interfering."

I could see Doug clinching his fists. He was really getting angry. I put my hand on his arm.

"She means well," I said.

He jerked his arm away. "The hell she does."

Kimberly Ann, aware that all eyes were on her, walked solemnly to the podium, reached behind it, and pulled out a small pitcher, like cream might come in. She then walked slowly back to our table, holding the pitcher out in front of her, like a holy relic.

"This is holy oil, Douglas. I will use it to anoint thee in the name of Jesus Christ." She touched her finger to the oil and then reached out and touched Doug's forehead. He jerked away and stood, knocking the pitcher out of her hand. It fell to the floor and broke into a thousand oily pieces.

"Jesus Christ, Kimberly Ann. Can't you just leave a guy alone? The only reason I came to godforsaken Patriot Christian is because my grandmother told my mother that the public school was worse. All I want to do is go to school and mark the days until I can get back to California. I don't need saving."

"Douglas, I care about you, and Jesus loves you."

"Cut the crap, Kim. The only reason you suddenly started being nice to Tim here was so he would get me to this ridiculous lock-in so you could make yourself the center of attention and save my soul. Well, guess what? My soul is just fine by itself, thank you very much. And I don't need any of your hillbilly religion."

Pastor Earl Don stood. "Now, see here, young man."

"No, you see here. I'm not a Christian, okay? I don't need it and I don't want it. And I don't need some fake, snooty girl like Kimberly Ann using my friend Tim to try to rack up gold stars for saving souls."

"Perhaps I should call your mother to come get you."

"Fine. She didn't want me to come, anyway. I should have danced out of here with the Vandellas." He turned to me. "Tim, I'm leaving. You coming?"

I wanted to say yes more than anything. I started to stand up. Pastor Earl Don sprinted over to me and put his hands on my shoulders.

"Timmy is a good Christian boy, and besides, he can't leave. He's on the planning committee."

Doug looked at me with a pained expression. "Last chance, Tim. Let's go."

Pastor Earl Don pressed hard on my shoulders. "Your mother would be so disappointed in you if you left, Timmy."

"I said I'd help," I said weakly. "I'm on the planning committee."

Doug nodded. "I gotcha." He turned and walked to the door. Just as he was about to leave, he turned and gave us all a salute. Then he banged the doors open and was gone.

I wanted to cry, but Kimberly Ann actually did. Big crocodile tears over Doug's lost soul. Pastor Earl Don left me and put his arms around Kimberly Ann. She broke away and stepped to the center of the room.

"Dinner's over, everybody. Time for the hell house. It's upstairs in the Sunday school rooms. Go! Now!"

I sat at the now-empty table by myself. I'd never felt so alone in my life. I regretted not leaving with Doug and considered dashing out and trying to catch him, but something held me back. If I'd left with him, everyone would have known we were boyfriends and then what? Kicked out of school? Kicked out of church? What would Momma think? It would kill her.

I stood and approached Kimberly Ann.

"It's okay, Kimberly Ann. I know you meant well with Doug."

She turned and stared at me, not like the Kimberly Ann of the past week who had wanted me on the planning committee, but like the Kimberly Ann who barely acknowledged my existence. I knew in that moment that Doug was right; she only wanted me on the planning committee because I could get him to come, and she could make a big display of saving his soul and become his girlfriend in the process. How could I be so stupid?

"Did you say something?" she asked.

"No."

"Good. Go make yourself useful. Go help the other girls clean up." And she stalked away.

The other girls.

I looked around the room and felt desperately sad. Doug was gone. Carleen and her crew were gone. Kimberly Ann and her friends had cast me aside because I was no use to them anymore. It was only nine thirty. What was I going to do all night? I saw a crowd of kids going upstairs to the hell house and thought maybe that would kill some time.

I hung back at the end of the line as small groups of five or so went into each Sunday school room at a time. I was in the last group of five with some kids from a country church. I didn't think any of them even went to Patriot Christian. That was fine with me. I was suddenly very tired of being around kids who didn't like me.

The hell house wasn't all too impressive. Each room depicted one of the seven deadly sins. Gluttony consisted of a guy with a pillow under his shirt with lots of Big Mac boxes scattered around. He was moaning and groaning about how fat and miserable he was and how he should have listened to Jesus and respected his body as his temple. "I just want to die," he said. Just then, a guy in a devil costume appeared from behind a curtain, holding a pizza box. He said, "Not before I stuff this whole pizza down your fat face."

Down your face? What does that even mean?

As we were escorted out, the devil approached the guy with the pizza, and the glutton yelled out, "No! No! Not pizza! Don't make me eat!"

Pride, envy, covetousness, anger, and sloth weren't much better. Lust was in the last room. We walked in, and I froze. The whole room was bathed in pink light while a guy in pink hot pants gyrated around the room while "Macho Man" by the Village People blared on the boom box. I felt like this whole show was directed at me and me alone. The guy pranced his way around the room crying out, "I love macho men, macho, macho men." Then, the devil appeared from behind a curtain, but this time, he had a real pitchfork in his hand.

"You want a poke, sissy boy?"

"Why yesssss," said hot pants guy, and he actually bent over so the devil could poke him in the butt with the pitchfork. As he did, he turned his face to the crowd. It was Jimbo! I didn't know he was at the lock-in.

"Ow, that hurths!" screeched Jimbo with an exaggerated lisp as the devil poked him into a billowing crepe paper hell. Jimbo pranced into hell with a limp-wristed, sissy walk. Then, he fell to the ground and rolled around, squealing like a little girl.

"Burn in hell, homo!"

Everybody cheered. Some zit-faced girl next to me said, "Yeah! Burn the homo!"

I started to back out of the room when Jimbo stood and pointed at me.

"You want to burn a homo? Burn the real homo!"

I took a step back and felt some hands on my arms. I think it was Tommy and several other boys from the JV football team.

"Who said you could go?" said Tommy. I smelled liquor on his breath. I struggled against them, but they were stronger. I could hear other kids gathering behind me and Kimberly Ann's voice saying, "Don't let him get away."

The boys threw me into the middle of the room as the kids cheered. I could clearly see Kimberly Ann in the front row pumping her fist saying, "Burn the homo! Burn the homo!" The other kids joined in. "Burn the homo!"

Jimbo grabbed the pitchfork from the devil and approached me with it. "You want it, don't you, fag. You want it in the butt, admit it." He started poking me with the sharp ends, and it really hurt. The pain jolted something in me. In one quick movement, I turned around, grabbed the pitchfork, and yanked it away from him. It clanked on the floor, and the chanting stopped. Everyone looked at it, surprised I'd fought back. I was pretty surprised, myself.

I seized the moment to break through the crowd and run out of the room. I ran down the hall and down the back steps to the rear entrance to the building. I burst through the door and kept running and running. There were woods behind the church, and all I knew was I had to make it to those woods. I knew in my soul that nobody at the lock-in would have helped me as Jimbo kept poking—certainly not Pastor Earl Don.

I passed the tree line and kept running. There were voices far behind me, calling my name. I ignored them. I didn't trust them. I ran and ran as hard as I could. I didn't stop until I tripped over a root and fell on my face. I had no idea where I was.

Curling up under a tree, I cried until I couldn't cry any more. Why did God make me this freak who everybody hated?

I'd have to run away from Edgewood. Doug would come with me, wouldn't he? I'd talk him into it. We couldn't stay in this town, and I certainly could never go back to school. It wasn't safe. I could wait until late tonight and sneak into the house. I made a mental list of the things I'd need: Clean underwear. My fashion drawings. The hundred dollars in birthday money stuffed in a sock in my bottom drawer. I'd gather all that and go throw pebbles at Doug's window. I'd apologize for not leaving the lock-in with him and beg his forgiveness. Then, we'd hitchhike to Columbia where we could get a Greyhound bus for California. Doug could call his dad from the road, and he'd take us in. We could live together in California with his dad. We could be safe. How far could a hundred dollars get us?

I startled to the sound of my name being shouted. The voice sounded like Daddy's! It was loud and clear and really close. Suddenly, a flashlight shone in my face, and Daddy grabbed me by my arm and hugged me tight.

"Son! What the hell! What the hell!" He kept repeating it and hugging me so tightly I could hardly breathe.

He drove me home in the wrecker, wiping his eyes. I think he might have been crying, which I'd never seen him do before. He didn't say a word the whole time.

When I got home, Momma rushed out and embraced me. She gushed and cried and felt me all over to make sure I was whole and not broken. She held me by the shoulders in front of her. "Are you okay?"

"Yes, ma'am."

"Pastor Earl Don called and said you'd run away from the lock-in, and everybody was looking for you."

"Yes, ma'am, I did."

"Have you completely lost your mind?"

"Yes, ma'am."

She stood and looked back at my father who was a few paces behind me.

"Thank you for finding him, Ronnie. That was good of you."

"Yeah, sure. No problem."

They stood there staring at each other for a moment.

"Okay, well, I guess I better go," said Daddy. "Got a transmission waiting for me in the morning. You do what your momma says from now on, you hear? You scared us all half to death." And he was gone.

"Go take a bath. I've never seen you so dirty," said Momma.

# Nineteen: Andie is a Girl Doll

AFTER MY BATH, I went to my bedroom and lay down. After a time, Momma came into my room with a tall glass of cold milk and a plate of chocolate-covered graham crackers. When I was little, I called them Grannies, and they were my favorite. At some point, I'd decided I was too grown-up for them. I hadn't had them in at least five or six years.

"While you were missing, Melanie called and asked what she could do. I asked her to go to the store and get some Grannies. It seems dumb, but somehow at the time, it seemed like a way to make sure you'd come home." She started tearing up. "I thought you'd enjoy some."

All I wanted right now was to eat Grannies and be with my mommy. I wanted to be a little boy again. But, I was the one who was supposed to be crying, not Momma.

"It's okay, Momma. I came home." With that, she cried harder. I went to the bathroom and fetched the tissues.

She blew her nose and got control of herself. "I was so excited for you being asked to be on the planning committee for the lock-in. I thought, finally, my son is popular with the nice kids from nice families. Then, this. What am I going to do with you, Timmy? I just want you to date cute girls and grow up into the man I know you can be."

I wanted so badly to tell her I wasn't ever going to date cute girls, and I was different in ways she'd always ignored. I wanted to tell her about Doug and what he really meant to me and about my first kiss and how amazing it was. But I knew she'd never understand all that, so I stayed quiet.

"When you were little, I indulged you with playing dress-up and buying you Barbies. I should never have done it. I blame Melanie. She always said it was harmless to give a boy a doll."

I suddenly felt weird and uncomfortable. I wanted her to stop talking. But she didn't.

"I thought it was all just a phase, and, pretty soon, you'd get excited about Little League baseball, but that never happened." She looked over at my desk where some of my designs were spread out. "Instead, you developed this fascination with fashion." She touched my cheek. "I guess you'll always be different."

I wanted to scream out to her that I never asked to be different, and she had no idea how hard it was to be different at a place like Patriot Christian. I wanted to explain to her that I was beginning to figure out it's not such a horrible thing to be different. I wanted to tell her that being different had led me to Doug, and I was in love with him.

I didn't tell her any of those things.

She smiled her best brave smile, stood, and smoothed out her blouse. "Eat your cookies, drink your milk, and go to bed. We'll all feel better in the morning." Then she left my room.

I bit into one of the cookies, but couldn't taste it. I put the plate and glass on my desk and crossed over to my closet. Rummaging around, I found her—my favorite rag doll from when I was a little kid. She had red yarn pigtails and a matching red dress. I could still remember the day I found her at a church tag sale Aunt Melanie had taken me to. She bought her for me. Momma wasn't happy when I showed it to her, so I told her I'd named the doll Andie. I thought if I used a boy's name, it would somehow make Momma happy. I was four. Andie was always my favorite stuffed toy, and I slept with her for years.

I turned out the light and curled up in bed with Andie.

# Twenty: A Sticky Mess

IN THE MORNING, I woke up feeling like I wanted to stay in bed all day. Around ten o'clock, Aunt Melanie showed up unannounced, which wasn't unusual for a Saturday. I could hear her talking with Momma because she was so loud.

"Hey, Jo, get yourself gussied up because we're having a girls' day out."

"Oh, Mel, no. I'm not..."

"Nonsense, it'll do you a world of good. When was the last time we had a day of shopping and lunch?"

"We've never had a day of shopping and lunch."

"Well then, we're overdue. Lunch is on me. There's this cute new place in Aiken I've been dying to try. Nothing but quiche. They have ten different kinds. It's called Quiche Me, Kate. Isn't that cute?"

"Melanie, you can't afford to treat me to lunch. You've been unemployed for months."

"Not anymore. I got a job."

"How wonderful. When did this happen?"

"Just yesterday. I didn't say anything because, you know. We were focused on Mr. Timmy."

"Tell me about this job."

"It's with Mr. Maurice Moray in his new boutique."

"Boutique Moray uptown?"

"The very same."

"Doing what? Are you going to be selling those beautiful clothes?"

"Me? Hell, no. I don't know a thing about fashion. I'm gonna do his bookkeeping for him. He was impressed with my accounting degree from community college."

"Degree? Since when do you have a degree?"

"I have an associate's degree. The equivalent anyway. Oh hell, school wasn't ever my thing, but I'm a wiz with numbers, and I'm about to make Maurice Moray wonder how he ever got along without me. Now get dressed so I can go spend all the money he's about to start paying me."

"I don't know."

"Tim could use some time alone. He's got a lot on his mind."

"I guess so."

"Great! You go get dressed, and I'll help myself to some coffee."

I stayed in bed until they left. I wasn't in the mood to talk to anyone. I got up and padded into the kitchen in my pajamas and slippers and found that Momma had left a pot of grits on the stove on low. There was also some bacon draining on paper towels. I spooned up a big bowl of hot grits, then cracked an egg and stirred, cooking it. For a final touch, I crumbled bacon on top.

I was seated at the breakfast table, scraping the bottom of the bowl when the doorbell rang. Ugh. I just wanted to be alone and almost didn't answer, but I looked out and saw it was Doug. I was in my little boy PJs and slippers and, for about a second, considered not answering. Then, I opened the door.

"Hey," he said.

"Hey."

We stood there for a moment. Everything was suddenly incredibly awkward.

"Mind if I come in?"

"Okay." I led him into the living room, and we both sat on my grandmother's settee.

"Nice room," he said, looking around.

"Thanks. This was my grandmother's."

"Oh, yeah?"

"Yeah."

We sat in silence. I felt terrible about not leaving the lock-in with him, but, at the same time, I was mad at him for leaving me there. I didn't know what to say and was hoping he did.

"This room's kind of formal—don't you think? I mean, I feel like you're about to serve me tea and crumpets or something."

I laughed. "I don't even know what crumpets are."

"Why don't we go back to your bedroom?"

"I would like that." We both got up and walked down the hall.

"Your aunt called my mother this morning and said she was taking your mom shopping all day and maybe you could use some company."

Aunt Melanie to the rescue, again.

"I sure could." We both sat on the bed.

"Listen, Doug, I feel bad that I didn't go with you when you left the lock-in."

"Don't feel bad, really. I shouldn't have flown off the handle and left. I should have stayed with you."

"You were right to go. Kimberly Ann is such a..."

"A bitch?"

"Yeah." I laughed. "She's a real B."

He laughed.

"Can we hug, please?" I asked.

He scooted over and wrapped me into a big hug. I started to feel warm and happy again. He released me, and we both scootched up against the pillows, holding hands, facing each other.

"So, it was Jimbo again, huh?"

"How did you hear?"

"Carleen called me."

"Really? I thought she hated us."

"She doesn't hate me. She doesn't hate you, either. She's just pretending."

"She's doing a convincing job of it."

"Well, anyway, she called me to tell me what happened. I think she believes she can still make me her boyfriend or something."

"She can't, can she?"

"Of course not."

"How did she even know? She and those girls left before it all happened."

"How could she not know? She's related to half the county, and everybody's talking about it."

I sighed. "I'll always be known as the guy who got poked with a pitchfork. It was really scary, Doug."

"I know."

"Yeah, I guess you do."

"Hey, I heard you actually grabbed the pitchfork away from Jimbo."

"Yeah, I did. It just kind of happened. I was shocked I actually got it."

"I bet it shocked the shit out of Jimbo."

"Yeah! I bet I did shock the, uh, poop out of Jimbo."

"Oh, for God's sake, Tim, say it. You've earned the right to cuss a little. Say shit."

"Okay, it shocked the shit out of him. Shit shit shit!"

Doug applauded. I laughed and blushed.

"I guess I'm going to hell now," I said.

"I think your God will forgive you this time." He shifted and reached behind his back, and, to my total mortification, he pulled out Andie the rag doll. "Who's this?"

I grabbed the doll. "Nothing. I don't know why she's in the bed." I got up to put her back in the closet, but he held me back.

"Let her stay. She's cute." He gave me that smile I couldn't resist, so I sat back and put my head on his shoulder.

He pointed to the drawings on my desk. "Hey, what are those?"

"Oh my gosh, those are my fashion drawings. I want to be a fashion designer. That's my dream."

He got up and picked up one of the drawings. "How did I not know this? Hey, this is really good. You did this yourself?"

"Yes! It's my latest creation. Let me show you some more." I pulled out some of my designs and spread them on my desk.

"You've really got talent."

"Gosh, thanks." I paused a minute while he studied my designs. "You're the first person other than Momma and Aunt Melanie who's ever seen them. I've got some others here, if you'd like to see them."

"Sure."

"Here's some I did last year. They're not very good, but I kind of like this one." I showed him a red chiffon gown I'd envisioned for Cheryl Ladd at the Emmys. "And then there's this one." I showed him a dramatic purple sequined number with a plunging neckline and a huge popped collar. "I designed it for Ann-Margret to wear to the Oscars. She could carry it off."

"You're really good," Doug said. "I can totally see Ann-Margret in the purple. Did you see her in *Tommy*?"

"No. Of course not. I'm too young to see grown-up movies like that. Besides, wasn't it all about drug addicts? Does your momma know you saw it?"

"Mom took me to see it. She's been taking me to R-rated movies for a long time. I saw *One Flew Over the Cuckoo's Nest* and *Midnight Express*. Those were both really good. She says most of the stuff Hollywood puts out for kids is propaganda to turn us all into little Republicans."

"I don't know about politics."

Doug put the drawings down and walked across the room. "I wish I could draw. I don't have that talent." He flopped onto my bed.

"Maybe I could give you a lesson, show you some tricks. We all have talents. We shouldn't keep them under a basket."

"That basket thing—is it from the Bible or something? Everybody around here keeps talking about it."

"Yes, it's from the Book of Mark. Jesus said it."

"You people around here sure do talk about the Bible a lot."

I sat on the edge of the bed. "I used to win all the Bible Bees when I was a kid. I know all the verses. What kind of stuff did you like to do as a kid?"

"Surfing, of course. I really loved it, and I was pretty good."

"I bet you were." I had a mental image of him in the surf in a tiny bathing suit.

"But Mom took me to the beach near Charleston right after we moved here. Folly Beach? I guess she was trying to make me not miss California so much. Didn't work. The Atlantic Ocean is like a lake. No waves at all. What was I supposed to do with myself, sit on the beach and sweat? It was so damn hot. They actually had surf shops, but for what? Were they waiting on a hurricane? Nothing like the beaches in California."

"I bet California's wonderful. I'd love to go there. Maybe we could go together."

"I'd love it. There's so much I want to show you."

"I'm so glad you came over here today. When you left the lock-in, I felt so awful. I thought maybe we were over, and I couldn't stand it. I think about you all the time, Doug."

"I think about you too, Tim. I didn't think I'd find someone like you here."

He pulled me closer and kissed me lightly on the lips. Then more urgently. Our mouths were open and our tongues were touching. We pressed ourselves together tightly, and I started running my hands up and down his back. I reached under his shirt and felt his warm, soft skin. His tummy was completely flat and hard. He broke the kiss and pulled off his shirt. Then he pulled off mine. He pulled me back into a deep kiss, and the sensation of our skin touching drove me wild. I pressed myself onto him and rolled him over onto his back with me lying on top. Then, he rolled back over, the weight of him on my body. He started kissing my neck, which sent shivers down my spine. He ran his hand over my chest and tummy to the waistband of my PJ bottoms. Then beyond. I didn't know I could be that hard. He put his hand on me and I moaned. As he touched me and kissed me all over, I became lost in the world of his skin and tongue and warmth and hands.

After a while, I had to take a break to pee. When I came back from the bathroom, Doug was lying on the bed, smiling at me, his arms behind his head. I stood in the middle of the bedroom, staring at him. "You're gorgeous."

Doug winked and stretched his arms out to me. "I bet you say that to all the guys."

I got on the bed and snuggled in next to him. "There's never been any other guy. Nobody but you, Doug."

"Really? You've never messed around before? Not with anybody?"

"Not with anybody else in the room."

After a beat, Doug laughed. He rubbed his hand across the bedspread. "So, is this the place? Is this where all the Tim solo action happens? This bedspread is nice and nubby. Perfect for rubbing around, right?"

"Maybe, but I don't think chenille bedspreads were made to take that kind of abuse."

Doug laughed again. "Tim, you're too much. I've never met anyone like you."

"And you never will," I said, feeling sassy.

He leaned in and kissed me, pressing our bodies together, and we began a new round of discovery.


I COULDN'T FACE church on Sunday. I expected to have to beg and plead with Momma to let me skip, but it wasn't so. All I had to do was ask, and she immediately said I could.

"I wouldn't want to go either, if I were you. I, on the other hand, have a thing or two to say to that pastor and youth minister about how to properly chaperone a lock-in."

That was another reason to be glad I wasn't going. When Momma got her dander up, it was best to step back and let her go.

She put a roast in the oven, gave me strict instructions to turn the oven off at eleven thirty, and she was gone.

I grabbed a Pop-Tart and went back to my bedroom with full intentions of working on my designs. Instead, I lay back on the bed and daydreamed about Doug and what we did yesterday. In fact, I didn't even eat the Pop-Tart. I thought about the moment when my hand slipped under his shirt and made contact with his skin—his warmth and the firmness of his muscles. I sprang to attention. Doug slipping off his shirt, then mine, then pulling me to him, our bare chests touching. He pressed his mouth to mine, our tongues playing. I rolled over onto my stomach and rubbed against the nubby chenille bedspread, my whole body flushing, remembering what we'd said to each other.

I went to the bathroom, again. I'd heard that cold showers killed raging urges. Turning on the cold water full blast, I braced myself and jumped under the icy blast— wow, what a bad idea—and jumped out as fast as I'd jumped in. I toweled off, and the friction from the terry cloth got me excited all over again. This was going to be a problem.

I got back in bed and, after a few minutes, heard Momma open the front door. Looking over at the clock, I was shocked to see it was 12:35. It wouldn't do for her to fine me completely naked, so I grabbed some shorts and a T-shirt. I was barely dressed when Momma appeared in my doorway.

"Can you not hear the oven buzzer? Do you know what time it is?" The timer had been going off for an hour. The roast!

We both ran to the kitchen. Momma opened the oven door, and smoke billowed out. She grabbed the oven mitts, pulled the roast out, and dumped it in the sink. It was ruined.

I braced for her to yell at me, but she didn't. She sat at the breakfast table and put her head in her hands. I didn't know what to do, so I just stood there.

"What am I going to do with you, Timmy?"

"I dunno."

Without saying another word, she stood, went to her room, and shut the door.

She stayed back there for a really long time, like three hours. I'd never seen her upset like that and decided I needed to do something to fix it. I looked at the burned roast and poked it with a fork. Maybe I could salvage some of it. I dug around in the pantry and found a bottle of barbeque sauce, some hamburger buns, and a can of butter beans. I could make it right.

When she finally came out of her bedroom, Momma found the table set with a steaming bowl of butter beans, toasted buns, and a platter of beef, chipped up like pork barbeque.

"We're having beef barbeque sandwiches for dinner, Momma. It's not exactly barbeque, but this sauce I found is pretty good."

"Oh, Timmy, you're such a good boy." She wrapped me in her arms and hugged me tightly.

Then, she released me, dabbed her eyes, and sat down. "This looks lovely. Thank you for salvaging dinner. I'm really hungry."

"Me too! I'm sorry about the pot roast."

"It's all right. I know you've got a lot on your mind right now."

She didn't know the half of it, but I didn't fill her in.

"You're probably wondering what I was doing in my bedroom all that time," she said. "I was on the phone. I talked with Pastor Earl Don, the new youth minister, and several of the mothers. I talked with Doris Mingees, and Annette Herlong, and I called Carleen's mother, Dot. I didn't know that Carleen and her friends got kicked out and Doug left. My goodness; the lock-in was a total disaster."

I couldn't disagree.

"So, the upshot of all this is, I've got a meeting at your school tomorrow at 9:00 AM sharp. I'm meeting with Mrs. Holt and Pastor Earl Don. I'm going to demand they expel that hellion Jimbo."

That reminded me I had to go to school the next day, and I suddenly lost my appetite. I didn't know how the other kids would react to me after everything that had happened. Having my mommy come to my rescue probably wasn't cool, but maybe getting Jimbo expelled would make things a little better.

# Twenty-One: Bunny the Bar Fly

THE NEXT MORNING, I walked into school and nobody bothered me. In fact, Jimbo and his partners in crime seemed to go out of their way to avoid me. It was weird.

When I walked into Good Citizenship, all the kids turned to look at me, then quickly turned away. All except Doug, of course, who smiled as I sat next to him. Nobody but us knew what we had done on Saturday, and it was exciting to share a secret. Carleen was sitting on my other side, but she was careful to avoid eye contact. I was getting really tired of her being my enemy. I looked over at Kimberly Ann, but she just stared straight ahead, an annoyed look on her face.

It was hard to pay attention because I knew Momma was going to be on school grounds at nine that morning. Sure enough, as we were changing classes, I saw her.

She walked into school with Daddy. I didn't think they'd both be there. She saw me in the hall and gave me a little wave. Daddy looked at me, but didn't wave or anything. He had a look on his face like something smelled bad.

Doug also saw them come in. "What's up with that?"

I leaned in. "Momma's trying to get Jimbo expelled."

"It'll never happen."

That worried me. In fact, I had no idea what happened in second period because I was too distracted. I don't know how I held it together to third period, but when we changed classes again, Mrs. Holt's door was still closed. What was going on? How could it possibly be taking this long? How could I be expected to handle so much stress?

Just before the end of third period, Miss Amanda interrupted the class to say I was wanted in Mrs. Holt's office. All eyes were on me as I gathered my books.

Miss Amanda put her arm around me and led me to the office where Momma and Daddy were waiting. I sat between them and glanced across the desk at Mrs. Holt, who was watching me. I felt like I was about to be expelled, even though I hadn't done anything wrong.

Momma spoke from my side. "Mrs. Holt said it was okay for us to take you to lunch, sweetie. Won't that be nice on a school day? Your Daddy's paying, aren't you, Ronnie?"

Daddy grumbled, "It'll have to be quick, like burgers at the pool hall. I have to get back to work."

"Well, I think that's real nice," said Mrs. Holt. "Just make sure he's back by one."

There was a bit of discussion between Momma and Daddy about which vehicle to take—the Lil' Ole Tow Truck or Momma's Catalina. Momma won, mainly because her air-conditioning worked, and she absolutely refused to ride in a hot truck cab in her new pants suit.

It was real cool in the pool hall, and old Mr. Baughtnight, who ran the place, told us to come on in. Momma had us sit as far away from the pool tables as possible. It was dark and smoky. A couple of old fellas were shooting pool, and a lone blonde woman sat at the bar nursing a Budweiser. An old Kitty Wells song played on the jukebox.

Momma pulled a bunch of paper napkins out of the dispenser and wiped down the table real good. She put one on the vinyl seat for me to sit on. Mr. Baughtnight called out and said he'd bring us three cheeseburgers, two Buds, and a Co'Cola for me. The pool hall didn't have menus. Momma said she'd have a Co'Cola too because she had to get back to work.

Mr. Baughtnight made change for the jukebox for the woman at the bar, then shooed away the flies from the raw hamburger meat that was sitting on the counter. He picked up the meat and formed three large patties. He dropped them on the griddle, and they sizzled like crazy. They smelled real good. It was my first time at the pool hall, and it was kind of scary, but I was suddenly hungry.

Momma began. "We had a long talk with Mrs. Holt. She agrees with me that what Jimbo did was really bad. And Kimberly Ann egged him on, which I found so shocking. I'd hoped both of them would be expelled, and I'd hoped your father would speak up about it, but..."

"Nobody's gonna expel the Mingees kid," said Daddy. "Her father pays the bills around there. Holt knows where her paycheck comes from." He took a long draw off his beer.

"But she wouldn't even consider expelling Jimbo. It was assault. He assaulted our son. I can't believe I have to explain it to you, Ronnie."

"Weak kids get picked on. If he weren't weak, he wouldn't get picked on. If you didn't send him to school with SlimFast bars and shit, he'd be better off."

"And what is that supposed to mean?" asked Momma.

"He needs to learn how to fight," said Daddy.

"But, Daddy, I grabbed the pitchfork from him."

"Nobody would have poked Jimbo the first time because he's a tough boy, and people know better. Hey, Baughtnight, where's them burgers?"

"Keep your pants on," said Mr. Baughtnight.

"I grabbed the pitchfork from him," I said quietly. I wanted to say, if you love Jimbo so much, why don't you adopt him? But I didn't.

The blonde woman from the bar approached our table with the burgers. Up close, I could see the bright lines of blue eye shadow and the deep-maroon lip liner. She'd left the rest of her lipstick on her beer bottle.

"Hey, JoAnne," she said. "You remember me, don't you? Lula from high school? Haven't seen you in forever. I go by Bunny now; so much more fun, don't cha think?"

"Yes, I remember you," said Momma. "So, you work at the pool hall now?"

"Naw. I just hang out here enough, and ol' man Baughtnight puts me to work sometimes. I get some tips."

"I'm sure you do," said Momma.

Bunny dropped her burger in front of her, scattering fries across the table.

"Ronnie's right, you know. Every boy's got to learn how to fight."

Momma glared at her. "This is a private conversation."

"Suit yourself," said Bunny. "All I'm sayin' is, Ronnie here could teach him a thing or two. He knows how to throw a punch." She paused a minute and held Momma's gaze. "And he certainly knows how to use his hands." Bunny flounced off to the bar and ordered herself another beer.

Momma redirected her glare to Daddy. "For God's sake, Ronnie."

THAT NIGHT, MOMMA retold Aunt Melanie about her exchange with Bunny. Melanie had come by with take-out dinner, and Momma started talking the minute she opened the door.

"It's actually not such a horrible idea," said Aunt Melanie. "It wouldn't be bad for Timmy to learn a little self-defense, but not from Ronnie, no way." She put the bags down, and I could smell food. I didn't recognize it, but it smelled delicious. "Ronnie hasn't ever won a fight in his life. He's usually too drunk by the time the first punch is thrown."

"Then who?" asked Momma.

"I don't know. I'll talk to Mr. Moray about it. I bet he knows something about dealing with redneck bullies."

"Mr. Moray? Well, I guess so. He certainly seems like a smart guy."

"Smart enough to hire me. Plus, I just got my first paycheck. I went all the way to Aiken to get Chinese food. What do you say, Tim?" She started pulling these cute little white boxes with wire handles out of the bag.

"It sure smells good," I said.

Aunt Melanie reached into another bag and pulled out a bottle of pink wine. "It's a little warm. Here, JoAnne, why don't you stick it in the freezer for a little flash chill."

Aunt Melanie set out all the food on the coffee table and told us to sit on the floor. "It'll be fun." There were even real chopsticks. Momma didn't try to use them, but I did. It wasn't easy, but I kept at it until I could eat a little. Mostly, I used a fork, though. I ate sweet-and-sour chicken and fried rice with little tiny shrimps in it. It was delicious. But the best part was the egg rolls. I had two, and they were real big. They came with a real sweet sauce that was perfect for cutting the grease of the egg roll.

Momma and Aunt Melanie drank the white Zinfandel with ice because they couldn't wait for the flash chill. Aunt Melanie suggested they pour me a glass.

"Yeah! Can I, Momma?"

"I don't know," said Momma.

"Oh, come on, JoAnne, just one." Aunt Melanie was already up, grabbing a third glass from the cupboard. "There's hardly any alcohol in this stuff anyway." She poured a glass and handed it to me without waiting for Momma to reply.

I tasted it. It was great. "It kind of tastes like Hi-C."

"Well, it's not, so be careful. Just little sips and only one glass," said Momma.

After a few more sips, I got an idea. "Oh my gosh, I've got to show you my new designs!" I ran back to my room to get them. The Emmys were coming up, and I was inspired. I ran back in and spread my new designs all over the shag carpet. Momma and Aunt Melanie freshened their wine glasses. Not mine.

"Well, I need to start off by saying some real glamorous ladies are nominated this year," I said. "Miss Patty Duke is nominated. She won an Oscar when she was just a little girl, and she wore a little girl's dress. Now that she's grown up, I think she needs to make up for it with something couture."

"Ko-what?" asked Aunt Melanie.

"Couture. It means high fashion made just for you. Now, look what I designed for Miss Duke." I pulled out a drawing of a dress made of emerald satin with long lace sleeves. It had a daring low-cut neckline. "I think this would be so flattering on her. Don't you?"

"I love it," said Momma. "I'd wear it in a minute."

"Where would you wear it? To the Bi-Rite?" asked Aunt Melanie.

"If I had a dress that beautiful, I'd darn sure wear it to the Bi-Rite, the Winn-Dixie, and anywhere else they'd let me."

"Now, pay attention," I said. "Miss Lee Remick is nominated, too."

"Oh, she's so pretty," said Momma. "I've always said so. Just like a perfect china doll."

"Yes, I agree," I said. "That's why I think she should wear something very simple. Basic black. Nothing to detract from her beauty. See?" I showed them my drawing of a simple black sheath, even more low-cut than Patty Duke's.

"I'd add a couple of stitches to that neckline," said Momma. "Seems a little much to me."

"What's the matter, JoAnne, afraid they'll fall out?" Aunt Melanie joked. I giggled.

"Besides," Aunt Melanie continued, "they have tape for that sort of thing."

"Tape? Really?" Momma asked.

"Yes, ma'am," I said. "When dresses are real low-cut, that's how they keep everything, um, in place."

"They call it titty tape," said Aunt Melanie. "What? Don't give me that look, JoAnne. I read about it in *Cosmo*. Go on, Timmy, what else you got?" She poured the last of the wine into her glass.

"Well," I said. "None other than Miss Bette Davis is nominated. You know she was robbed at the Oscars in '63."

"How do you know that? You weren't even born yet," said Momma.

"I read a lot. I know a lot of stuff."

"I wouldn't doubt his word when it comes to Hollywood glamour gals," said Aunt Melanie. "What have you got planned for Miss Davis?"

"Look." I brandished my favorite design of my entire Emmy collection. I'd drawn a regal lady in a flamboyant, bright-red ball gown. "It's inspired by the red gown in *Jezebel*, but modern."

"That's the most beautiful thing I've ever seen," said Momma. "Timmy, you are becoming more and more talented every day."

"Yeah, forget self-defense. He needs to be studying fashion design," said Aunt Melanie.

I beamed and gently ran my hand across the drawing.

"In fact," said Aunt Melanie, "I need to introduce you to Mr. Maurice. You need to learn from him. You need a fashion mentor, and nobody knows more about fashion than Maurice Moray. Come hang out with me at his shop. He'd love it. In fact, I've been telling him he needs some more help, someone to run errands or open boxes or help clean up, stuff like that. I think you'd be perfect."

"Are you serious? I could actually work at Mr. Maurice's beautiful store?"

"Just leave it to me."

"And he'd get paid?" asked Momma.

"Maybe. Probably. Definitely. Maurice loves me. I'll set it up." She lifted her glass. "Let's drink to the start of Timmy's fashion career!"

We drank, and I felt a warm buzz from the wine.

"Hey, Tim," said Aunt Melanie. "I saw your friend Carleen this afternoon. I stopped by the dime store, and she was in there with these two girls I didn't really know."

"Jaime and Patti," I said.

"Yeah. They were in the makeup aisle, and I think I surprised Carleen when I said hi. Actually, I think those two girls were about to shoplift some lip gloss. They both had some in their hands, and there was something about the way they carefully put them back when they saw an adult."

"Carleen shouldn't be hanging around with a bad crowd," said Momma.

I frowned. "Carleen and I haven't been seeing each other so much lately. She's got these new friends."

"Maybe you should give her a call," said Aunt Melanie. "You two have been friends for a long time."

"I'll see her at school. Hey, there is someone I want to call, though. Can I be excused?"

"Who do you want to call?" asked Momma.

"He's going to call his new best friend, Doug," said Aunt Melanie, giving me a knowing look.

"Doug is such a nice boy," said Momma.

# Twenty-Two: Baby Love

I STRETCHED THE phone cord from Momma's room to mine and shut the door.

"Hey, Doug, it's Timmy, I mean, Tim."

"Hey, baby. I was just thinking about you. I'm lying on my bed wishing you were here."

He called me baby!

"I wish I was there, too."

"What would you do to me if you were here?"

I giggled and blushed and had absolutely no idea what to say.

"Cat got your tongue? I wish I had your tongue...in my mouth."

"Me too," I whispered. "But that's not what I called about. I've got really important news."

"Okay, spoilsport. Spill."

"I'm getting a job!"

"Really? Where? Your dad's garage?"

"Oh, gross, no. At Boutique Moray."

"That fancy dress shop on the square?"

"The very one."

"That's great. That suits you a lot more than some greasy garage."

"No kidding."

"What will you be doing?" he asked.

"I'm not completely sure. I don't technically have the job yet."

"What did Mr. Moray say?"

"He doesn't technically know about it yet."

"Then how did you get this job? Technically."

"Aunt Melanie works for him, keeping his books. He loves her like everybody does, and she said she'd tell him he has to hire me. I'm so excited! I just love that place, although I've never actually been inside."

"Technically."

I giggled. "It's way too expensive for Momma to shop there. It's probably too expensive for Mrs. Mingees. I think his customers are all rich ladies from Columbia and Charleston and Atlanta."

"Why would women drive that far to shop in Edgewood?"

"Because he has things nobody has outside of New York. Did you know he single-handedly introduced Halston to South Carolina?"

"Somehow, I missed that."

"It's true. It was about three years ago, not long after he opened. I'd invent excuses to go uptown just so I could look in the windows. They were so beautiful. This one time, he actually had Halston in the window. Real Halston. Nobody in this town knew what it was, but I knew because I read *Vogue* religiously, of course."

"Of course. But I wonder why he ever chose Edgewood for his shop? It seems like it belongs in a city. Charleston maybe. I wonder what his story is."

"Oh, I know all about it."

"Why am I not surprised?"

"For years, it was known as McDonald's Mercantile and was run by a lady named Miss Inez McDonald. She inherited the business from her daddy, so it was there for a really long time keeping all the local little old ladies in corsets and supp hose. When Miss Inez finally died, everybody wondered what would happen to it. Then, Mr. Maurice showed up at her funeral.

"He said he was Miss Inez's great-nephew, and he'd inherited the business. He came from Alabama where he said he had a shop that served the Mobile carriage trade. Everybody knows Mobile is real fancy and has lots of grand ladies. I think it's like Charleston but with more big cotton money.

"Mr. Maurice said he had a vision to bring high fashion to the South Carolina Upcountry, and Miss Inez's store was such a great opportunity, it was worth giving up his business in Mobile. People gossiped, for sure. Everybody wanted to know why he'd give up a thriving business in a city to come to this Podunk town.

"There were rumors of some kind of trouble in Mobile, something vague about a college boy, but I couldn't imagine what."

"I can," said Doug.

"Well, maybe I could if I listened to gossip, but I don't. The Bible talks about that, you know."

"Let's pretend I do and keep moving."

"People were just jealous of Mr. Maurice's flair and style. That's what Momma said he had—flair and style, just like she said about me. Anyway, after Miss Inez's funeral, he closed the store down for two months and put brown paper over the windows. When it reopened, all the corsets and supp hose were gone. It was renamed Boutique Moray, and from the window displays to the dressing rooms, everything was high fashion and sleek."

"And now you get to work there. Congratulations."

"Thank you! I'm so excited!"

"I can tell. When do you start?"

"I don't know. I should probably go ask Aunt Melanie. I vote for Monday after school. Oh, hey, speaking of Aunt Melanie, guess who she saw at the dime store today?"

"Tom Selleck?"

"No, silly. Carleen with her new crew."

"What were those bad girls up to?"

"Aunt Melanie thinks they were shoplifting lip gloss."

"See what happens when you're no longer in her life? She becomes a criminal. Next stop, reform school."

"I kind of miss her sometimes."

"I know you do. She'll come around. I promise."

"If you say so."

"I say so. Hey, I need to go. I'm about ready to go to bed."

"I wish I was there."

"I wish you were here, too."

"Good night...honey," I said.

"Good night, babe..."

"One of us has to hang up first," Doug said, after a pause.

"I can't! You hang up first."

"Okay."

"No! Okay, go ahead," I said.

"How about we hang up together. One, two, three..."

# Twenty-Three: Mr. Maurice

AUNT MELANIE CAME up with a plan to keep her word about getting me hired at Boutique Moray. Once she sobered up from her white Zin buzz, she decided she couldn't just waltz into the store on Monday and demand I be hired. Instead, I was to come by after school and drop some hints here and there about my fashion knowledge.

"He needs an extra hand around there, and once he realizes you're a fashion star in the making, he'll snap you up."

She had total confidence in her plan. I didn't. In fact, as I approached the store on Monday afternoon, I was a nervous wreck. But as soon as I walked in, my nerves evaporated and I was transported to a world of beauty and magic. There was soft classical music playing. Real white roses filled gigantic vases, scenting the air. It was even more beautiful than I'd imagined.

"There you are. Let me introduce you to Mr. Maurice Moray," said Aunt Melanie, turning me toward a handsome, slightly portly man with perfectly groomed salt-and-pepper hair. He reached out his hand, and I took it. He gave me a firm handshake and spoke in a rich, confident voice.

"Well, hello, young man. You must be Melanie's nephew, Tim. She's told me so much about you."

"Hello, sir."

His suit was expensive and obviously tailored for him. I'm pretty sure the shirt was real silk, and it had a little *P* above the pocket, which I knew stood for Pierre Cardin. That meant it was French. His tie was in a bold paisley pattern. He smelled good, too, kind of like the woods on a fresh, sunny fall day.

"I understand you're interested in fashion, is that right?"

"Yes, sir." He was so handsome, and his voice was so commanding I couldn't think of anything else to say.

"Well, that's just great. Not very many boys your age are interested in fashion. I think that makes you very special. Don't you agree, Melanie?"

"Timmy is the most special boy in town. He reads *Vogue* cover to cover each month."

"Good for you. *Vogue* is the bible, you know."

I thought Doug would get a kick out of that line. "It's important," I said.

"Yes! Important is the word."

Just then, a tall blonde lady walked into the store, and Mr. Maurice excused himself to assist her. Aunt Melanie took me back to her office. It wasn't an office so much as a storage room with racks of clothes and a few old mannequins and, in the corner, a desk and some file cabinets. That was where Aunt Melanie kept the books.

"Good job impressing him," she said. "Right now, I have some work to do, so why don't you sit and do your homework while he helps that client."

I sat and tried to concentrate on my algebra homework, but those racks of clothes kept calling my name. I walked over to them and ran my hands across them.

"You better have clean hands," said Aunt Melanie, without looking up. I'd never felt fabrics like them. There was no polyester at all. They felt rich and fine. There were silks and satins and sequins. I never wanted to think about geometry again.

I didn't notice Mr. Maurice standing there until he spoke. "You think those are nice? Come with me, kid." He put his arm around my shoulders and ushered me out of the back room.

"Mr. Maurice, I'm so sorry," said Aunt Melanie. "He was supposed to keep his seat and do his homework."

"Nonsense," said Mr. Maurice. "The young man is curious about beautiful things, and that should be encouraged. What sort of homework were you doing, anyway, Master Timothy?"

"Algebra," I said.

"Thank God I rescued you. Trust me when I tell you you'll never need algebra in your entire life. Now come with me." He led me over to the storeroom. "We just got a new shipment in from New York. There's nothing more exciting than a new shipment." My head was swimming. Those clothes had come all the way from New York!

"Hey, Mel, do you mind if I use your nephew to help me get these garments out on the floor?"

"Feel free to put him to work."

He led me to another back room where his sales girl, April, was hanging up dresses. I recognized them immediately as Diane von Fürstenberg wrap dresses.

"*Women's Wear Daily* says these are over," he said. "I don't believe it. They're modern classics, and Boutique Moray will always stock them. Don't you agree, Timothy?"

Nobody ever called me Timothy, and I started to correct him but instantly decided I liked it. It fit the professional atmosphere of the store.

"Now, Timothy, help me choose the right dress for the window. I'm doing a special Diane von Fürstenberg trunk sale and need the perfect dress to set the mood."

April held up a gown and said, "This is the one I would put in the window."

It was stunning and completely unexpected. It was a long wrap maxi-dress in a print that was sort of animal, but not quite. It was like abstract art. The colors were chocolate and taupe and cream with pink around the neckline. You wouldn't think pink would work with chocolate and taupe and cream, but it was gorgeous. I touched it. It was such fine silk that it was like putting my hand in a mountain stream.

"You can't put this in the window," I said.

"Why not?" asked Mr. Maurice, smiling.

"It's too special. The average person walking by this store wouldn't understand it. There's one woman for this dress, and you need to find her. No one should see it before she does."

Mr. Maurice smiled. "I do believe fashion is your calling."

He called for Aunt Melanie. "This is a creative boy. You cannot stifle his muse with algebra. I believe we should find something for him to do around here—don't you think? Perhaps April could use an assistant."

"That's a great idea," said Aunt Melanie. "Timmy could be really useful." April nodded but didn't smile. I think she was a bit stung that Mr. Maurice liked my idea better than hers.

That was the beginning of my life in fashion. I ran errands, opened boxes of new shipments, put out clothes—whatever April needed. When Mr. Maurice had clients, I would hang out in the back and listen to him. He knew so much about fashion and could size up a woman in a minute. The moment she walked into the store, he knew what sort of silhouette would work on her and how much she'd be willing to pay.

So many women didn't know how to dress, especially those who dressed too young. There were women in their thirties who tried to wear cute little numbers like they wore when they were cheerleaders. Thirty-five was too old for a crop top, not that Mr. Maurice would sell such a thing. Mr. Maurice would never come out and tell a client she was too old for something, though. He'd gossip and chat and flatter until the customer was putty in his hands. Then, he'd start showing her the right clothes to maximize her assets. It worked every time. He transformed women every day. I had so much to learn from him.

During my second week, I reported to work to find Mr. Maurice in a real tizzy. He was rushing around the store, plumping pillows, rearranging flowers, and generally making everything even more perfect than it already was. Aunt Melanie pulled me back into her office and told me to stay out of the way and quietly do my job.

"Our most important client is coming today," she said. "Her name is Maureen Hamilton, she's from Mobile, and she owns half of Alabama. She shopped with Maurice when he was in Mobile, and she's followed him here. With any luck, she'll buy scads of clothes."

I was incredibly curious, so I decided it was important that I dust the handbags at the front of the store at Lady Hamilton's scheduled arrival time. Just as I was about to get bored with dusting the same bag over and over, a gigantic new Mercedes with Alabama plates pulled up to the curb. A driver in uniform—no kidding!—got out and opened the back door. He was black and tall with broad shoulders and was pretty darn handsome. He reminded me of the black guy on *Mission: Impossible*, but better looking. A tall lady in a full-length fur coat got out. It was November and probably about seventy degrees, but that coat was so gorgeous I would have worn it in August. A great big black standard poodle on a jeweled leash followed her, and the two of them walked right into Boutique Moray.

Mr. Maurice rushed up to her and kissed her on both cheeks. Then he quickly locked the front doors—in the middle of the workday!

"Maureen, my dear, you look lovely as always. I'm absolutely delighted you agreed to come visit with me out here in the provinces."

Mr. Maurice removed her coat, revealing a lovely and expensive-looking royal-blue silk dress.

"I had no choice but to come here, Maurice," she said, smoothing out her dress. "Look at what I'm reduced to wearing without you, some cheap frock from God knows where."

"Not to worry, my dear. You're in good hands." He actually snapped his fingers, and April came out bearing a tray with a bottle of champagne and two flutes. She struggled for a minute, trying to figure out how to open it before Mr. Maurice impatiently took it from her, expertly opened it, and filled the flutes.

"A toast," he said.

"To good taste," Lady Hamilton said. "Now, let's get to work."

After seeing and rejecting more gowns than I realized we had, Mr. Maurice brought out the special Diane von Fürstenberg in chocolate and pink.

"I've been holding this back just for you, my dear."

Mrs. Hamilton coolly appraised the breathtaking gown. She touched the fabric.

"Nice. Now we're making progress. That will be perfect for the Johannsson wedding. You know my measurements. Now, on to the symphony gala." I felt a surge of pride. It would look amazing on her.

Mr. Maurice motioned me over. "Maureen dear, this is Timothy, my new intern. He has quite the eye for fashion, and I believe will make quite a splash one day. In fact, he recognized the importance of this DvF gown almost as quickly as I did and knew it was meant for a special client."

"A young man mature beyond his years. What a find, Maurice. And in *this* town."

I was downright giddy, but didn't know what to say other than "Thank you."

"Now, Timothy, please take Katie Scarlett out so Mrs. Hamilton's driver can take her for a walk," said Mr. Maurice.

I assumed Katie Scarlett was the dog. I bent down to take the leash and got my first close look at Mrs. Hamilton. She was very pretty and must have been Miss America–level beautiful at one time. She wore a lot of makeup, so, at a distance, her face appeared lineless. Up close was another story. I also couldn't miss the gigantic solitaire diamond on a gold chain just long enough that the stone nestled between her breasts. It matched her simple diamond earrings. Those, and a Cartier tank watch were her only jewelry. Together, they were probably worth more than Momma's house.

I took the dog out, and the driver got out of the car and took the leash.

"She's a nice dog," I said. "I bet that lady's gonna buy a lot of beautiful clothes."

He laughed while I petted Katie Scarlett. "She'll leave here without a thing. Then, in a few days, a ton of packages will arrive. Maybe she'll remember, maybe not. What a life."

I noticed he had pale, hazel eyes. He smiled. I felt a little weak in the knees.

"What's your name?" he asked.

"Tim. Timothy." I decided in that moment to use Timothy as my professional name.

"How do you do, Tim Timothy. My name is Shane, and I'm pleased to make your acquaintance." He shook my hand. His hand was huge and strong.

Shane. It was a sexy name.

"I've got things under control with the dog, so you can go back to your job now, Timothy."

I went back into the store and debated telling Doug about Shane. Would he be jealous that I found another man attractive? Was it okay to talk to your boyfriend about good-looking guys? There was so much to figure out now that I was gay. Not that I was complaining.

After a while, the lady left in a swarm of air-kisses and *darlings* and promises for lunch. Shane helped her into the Mercedes, gave me a quick tip of the hat, and they were gone. Mr. Maurice and April stood there, waving until the big car turned the corner.

As they turned to go into the store, Mr. Maurice looked in my direction and smiled. "Excellent job, Timothy. Thank you for your help. Mrs. Hamilton just bought so much that everyone will get a Christmas bonus."

April clapped, and I immediately wondered what I could buy Doug with my Christmas bonus.

Mr. Maurice put his arm around me. "Timothy, you behaved yourself beautifully today. I have an idea, and I believe you'll be perfect. I'm throwing a party in a couple of weeks. It's a thank-you for my most important clients. In other words, it's a very important business party, and I need a mature, well-behaved young man or two to help me. I would need you to take ladies' coats and wraps, keep track of them, and return them."

"Gosh, Mr. Maurice, I'd be happy to. But it's still so warm; do you think very many ladies will wear coats?"

"It's late fall, and the ladies will wear their furs," he said, "even if it's a hundred degrees. Now, do you have a friend who could help collect coats? Someone polite and presentable and attractive who you wouldn't mind spending the whole evening with?"

Did I ever! Doug would be perfect for the job.

"Yes, sir, I know just the guy."

Mr. Maurice winked at Aunt Melanie who smiled back. "Could this guy be young Mr. Appleby?" asked Mr. Maurice. "Your new special friend?"

"Yes, sir, how did you know?"

"Why, everyone in town is talking about the new boy from California. I believe he'd be perfect. Talk to him and set it up."

# Twenty-Four: Soirée Chez Maurice

I CALLED DOUG as soon as I got home, but he already knew. It turned out Aunt Melanie had called Doug's momma that day. Doug wasn't as super excited as I was to go to a glamorous party with rich, fashionable people, but he was going, and that was all that mattered.

Aunt Melanie was also going to be there, and I told her I'd help her pick out what to wear. I knew I could find just the right silhouette for her, but Mr. Maurice beat me to it. He was going to let her borrow a dress from the boutique. She'd be like a model, working the party. It was all just too exciting and chic!

On the big night, Aunt Melanie looked so pretty. Momma had suggested she go to Merle Norman in Greenwood to have her makeup "professionally done," but, thankfully, Aunt Melanie talked her out of it. Every bride at First Baptist got her face done at Merle Norman, and they all looked like Japanese geisha girls. Makeup was supposed to be light and natural now, and thank goodness, Aunt Melanie had the right touch.

The dress she borrowed from the boutique was a knockout. It was a simple halter dress, just like Marilyn Monroe over the subway grate, but sexier and in red. With her dark hair and good makeup, she'd transformed herself from cute small-town girl to Jaclyn Smith look-alike. Aunt Melanie said there'd be rich men from New York at the party, and she was man-hunting.

When it was time for me to get dressed, Momma had a big surprise. I was planning on wearing my blue blazer like I wore to church every Sunday, but she pulled out a new camel blazer! It was gorgeous.

Her eyes teared up a little bit when she told me about seeing it at Belk's and deciding it had my name all over it. She even said Daddy helped her pay for it. Daddy!

Momma straightened my lapel and said, "Your daddy's been feeling bad about how things have been going lately, what with those white trash boys at school being so mean and all, and he's been wanting to do something for you. You be sure and tell him thank you, you hear?"

Aunt Melanie then presented me with a paisley silk tie in shades of dark green. The look was straight out of *GQ*, and I felt very sophisticated.

"We're just so proud of you for being a big, grown-up man, starting your career in fashion," Momma said. "You're growing up so fast I can't believe it!" She grabbed me and hugged me hard. I hugged back.

About the time I finished getting ready, Daddy drove up in Momma's Catalina, and we all went out to the front yard. He'd taken it to wash and wax and clean up inside for our big night. It looked showroom fresh even though it was a '72.

"The car looks good, Ronnie," said Momma. "Thanks for doing all that."

"I couldn't let 'em go to a fancy party in Mel's ratty old Vega with no AC."

"Thank you for the jacket, Daddy. It's really nice."

"It looks good on you," Daddy said. "Your momma said it would. She always knows about things like that. I don't know nothin' about clothes and shit."

"Ronnie, language."

"Sorry. It's just that I wanted my son to look as good as any of those fancy people at that fancy party." He'd never actually called me his son before. Ever. I stepped up to maybe give him a hug or something, and he stuck out his hand for me to shake. It felt grown-up to shake my Daddy's hand.

"Now, don't you spill nothin' on it."

"I won't, Daddy." I wouldn't dare. I wanted to cry all of a sudden, and I chewed on the inside of my cheek to stop it.

"All right," Daddy said. "Well, I gotta go. I can't stand around here flapping my gums all day. I got a transmission to rebuild before the day's out. JoAnne, you still gonna drive me back to the Amoco?"

They took off in the Vega, and Aunt Melanie put her arm around my shoulders. "Let's go party with the rich folks."

We went to pick up Doug, and he looked amazing. He was in the same blue blazer he wore when he went to church with us, and his mother had put some sort of gel in his hair that made him look real grown-up. He sat next to me in the back seat of Momma's Catalina and took my hand. I caught Aunt Melanie's eyes in the rearview mirror, and she smiled warmly. Our first PDA. I squeezed his hand. I almost leaned over to kiss him but decided not to push my luck.

"You look like you could be on the cover of *GQ*," I said.

I couldn't wait to see Mr. Maurice's house. He'd bought this ultramodern place that had been built a couple of years ago by a peach farmer who thought he was richer than he really was. A late freeze killed that year's crop, the bank took the house, and Mr. Maurice picked it up for a song, or at least that's what Aunt Melanie said.

The house was set far back from the road, and there were stone pillars flanking the driveway with "Creekside" written on one of them. We drove down the long, twisting drive, and the house came into sight. I'd never seen anything like it. It was sleek and modern, yet rustic. It was built of cedar and seemed like it grew out of the hillside.

Mr. Maurice answered the door, and he looked superhandsome. He wore the latest double-breasted blue blazer, and it was tailored perfectly. I never noticed before how broad his chest was. I decided he must lift weights. He'd found a pocket square that matched his blue-green eyes perfectly. Only Mr. Maurice could pull it all together.

When he saw us, he clapped his hands. "Fabulous! Our handsome young men are here!"

I entered the home by crossing a faux footbridge over a dry creek bed *inside the house*. We walked down slatted stairs into the great room. There was a huge wall of glass revealing a perfectly lit stream flowing beyond the terrace, with giant, carefully placed boulders and a footbridge like the one in the entrance hall. The furniture in the great room was mostly sleek white leather, with occasional *objets d'art* expertly placed here and there.

To the side was a large fireplace, and over it hung a huge portrait of an elegant lady dressed in a white gown, lounging on rocks beside a stream. It looked just like the rocks and stream outside the window.

"Who's the lady in the portrait?" I asked.

"I have no idea," said Mr. Maurice. "But I tell everyone she's Mother Dear. I found the painting in an antique store in London and modeled my landscaping after it."

"Whoa," said Doug, finally impressed with something. "You modeled your landscaping after a painting. Really cool."

Beside the painting stood a man holding a martini and looking very sophisticated. He appeared older than Mr. Maurice, but was just as good-looking. He was well groomed with his hair combed straight back from his forehead and gelled. He was in a single-breasted blue blazer and a bright-red bow tie.

"This is Georges," said Mr. Maurice. He pronounced it the French way. "He's the proprietor of the famous Jean Georges gallery in New York."

Aunt Melanie made a beeline to the New Yorker and introduced herself. Doug and I followed Mr. Maurice into the huge kitchen where the bartender was setting up. It was Debbie Abernathy, Jimbo's cousin from the dime store. What was she doing there? I should have known she was a bartender.

"Hey, Mr. Maurice," said Debbie. "Ready for a fresh one?"

"Just a light one, Debbie. I need to pace myself since I'm the host. Do you know these two young men? They'll be collecting wraps this evening."

"Sure, I know them," said Debbie. "How you boys doing?"

"And this is her bar back," said Mr. Maurice as Jimbo walked in carrying two bags of ice. My stomach dropped down to my shoes. Jimbo saw Doug and me and looked as surprised as we were, but he didn't say anything.

"Do you boys know each other?" asked Mr. Maurice. "I believe you all go to the same school? The patriotic one?"

"Yes, sir," said Jimbo, shifting from one foot to the other. "Hi, Doug. Hi, Tim."

"Hey," said Doug. I mouthed the word *hey* but no sound came out.

"If your wrap-gathering duties slow down during the night, feel free to help Jimbo out in the garage. He'll be lugging ice and bottles back and forth," said Debbie.

"No, no, these boys will be fully employed tonight," said Mr. Maurice. "We wouldn't want to keep a lady waiting for her wrap, would we? Now, come with me and I'll show you to your station." I was relieved he had saved us from having to work with Jimbo.

He walked us back past Aunt Melanie just as she grabbed Georges' bicep and threw her head back, laughing at something he said. Mr. Maurice showed us a small sitting room just off the rustic footbridge where he'd wheeled racks set up with wooden hangers. There was also a tray with sandwiches, cookies, and Cokes on ice, just for us. Mr. Maurice had thought of everything. He left us alone to await the start of the party.

"Shit, Jimbo's here," said Doug.

"I know! He ruins everything."

"Who's going to show up next? Carleen and the Vandellas?"

I laughed. "Maybe they're the live entertainment."

Doug stuck his finger in his mouth. "Gag me."

I laughed.

"Don't worry about Jimbo," Doug said. "He's not going to pull any crap at a fancy party like this. He's just trying to make a buck or two; that's all. We'll stay out of his way."

"Okay. If you say so."

He smiled at me, and I felt better.

Pretty soon, people started arriving, although at first it was mainly local folks. Aunt Melanie always said country people show up early, especially if there was free food and booze. Doug and I took turns helping ladies with their coats and hanging them up.

I was getting the hang of it and feeling good about the night ahead when the door opened and in walked Kimberly Ann with her parents, Dr. and Mrs. Mingees.

"What's she doing here?" Doug whispered to me.

"I have no idea. I thought this was a grown-ups only party."

Kimberly Ann and Mrs. Mingees pretended like they didn't notice us, but Dr. Mingees gave us a big smile. "Well, if it isn't Annette Herlong's boy," he said as he grabbed Doug's bicep. "You've got quite a muscle there, young man. You lifting weights? And hello there, young Mr. Thompson. Nice jacket. Is your pretty mother here?"

"No, sir," I said.

"A pity."

Mrs. Mingees and Kimberly Ann were standing on the landing, scanning the crowd. Kimberly Ann was in a red dress that looked like a bad Halston knockoff. Mr. Maurice came up to greet them.

"Well, if it isn't the good doctor and his pretty wife." He air-kissed Mrs. Mingees. "And you brought your daughter along, too. What a nice surprise."

"We thought you wouldn't mind," said Mrs. Mingees. "She's been dying to meet you. Say hello, Kimberly Ann."

"Hello," said Kimberly Ann shyly. I'd never seen her act shy before. She even gave Mr. Maurice a little curtsy.

"No need to curtsy, dear. I'm not the Queen. Not *that* queen, anyway."

Doug chuckled.

"Aren't you funny," said Mrs. Mingees. "I was thinking you might want Kimberly Ann to model for you and maybe appear in some of your ads. Isn't she pretty? She's a size four and was All American Teen for two years running. She'd be a wonderful representative of your business—don't you think?"

"All American Teen?" said Mr. Maurice.

"It's a competition sponsored by the Daughters of the American Revolution to find the perfect teenager who exemplifies citizenship, patriotism, and popularity. Kimberly Ann always wins, of course."

"Of course," said Mr. Maurice, looking bored. "Now, Kimberly Ann, do you know young masters Timothy and Douglas, here? Perhaps you go to school together at— what's it called?"

"Oh, yes, I believe they do go to Patriot Christian," said Kimberly Ann, without looking in our direction.

"We've been in every class together since kindergarten," I said, feeling emboldened standing next to Doug.

"Well, then," said Mr. Maurice. "Would you like to hang out with your friends?"

"Certainly not," said Mrs. Mingees. "She's a guest, not the help." She turned to her husband. "What does it take to get a white wine spritzer around here?"

"Right this way," said Mr. Maurice. "And I suppose the doctor would like a double scotch?"

"Triple," said Dr. Mingees with a smile.

"Kimberly Ann, I can't help but notice your dress," said Mr. Maurice.

"Thank you. Mother said it's a Halston." She beamed and twirled, almost falling off her heels.

He looked her up and down and glanced quickly at me. "My dear, mother doesn't always know best."

The Mingees disappeared into the crowd with Mr. Maurice.

A few more local people showed up, and then the out-of-towners began to arrive. Mr. Maurice had been right when he said ladies would wear wraps even though it was a warm night. Everyone wore some sort of coat or wrap or stole.

I recognized most of the people as clients from the boutique. Miss Pringle from Columbia, who was one of the boutique's best customers, arrived in a full-length mink coat that she wouldn't let me take. She strode to the landing, surveyed the room below, then dramatically whipped off the coat and walked down the stairs, dragging it behind her. Underneath the coat, she was wearing a little black dress so skimpy I told Doug I hoped she had some of that titty tape.

When Miss Pringle reached the bottom of the stairs, Mr. Maurice rushed up to her and took her hand and said, "My darling, you are a vision."

"I'm fresh from the divorce court where I fleeced my husband for everything before his twelve-year-old girlfriend could get her claws into it. Why is there no champagne in my hand yet?"

Mr. Maurice snapped his fingers at Debbie, who scurried up with a perfect flute of bubbly. Miss Pringle took it without looking at her and plunged into the crowd.

A lady from Charleston arrived in a stylish satin wrap that had been shipped directly to her from New York just days before. She wouldn't let me take it either and spent the entire evening dramatically wrapping herself and unwrapping herself, depending on her audience.

Then, Maureen Hamilton arrived. The front double doors swung open, and I was practically blinded by all the diamonds...on the dog! They both wore diamond-studded collars and glorious white fur coats. She had dyed her poodle to match her coat! Katie Scarlett was white! She was trimmed and groomed like a show poodle with balls and fluff. She somehow managed to look majestic and ridiculous at once.

Mrs. Hamilton had bleached out her own hair several shades blonder than before, and her updo was as elaborate as the dog's. The two of them stood at the top of the landing, surveying the crowd, looking completely bored. I was enthralled.

Mr. Maurice made a beeline up the staircase to greet them, champagne in hand, and kissed the lady on each cheek. "Katie Scarlett is fabulous," he said, gesturing to the dog. "And so are you, Maureen, my dear."

"Her name is Blanche tonight, not Scarlett. Can't you see?"

"Of course, my dear. How clever. Boys, be very careful with Mrs. Hamilton's stunning coat."

"Never mind," said Mrs. Hamilton. "I prefer to keep it with me."

"As you wish," said Mr. Maurice with a little bow, and he ushered them down the stairs. Mr. Maurice took Mrs. Hamilton to a white leather chair in the center of everything, and she sat, spreading open her white coat. Underneath was a blood-red gown that could have been worn by Jean Harlow. It clung to every inch of her toned body, including her smallish, free-hanging breasts. Blanche/Scarlett jumped up on a white leather sofa, running off two ladies who were sitting on it. She growled at anyone else who tried to sit there for the rest of the night.

But the most dramatic arrival was yet to come. Four men came in together. They must have been from New York because I'd never seen men like them in South Carolina. They were all in their twenties and wearing expensive-looking tuxedos. Doug caught my eye and mouthed *Wow*.

One of the men had blond hair and looked a lot like Björn Borg. Another had dark hair and a moustache and wasn't wearing a tie. Instead, he had a couple of shirt buttons unbuttoned, showing off his chest hair, just like Tom Selleck. The third guy looked like Lorenzo Lamas, and he had Dippity-Doo in his jet-black hair. The last one looked like he was Chinese, and he had a body like Bruce Lee. I could tell because his suit fit him so tight I didn't know how he could breathe. His shirt was obviously pure silk, and, just as obviously, he wasn't wearing an undershirt.

Actually, none of the young men were wearing undershirts. Their shirts were tight, and I couldn't stop staring at their nipples.

"Those nips could put an eye out," whispered Doug. I put my hand over my mouth to stifle a laugh. I was tickled and turned on at the same time.

The guys all stood on the landing for a few moments. Björn Borg nudged Tom Selleck, and they looked at me and Doug staring back at them. They smiled, and Lorenzo Lamas said, "Leave it to Maurice to find the cute HITs."

"We're not in training—not anymore," said Doug, taking my hand.

The guys all laughed, and Bruce Lee clapped.

"Who would have guessed, in this little town," he said.

Suddenly, I heard Maurice's booming voice. "BOYS! Come in, come in. Everyone, I want to welcome four of the hottest young actors from New York!"

They were actors! From New York! I wondered what they'd been in. Maybe soap operas, although it couldn't be *All My Children* because I knew everyone who was in *AMC.* Maybe they were on Broadway. Maybe they were in *A Chorus Line.* I wanted to ask them about *A Chorus Line* and Susan Lucci, but Mr. Maurice was already ushering them down the stairs. I wouldn't have dared, anyway. How do you even approach someone that handsome and sophisticated?

"Which one's your favorite?" asked Doug.

Maybe it was okay to talk about cute guys with your boyfriend, after all. I hadn't actually told him we were boyfriends yet, but we were, just the same.

"You go first," I said. "Your choices are Björn Borg, Tom Selleck, Lorenzo Lamas, and Bruce Lee."

He laughed. "I can't decide. Lorenzo Lamas is gorgeous, but Bruce Lee's body! I want to lick his nipples."

I blushed. "I do too. But I pick Tom Selleck."

"You want to bury your face in his chest hair, don't you?"

"Stop!" I said, blushing. "Okay, yes."

We watched as Mr. Maurice introduced the guys to his clients. Miss Pringle's tongue practically hit the floor when she laid eyes on them. Georges suddenly appeared to rescue them from the Columbia divorcée.

"Thank God you're here!" Georges said in a loud voice. He kissed them on each cheek just like they were French. "Now come let me introduce you to the most delightful young lady who works for Maurice, and help me convince her to move to New York. She's simply wasted in this burg." He was talking about Aunt Melanie! Debbie brought them champagne, and soon, the six were laughing loudly.

In between arrivals, Doug and I would sit at the top of the landing, drinking Cokes and watching the whole party unfold before us. Miss Pringle kept trying to break into the group of six and get the actors' attention, but they hardly noticed her. At one point, Lorenzo Lamas left the group to get more champagne, and I swear Miss Pringle dropped her purse on purpose right in front of him. She bent over, and I actually saw her little booby. Gross! She probably wasn't wearing titty tape after all. Lorenzo just handed her purse to her and kept walking.

Dr. and Mrs. Mingees had long since separated and were mixing and mingling. Kimberly Ann was nowhere in sight.

Mr. Maurice must have told Debbie to keep Mrs. Hamilton's glass full because Debbie refilled it every time it got low. She didn't do that for anyone else. Mrs. Hamilton never noticed; in fact, the only time she changed her bored expression was when Georges excused himself from Aunt Melanie and the actors and went to her. He kissed her hand and actually knelt at her feet. He was describing something with dramatic hand gestures, and she actually smiled. A little.

"Looks like we'll be getting a shipment of art from New York soon." I turned, and it was Shane, the driver. He stood behind us, holding a sandwich. "I know that guy Georges. He has an art gallery in New York, and he's sold her a lot of expensive pieces over the years. I'm guessing large, abstract outdoor sculpture. She's going through an abstract sculpture phase." He took a bite of his sandwich. "Hey, this ham and cheese is pretty good. Is this Gruyère? I was told there were snacks in the guest room. Mind if I camp out with you boys for a while?"

"No, sir," said Doug.

"I don't mind," I said, taking in Shane's tall, athletic body.

We followed Shane into the coatroom and each grabbed a fresh Coke.

"So, how long have you guys been an item?" he asked.

How had he figured that out? He must have read my surprised expression. I was probably red as a beet.

"Don't worry," he said. "Your secret's safe with me. I realize you have to be discreet, especially in the small towns. Even in Atlanta, for that matter. It's not like I'd bring my guy around to meet Mrs. H."

"You have a guy?" asked Doug.

"We've been together eight years. He teaches at Georgia Tech. We met when I was in school there."

"You went to college?" I asked and then felt embarrassed. "I mean, it's just that..."

"No problem, buddy. You're probably wondering why a college grad is driving around a white lady. Number one, the pay's good. Number two, the big companies in Atlanta aren't exactly lining up to hire black homos like myself." He chuckled to himself and took a big swig of his Coke.

"That really sucks," said Doug.

Shane shrugged. "Don't worry about me, boys. I'm doing all right. Mrs. H can't get along without me. Besides, as soon as my man finishes his fellowship, we're heading out. Maybe New York. Maybe LA."

"I'm from LA," said Doug. "Just moved here in August."

"You moved here from LA? Why?"

"My mother's family is from here. She and my dad split up, and she dragged me here."

"It doesn't look like things are all bad here in South Kakalaki," said Shane. "You got yourself a cute fellow."

I blushed even deeper. "You're from South Carolina, aren't you?"

"Orangeburg born and bred," he said.

"How did you know he was from South Carolina?" Doug asked me.

"Nobody but a native would say South Kakalaki."

"You people are weird," said Doug.

Shane laughed. "You got that right, man."

The party went on and on, way past the time I expected Aunt Melanie to come get us and go home. She was still laughing it up with Georges and Lorenzo Lamas. Björn Borg and Bruce Lee were circulating. Debbie was pouring drinks as fast as she could.

At about eleven, the party crush was on, and Mr. Maurice rushed up the stairs and said, "Boys, I need you to go help Jimbo for a bit. This crowd is boozing it up so fast he can't keep up. Shane, would you mind helping any ladies who leave find their wraps? Not that anyone is showing any signs of leaving." Shane agreed to the new arrangement, and Doug and I plunged into the party. When we passed Georges, he had his arm around Lorenzo Lamas's waist, pulling him in close. Both men were all ears for Aunt Melanie, who called to us.

"Timmy! Dougie! Hey, you two! You know Georges and Raul, don't you? They're my new best friends. Guess what they've been talking me into all night long? Go on, guess! You'll never guess, so I'll just tell you. I'm going to New York! They talked me into it, so I'm just gonna do it. And soon. What do you think? Isn't that amazing?"

Before I could answer, Miss Pringle stumbled into Doug. He handed her off to Dr. Mingees who was standing behind us. She hung on to his lapels for dear life to keep from falling onto Blanche, the dog, who growled every time Miss Pringle swayed in her direction. She pressed her glass into Doug's hand.

"Oh, boy, get me another drinkie."

"Make it a double," said Dr. Mingees, and Miss Pringle laughed like a hyena.

Mrs. Mingees was across the room and seemed to have abandoned her white wine spritzer for bourbon and Bruce Lee. She was holding on to his arm and kept saying in her upcountry drawl, "Say something in Chinese, come on, say something."

Mr. Maurice deposited us with Debbie and said, "The cavalry is here! Would you mind freshening my drink just a bit?" Debbie poured straight Scotch into his glass, and he was off, pausing just long enough to air-kiss Mrs. Mingees and Bruce Lee.

As soon as he was gone, Debbie's bright smile turned into a scowl. "I asked for help thirty minutes ago. I guess he had too much rich bitch ass to kiss." She motioned to several boxes of liquor behind the bar. "Jimbo already hauled in all I need for now. You might as well go to the garage and see if he still needs anything. He's been back there a while. He's probably worn out."

I braced myself, and Doug squeezed my arm. He wasn't afraid of anyone, even if I was. We went into the garage, shutting the door behind us, and didn't see Jimbo anywhere. I started to call out for him, but Doug put his hand on my arm to stop me.

"You hear that?" Doug whispered. I did. It was the rhythmic sound of something scraping on cardboard and, very lightly, a girl's voice moaning in time with the beat. Doug pointed to something on the floor in front of some stacked boxes. It was a pair of girl's underpants. They were pink.

We quietly moved toward the boxes, and I saw it. Kimberly Ann's legs were in the air, and Jimbo's pants were around his ankles, exposing his pimpled butt. He was rutting her, furiously. I stepped back in shock, kicking an empty bourbon bottle. They turned and saw us. Fear flew all over me.

"What the fuck," Jimbo said.

"Get off me!" Kimberly Ann yelped, pushing him off with surprising strength. "What are you two doing here?"

"We were sent to help Jimbo with the liquor," said Doug.

"You didn't see any of this," she said as she grabbed for her underwear. "One word and I'll ruin you both. You know I can do it."

"And I'll beat your fucking asses," said Jimbo. He pulled his underwear up over his still-hard member. He was wobbling a little and reached over behind Kimberly Ann and grabbed a half-empty Jack Daniel's bottle. He took a long swig from it and handed it to Kimberly Ann who drained it. I couldn't believe what I was seeing.

"Kimberly Ann, your parents are here," I said.

"They're too drunk to give a shit." She handed the bottle back to Jimbo.

"My grandpappy drank Jack." Jimbo took a swig straight from the bottle, his face flushed. "He said it's the only thing a man should drink." Doug moved closer, and Jimbo held out the bottle and then quickly pulled it back.

"You gotta swear you won't tell. If Debbie finds out, she'll tell my daddy, and he'll beat the shit outa me again. Ya swear?"

"I swear," said Doug.

"You gotta swear too, Thompson, or I'll beat your ass," said Jimbo. "*Swear.*"

Doug looked at me and nodded.

"I swear," I said.

Doug took the bottle and drank from it. It didn't seem to affect him. Doug handed it back to Jimbo.

"You afraid to drink, Thompson?" said Jimbo.

"No."

"Don't bother him; he's harmless," said Kimberly Ann.

Jimbo stared at me. "You think you're hot shit because you grabbed that pitchfork away from me? Fuck you. I let you take it. Pussy."

"Shut up," said Doug. Amazingly, Jimbo did.

I grabbed the bottle from Jimbo and took a little sip. It was gross. I wanted to spit it out, but it was already burning its way down my throat. It wasn't anything like Aunt Melanie's white Zinfandel. I felt my whole body turn red. I thought Jimbo would laugh, but he didn't. He took the bottle from me and took another swig.

We passed it around like that, and the second time, it wasn't so bad. It still tasted like turpentine, but in a good way. By the third sip, I was beginning to understand Jimbo's grandpappy. This was what men drank. It was with the fourth sip—well, more like a gulp—that the world suddenly started to spin. Maybe I was the one spinning, but it was all I could do to hold on and pass the half-empty bottle back to Doug.

"I think that's enough. We don't want to get caught," he said.

"I shoulda known the faggots would pussy out," said Jimbo. He grabbed the bottle from Doug. "I been stealing booze from my daddy's liquor cabinet since fifth grade.

Mostly cheap shit, though. He don't buy the good stuff like Jack. Grandpappy said a man's gotta learn to handle his drink, so that's what I'm a-doin'.'"

"Doesn't your daddy notice you're taking his liquor?" I asked.

"Naw," said Jimbo. "He ain't never sober long enough to notice."

"I need to get back to the party," said Kimberly Ann. "I'm not the hired help, like you all."

"You wasn't complaining about me being the hired help when I was making you come," said Jimbo. "You were begging me for it."

"Shut up," she said and left the garage.

"Nobody out there cares about us hired hands," said Jimbo. "'Cept maybe that big ol' buck you been hanging out with all night. Is that what you faggots like? Big black dick?" He slid down the wall, taking a deep drag from the bottle on the way, and plopped on the floor.

"Damn, drinking makes me horny," Jimbo said.

"You haven't had enough for one night?"

"Shit, ain't never enough pussy for me. I been fucking every girl in this town."

"You're full of shit," said Doug.

"I must've fucked Kimberly Ann a hundred times. She loves it. Can't get enough. The only reason she came tonight is because she knew I'd be here. We started last summer. Fucked all summer long."

"Even when she was dating that senator's son?" I asked.

"Especially then. Pencil dick couldn't satisfy her, not like I can." He took another swallow. "I even fucked Carleen once or twice. Damn, fat girls are good."

"I don't believe you," I said.

"Don't much matter if you believe me. Hell, she fucked half the football team and some wetback on her grandaddy's farm. Why not me? You think I'm no better than a fucking wetback?"

I didn't reply. I felt so badly for Carleen.

Jimbo started to rub himself below his waist through his pants. "Mmmm, thinking about Carleen makes me hard." He kept rubbing himself and looking at Doug. I could see Jimbo's member growing in his pants. He kept rubbing it and looking at Doug, rubbing and looking, rubbing and looking. Always at Doug.

"What makes you horny, Doug?" Jimbo was breathing heavy and rubbing himself. "Nigger dick like ol' Tim here?"

Doug met his gaze but didn't reply. After about a minute, he reached down to help Jimbo up and said, "We should go."

"Touch it," said Jimbo, unzipping. He grabbed Doug's hand and put it right on his hard penis. "Suck it, boy."

The room suddenly spun out of control, and everything I'd eaten all day came up and out like a geyser all over Jimbo, covering him in ham and Gruyère and Jack Daniels vomit.

Suddenly, he lunged at me, screaming, "You dirty faggot!"

Jimbo rammed me full in the chest, and we both fell to the floor, my head hitting the concrete with a *thunk*. Jimbo held me down and glared at me like an animal. He had his hands on my throat, squeezing. I was terrified. His penis was pressed against me, hard as a rock. He was choking, pressing harder and harder. I was using my hands to push against his shoulders, trying to push him off. He was too strong and heavy.

Just as I was about to pass out, I was suddenly filled with rage, and in one quick move, I grabbed his ballsack. I squeezed and twisted and tried to rip it off. I wanted to crush his nuts into dust. For a flash, he looked at me with shock, and then he screamed and rolled off me, onto the concrete and into a fetal position.

Doug grabbed him by the collar and pushed him against the wall and was drawing back to punch him when the door slammed shut. Debbie was standing there.

"What the hell?"

Doug let go of Jimbo, and he crumpled back to the ground. Debbie made no move to help him. She eyed his open pants, his erection in full view, and me on the ground, my own vomit on my new camel jacket. Jimbo's face went pale, and he stood up. In a flash, he pulled open the garage door and ran out. Just like that, he was gone.

"Should we go after him?" asked Doug.

Debbie shrugged. "It's not the first time he's run off. When he sobers up, he'll show up at home, probably before anybody misses him." She looked around at the pool of vomit and picked up the mostly empty Jack Daniel's bottle. "Your first drink of bourbon, Timmy?"

"Yes'm," Doug and I both said.

"Timmy—I believe; I'm not so sure about Mr. California Dreamin'," she said.

Debbie found a mop and some rags and put us to work cleaning up the vomit.

"Your momma will kill you and me both if she finds that mess all over your new jacket. I know she spent a lot on it. Hand it over." Debbie took my jacket and cleaned off the excess, working it over with seltzer water and a dishcloth.

In the end, there was no stain. It was just a little damp. She sprayed about a whole can of Lysol around the garage, and you wouldn't have known I'd upchucked at all.

"Tell your momma you spilled some water on it, and she'll never suspect a thing. Go get yourselves a couple of Cokes. It'll settle your stomach and hide your breath. By the way, Timmy, nice move with the balls. I've used that myself a few times."

"How much did you see?" asked Doug.

"I heard something hit the floor and opened the door just as Timmy here reached for the nads. I figured I should probably stop you before you punched him since he'd had enough from the human nutcracker, here. Now, you guys go on. I've got to get back to the bar and keep all these rich drunks happy."

As we were leaving the garage, Mr. Maurice appeared in the doorway. "There you are, Debbie. Everything all right in here? The natives are getting restless. Say, where's that boy you hired?"

"I sent him home. Past his bedtime," said Debbie as she hurried back to her station.

"He must have been in a hurry to get to bed." I turned around just as Shane entered through the still-open garage door. "He went running off into the woods."

"Debbie says he'll be fine; he knows his way home," said Doug.

"Well, I suppose Debbie is responsible for him." Mr. Maurice pushed his hair off his forehead. "You boys go on and enjoy the party. Debbie has a river of booze at her bar, and the party is past its peak, so I think you're through here. You may sample the buffet table on the way out. I obviously ordered far too many mini quiches and crab puffs. Please eat some."

The thought of mini quiches and crab puffs turned my stomach, and Doug pulled me into the bathroom where I upchucked again. I threw up so hard it made me cry, and I sat there on the floor of the bathroom for what seemed like a long time. Doug didn't say a word. He just kept handing me Kleenex and flushing the toilet.

When he sat next to me and held me in his arms, I started crying for real. "It's all right, baby. Really, it's all right. I'm here, and I love you."

"You what?"

"You heard me. I love you, Tim Thompson."

"I love you, too, Doug. I've loved you since the moment I saw you on the bleachers on the first day of school."

"For me, it was the moment you tripped over your laces and fell on your face on the ball field."

"Oh no! Not that!"

"Yeah, that. You were just so cute and goofy and clumsy. I fell for you hard, right then and there. Plus, seeing you fight back against Jimbo made me hot for you, stud."

I blushed. "You came to my rescue. You're the stud."

"You didn't need rescuing. You can take care of yourself. I am so in love with you, Tim."

"I want to kiss you, but I just threw up."

He laughed and held me tight until there was a pounding on the door, startling us.

"What's going on in there? A girl can't hold it all night."

"Shit, it's Kimberly Ann," said Doug. "Let's get ourselves a couple of Cokes so we can kiss." He handed me a damp towel to wash my face. I buried my face in it and started crying again, but this time, it was tears of happiness. I couldn't seem to stop crying. But somehow, crying in front of Doug seemed okay.

When the tears finally stopped again, I lowered the towel. "I'm so sorry I'm such a crybaby."

"You're not a crybaby. It's okay to cry."

Kimberly Ann pounded on the door again. "What're you boys doing in there? As if I don't know."

We quickly hung up the towels and opened the door. Kimberly Ann glared at us and stood in the way. "Debbie told me everything. Plus, I know what you were doing in the bathroom. If anyone says one word about me and Jimbo, then this entire town will know that Doug and Timmy are a couple of fags, get it?"

"I wouldn't threaten Tim if I were you," said Doug. "He fights back." He pushed her aside, and we walked out of the bathroom. I swear she looked scared. Of me!

Doug and I headed straight for our station and grabbed the last two Cokes. I took a deep draw as Doug shut the door. He clicked the lock and motioned for me to come over. I lunged at him, grabbed him, and kissed him with a frenzied passion I'd never felt before. We were practically choking each other with our tongues. We fell on the floor and made out like crazy. I pulled up his shirt and kissed and licked and bit his nipples. He cried out in pain and pulled me up to him, and we kissed so hard our teeth clicked. I didn't care—I plunged my tongue deeper.

Then, there was a knocking on the door, and a familiar voice said, "Boys, you should let me in."

Doug broke the lip-lock and said, "It's Shane." I rolled off him, and he jumped up and opened the door.

Shane came in, shutting the door behind him, and surveyed the scene. Two out-of-breath boys with disheveled clothes, hair sticking in all directions, me on the floor, lips beginning to swell, and two spilled Cokes on the carpet. "Guys, I get it. I was your age once, but ladies are asking for their coats. Tuck your shirts in, do something with your hair, and catch your breath." He gave us a minute to do just that. I looked at myself in the mirror and tried to smooth down my hair. I touched the place where my head had met the concrete and cried out in pain.

"You okay?" Shane came over and felt the fast-growing knot on the back of my head. "Damn, where did that come from?"

"Um, I fell in the garage."

"And what about those red marks on your neck? You didn't get those from falling. You boys want to tell me the real story?"

Doug shut the door and told Shane all about the fight. He left out the declarations of love in the bathroom and the frenzied make out.

"I'm impressed," said Shane. "That's the only way to deal with a bully. You done good, but I think you two have had enough excitement for one evening, and you should probably go home. Who did you come with?"

"Tim's aunt Melanie. Red dress."

Shane went to find her and returned in a few minutes, Aunt Melanie in tow.

"What happened? Was there a fight?" She looked from me to Doug, wildly. "Timmy? You were in a fight?"

Shane spoke up. "It sounds to me like Timmy was a hero tonight, ma'am, but it's probably time for them to go to bed. I can help the ladies with their coats."

"Thank you, Shane. I'll just tell Mr. Moray I have to leave."

On the ride home, I was suddenly exhausted and quiet.

"If there's anything you want to tell me before we get home, we've got about ten minutes," said Aunt Melanie. "You can trust me, you know."

"I know we can," said Doug, taking my hand.

"A lot happened," I said.

"It was Jimbo, wasn't it?" Aunt Melanie looked at me in the rearview mirror. "There's a knot on the back of your head getting bigger by the second."

I felt my head and realized I had a thunderous headache.

"Loosen your tie," she said. I did, and she gasped and pulled the car over.

"Are those choking marks? Did Jimbo try to choke you?"

I was silent. Doug spoke up. "We caught him having sex with Kimberly Ann."

"That doesn't surprise me."

"They'd both been drinking. When she left, Tim got sick, and some of the vomit hit Jimbo."

"What made you sick, Timmy?"

"Uh, too many crab puffs."

"Uh-huh," she said, meeting my eye in the rearview mirror.

"When he threw up, Jimbo pushed him down, got on top of him, and tried to choke him."

"Oh my God, Timmy."

"And Tim fought back. He was amazing. It all happened really fast before I could get to them," said Doug.

"What did you do, Timmy? Punch him?"

"No, ma'am. I grabbed his...um..."

"He grabbed Jimbo by the balls," said Doug. "I thought he was going to pull them right off him."

Aunt Melanie got wide-eyed and then started laughing. "Holy crap, Timmy, that's perfect!"

"Then Debbie walked in on us, and he ran off."

"Jesus Christ."

"He's an asshole," said Doug. "He'd been stealing liquor all night."

"Shoulda known," said Aunt Melanie. "His father was a drunk and his grandfather before him. So, Mr. Tim, we can't exactly keep these marks secret from your mother. I think we have to tell her, don't you?"

"Yes, ma'am."

"You know she's going to go ballistic," she said.

"Yes, ma'am."

"We just won't try to explain the swollen lips." She winked at me.

I put my hand to my mouth, my face flushing.

"I saw Kimberly Ann pounding on the bathroom door and you two coming out." She smiled at both of us. "I think you make a cute couple."

Doug smiled and put his arm around my shoulder, pulling me close. "I think we're the cutest couple at Patriot Christian Academy."

She pulled to the curb about a block before we got to Doug's house and announced she was going to get out of the car and give us five minutes of privacy. "I need to smoke a cigarette before I get to JoAnne's, anyway."

After she left, I told Doug, "Thank you for coming to my defense tonight."

He stroked my cheek. "And thank you for jumping my bones."

I blushed. "I'd kiss you, but my lips are swollen."

"Screw it," said Doug as he pulled me in for a deep good-night kiss.

"I love you, Doug."

"I love you, Tim."

# Twenty-Five There's got to be a Morning After

WHEN I WOKE up Sunday morning, Momma was in the kitchen, stirring a pot of grits. She glanced over at me as I stepped up to the fridge.

"How's my little hero this morning?"

"I have a headache." I gingerly touched the lump on my head.

"I've got grits and eggs and fried bananas for my big strong man today."

The sticky sweet smell of fried bananas made my stomach turn, but I didn't say anything because I didn't want Momma to catch on that I'd been drinking. Aunt Melanie had told her about the fight when she dropped me off last night. She said Jimbo had been drinking and messing around with Kimberly Ann when Doug and I walked in on them. She told her I got sick from the fancy finger foods and upchucked on Jimbo who pushed me down and choked me. She described how I'd fought back by grabbing Jimbo's "nuts" and how Doug pulled Jimbo up and was about to punch him when Debbie walked in on us. Thankfully, she left out the drinking and the romancing.

"How are you, sweetie?"

"It hurts a little." I drank down my orange juice to settle my stomach. It didn't work.

"I should have called the police last night. I still can."

"No, Momma, don't. It's okay, really."

"How is it okay when you could have been choked to death? Jimbo is a thug who should be in jail."

"I can handle it."

"You sure can, my big boy." She brought two plates to the table, and I caught another whiff of bananas and eggs.

"I'm not real hungry."

"You're not? Well, of course you're not. You got sick last night on those crab puffs and all, silly me. I'll take this right away. What can I get you instead? Dry toast? Maybe whip up some plain oatmeal?"

"Nothing really. I'm okay." I looked up at the clock. "Did you see the time? We're about to miss church."

"I know, baby. I let my big strong boy sleep in today. You earned it."

"Thanks, Momma." I was glad I didn't have to go to church. I couldn't handle my first ever hangover and Pastor Earl Don at the same time.

"I wonder if the Mingees will dare show their faces after what your aunt told me about Kimberly Ann. I'm still in shock. I always thought she was such a nice girl."

"All the grown-ups think she's a nice girl."

"Poor Doris Mingees. Her only child is a fallen woman at fifteen."

"Would you mind if I got back in bed? My head hurts."

"Of course, baby. This is your day to do whatever you want. You go on back to bed."

I slipped under the covers, thinking about how my life was completely different this morning. I'd been in my first ever fight, and I'd won. I'd made out with my cute new boyfriend. I'd had bourbon for the first time. And last time.

I lay back and thought about the sermon that must have been about to start. It was to be on the Good Samaritan, one of Pastor Earl Don's favorites—after the sin of Sodom, that is. I wondered what I would do if I saw Jimbo by the side of the road, beat up by bandits. I imagined him lying on the stony ground, baking in the hot desert sun. He was naked because the bandits had taken all his clothes. He was beaten and broken and bloody. He had disgusting sores with bugs crawling all over them. Along I'd come in my fine cloaks, with food, water, and bandages, which a smart person takes with him if he's traveling the road to Jericho because of all the bandits. Jimbo would call out to me, "Help me, Timmy! Help me in the name of Jesus! I've been robbed and beaten, and I'm helpless and naked!" I'd stop and looked down on him, lying there in his nakedness and filth...

"Honey, are you feeling better? You need to get up." It was Momma in my doorway. I sat up in bed. "You'll never guess who just called and said she was going to drop by. Annette Herlong and Doug. Won't that be nice?"

I hopped out of bed. "How much time do I have to get ready?"

"Not long, so get a move on."

I'd showered and dressed in record time when I heard the doorbell ring. Momma and I opened it to Doug and his mother, holding a tray.

"I brought hummus." She handed over the tray with a bowl in the center surrounded by little pieces of bread.

"My goodness, thank you." We both stared at the brown, viscous paste.

"It's chickpeas and olive oil, basically," said Doug's momma. My stomach did another backflip.

"How delightful." Momma ushered them in and handed the plate to me. "Y'all come on in. Timmy, why don't you take Doug into the living room. Annette, would you mind helping me in the kitchen?"

Doug and I went to the living room, and he immediately pulled me into a deep kiss. "I missed you."

"Me too." I was excited by the danger of kissing with Momma in the next room.

"How'd you sleep?" he asked.

"I had a nightmare about Jimbo, but then I started thinking about you and went right back to sleep."

Doug made a little heart with his fingers, and I just about melted. Our mothers walked in with trays of hummus and iced tea.

"Doug told me everything that happened last night, and I wanted to see how Tim was doing today. I understand you were a brave young man last night," said Doug's momma.

"He sure was," said Doug. "He grabbed Jimbo right in the—"

"That's fine, son," said his momma. "I'm sure we all know where he grabbed Jimbo."

"Did Doug tell you the whole story?" asked Momma.

"Oh, yes, my son tells me everything."

I shot Doug an anxious look and wondered if he'd told his mother *everything*.

She continued, "Doug told me he and Timmy walked in on Jimbo *in flagrante* with Dr. Mingees's perfect little girl. Then, Jimbo jumped on Timmy, knocking him down, and tried to choke him."

"And Timmy showed him," said Momma. "And your son was very brave, too. Thank you, Doug."

Doug nodded but didn't say anything.

"And Kimberly Ann!" said Momma. "I am so disappointed in her. I always thought she was such a good Christian."

"She's just like her mother. What a bitch," said Doug's momma. "Oops, sorry. I guess I shouldn't use such language in front of the boys."

"Why not? You talk that way around me all the—"

"That's enough, Doug," said his momma.

"You're forgiven, Annette, and I agree. I also think something must be done. I wanted to call the police last night and have that white trash hellion Jimbo arrested and sent straight to reform school, but Timmy talked me out of it. I still might. At the very least, however, he should be expelled from Patriot Christian."

"How do you intend to do that?" asked Doug's momma.

"By getting all the mothers involved. We'll call a special meeting of Patriot Christian Moms in Prayer. Everyone needs to know what happened."

"Don't, Momma, please," I said.

"Tim and I should handle it, ourselves, Mrs. Thompson," Doug said.

"Absolutely not! I already let you talk me into not calling the police, but I'm not going to yield on getting the boy expelled."

"It'll just make things worse for us," said Doug.

"I think I have to agree with the kids," said Doug's momma. "The only way to deal with bullies is to stand up to them, and your son has. Bullies are everywhere, and sending them away or running away doesn't solve anything." She looked at Doug. "I brought Doug out here to escape bullies in California, and it's no better here. I'm sorry, dear, for taking you away from everything you knew."

"It's okay, Mom."

Momma looked alarmed. "What are you talking about, Annette?"

"Just as I was going through my divorce, Doug was attacked by some boys at the beach. I made a rash decision to uproot the both of us and drive across the country. I realize more every day that it was a mistake."

"You were protecting your child. You were being a good parent."

"You can't protect them from everything."

Momma put her glass down. "Boys, why don't you take your tea back to Timmy's room. Mrs. Herlong and I need to have a serious discussion."

BACK IN MY room, I shut the door, and we put our glasses on my desk. We plopped onto the bed and snuggled.

"I wish I knew what they were saying," I said.

"Then open the door and listen."

"I can't cuddle with you with the door open. Momma might walk in on us."

"You should tell your mother the truth about being gay. I told mine last night."

I sat up. "You did? Really? What did she say?"

"She said she wasn't surprised. My dad's gay. That's why they got divorced. He came home one day and announced he was in love with a man."

"Oh my gosh, how did you mother react?"

"She had a total meltdown. I was afraid to tell her about me for the longest time, but after last night, I felt like I had to."

"How do you feel about it?"

"I'm really glad I did it. It feels good to be honest with her. I don't have to watch what I say anymore. It's a relief."

"You don't think she'll tell my mother, do you?"

"No. I made her promise. She should hear it from you."

"No way! I could never tell her. She'd never understand. Never."

"You may be right, or you may not be. But at least she'd know who you really are, and you wouldn't have to pretend anymore."

"You're making my head spin. Can we deal with one crisis at a time, please?"

He smiled. "Sure. Makes sense."

I lay back down and put my head on his chest. I could feel his heart beating. It made me feel safe.

"I don't want to go to school tomorrow. Or ever again," I said.

"It's not as bad as you think."

"How is it not bad? Jimbo will be there waiting for me. He wants to kill me. I thought he was going to last night."

"Yeah, but Jimbo knows you'll fight back. For the second, no, third time. You got the pitchfork away from him too, remember? You stood up to him."

I thought about that. "He won't give up. He can't let the school sissy get the better of him."

"He already has. I bet he leaves you alone. In fact, I'd be surprised if he even comes back to school."

"Why do you say that?"

"Because he's got a secret, and now we know."

"What's his secret?"

"Tim, think about it. He showed it to us. Literally."

"Huh?"

"Tim, he pressed his hard dick onto you. He put my hand on it and told me to suck it."

"Holy moly! You think he's gay like us?"

"Not like us, but, yeah, I think he's a big old homo and can't admit it. His daddy would beat the crap out of him, and he knows it."

I lay on the bed again and slapped my forehead. "I never would have thought of that, but it makes sense. That's why he acts all tough and makes fun of me all the time."

"Exactly. He's trying to take the focus off himself."

"Wow. That's all so crazy." I sat up. "Hey! I have an idea. What if we talked to him and told him how nice it is to admit to yourself that you're gay? It's the best! You get to have a cute boyfriend and kiss and stuff. We could help him."

"You are nuts. There's no way that would work. He's way too scared of what he is to ever acknowledge it. If you ever suggested such a thing to him, he really would kill you."

I stretched out and put my head on his chest again. "Yeah, I guess so. It was just a thought."

"Besides, Kimberly Ann is the real problem."

"You think?"

"Of course. Jimbo's just a dumb bully. Kimberly Ann's smart and clever; plus, she's popular, and all the adults love her."

"She's the queen of the snow jobs."

"She set you up at the lock-in and cheered when Jimbo made you the butt of the joke. She treats her friends like crap. Just look at those Anns and former Anns. She's a terrible person."

"And she knows about us."

"Which is a good reason to tell your mother. That takes away Kimberly Ann's power."

"I just couldn't. It would kill Momma, and she'd forbid me from ever seeing you again. I'm sure of it."

"Baby, nothing's going to come between us, and I'm not trying to pressure you."

"Let's just concentrate on what we're going to do about Kimberly Ann. Her reign of terror needs to end, but what can we do about it? She's the queen of Patriot Christian, and we're just a couple of nobodies." I sighed. It felt like a dead end.

But then, Doug smiled. "Maybe it's time we stopped being nobodies and became somebodies."

"What do you mean?"

"I'm getting an idea. What is Kimberly Ann most afraid of?"

"I don't think she's afraid of anything."

"Think about it. Let me put it another way. What's most important to her?"

"That's easy. Being popular."

"Exactly. So, what's she most afraid of?"

"Not being popular?"

"That's right. Without that, she's no threat to you, me, or anyone. Her popularity is her power."

"But how do we make the most popular girl in school unpopular?"

"We start with the Anns."

"Her best friends?"

"Her best servants is more like it. She treats them like crap. But we have an edge with them. I believe they're gay. Like us."

"Whoa. Really? Why do you think that?"

"Remember their presentation at the lock-in?"

"Sure. Naomi and Ruth."

"All that talk about love between women?"

"Oh my gosh, do you mean that Naomi and Ruth are like David and Jonathan?"

"Exactly. Lesbians celebrated in the Bible for their love."

"Lesbians in the Bible?"

"And at Patriot Christian."

"So, we might not be the only gays?"

"Exactly."

Just then, there was a knock on the door, and the knob started to turn. Momma! I was off the bed and into my desk chair before the door cracked.

"Timmy dear, you didn't hear the doorbell? Look who's here to visit." She opened the door all the way, and there stood Carleen. She had a six-pack of Cokes in eight-ounce bottles in one hand and a jar of peanuts in the other. I knew immediately she was here to make up. She and I'd shared Cokes and goobers a million times.

She put the six-pack and the jar on the desk next to the uneaten chicken dinners.

"I heard what happened," she said.

"How did you hear?" Doug asked.

"Debbie Abernathy is my mother's second cousin once removed. They're practically sisters. Debbie came over for Sunday dinner today and told Momma all about it. She was so upset about Jimbo because if word got out, she might not get any more bartending gigs, you know? She must have smoked two packs of cigarettes telling Momma about what a trashy little redneck that Jimbo has become."

"Of course, he is. Look at his family. They're all trash," I said.

"Hey! That's my family you're talking about. Are you saying I'm white trash?"

"No! No! No!" I said. "I didn't mean you and your momma and daddy. You're not like Jimbo and his people. Everybody's got trash in their family if you look hard enough."

"I don't have to look any farther than the Amoco to find some trash in your family." Carleen knew how to twist the knife.

"If you're here to make up, you're doing a bad job of it," said Doug.

Carleen smiled and started pulling Cokes out of the carton. "You're right. Timmy, when I heard what happened and I realized you weren't going to call me to gab about it all night, it made me really sad. We've been friends way too long to continue like this."

"I know," I said, starting to choke up. "But you were really mean to me."

"Yeah, I know. But I had my reasons."

I sat on the bed next to Doug, and Carleen took the desk chair, facing us. Carleen opened the Cokes, poured a handful of nuts into each, and handed one to me.

"What are you doing?" asked Doug.

"It's Cokes and goobers," said Carleen. "It's the best. Try it." She handed him one. We all clinked bottles.

"To good friends," said Carleen.

"To ruining a perfectly good Coke," said Doug. Then he took a sip.

"Well?" I asked.

"It's actually not completely disgusting," he said, and we all laughed.

"So, are you two officially a couple yet?" asked Carleen.

"Yep," said Doug, pulling me in close. I eyed Carleen, looking for her reaction, but she only smiled.

"I figured. I knew it was going to happen when I saw Timmy's reaction to you that first day in assembly. I thought he'd cream his jeans right there."

"Carleen! You're so dirty," I said.

She and Doug laughed. "You know it's true," she said.

"Yeah, but you had the same reaction," I said. "You called him a fox."

"I sure did. You are a fox, Doug."

"Thanks. Small pond."

She put down her Coke. "I hoped you would be this crazy, different kind of guy from California who might want to date a fat, fun chick. Every other boy in this town has wet dreams about Kimberly Ann and only Kimberly Ann. I thought you might be on Timmy's team, but I held out hope. I guess I felt like me and Timmy were in competition for you. We've never been in competition before."

"But, Carleen, you were bragging about those other boys—Juan and Dean and the other guys."

"Those boys didn't want to be with me. I was just a lay. The day before you and me had our big argument in the library, I'd asked Dean if maybe he wanted to go to a movie sometime. He just laughed. He said he only takes pretty girls to the movies. He said I was just a fuck. He said he knew I wouldn't say no because I was fat and easy."

"Wow, Carleen, that's messed up," said Doug.

"For the first time in my life, cute boys were paying attention to me. I actually thought I might have a boyfriend. But I was just a fuck. A nothing. I was nothing."

I reached over, took her hand, and pulled her onto the bed with us. I gave her a big hug. "Those boys were nothing. Not you. You're Carleen. They're jerks who took advantage of you."

She released me and sat up on the bed. "I know you're right, but it still hurts. Then, when I saw you guys together and realized you had something really special, I just went crazy. I want what you have, and I feel like I'll never have it." The tears started, and Doug joined her in the group hug.

"I need more Coke," said Carleen, and she took a big swallow. "All any boy in Edgewood wants is to screw Kimberly Ann."

"Apparently that includes Jimbo," said Doug.

"Debbie told me she saw Jimbo sneak her into the garage and then saw her come back out with her dress all wrinkled and sideways. Debbie knew exactly what that meant. Yuck, that is so gross. Even I wouldn't stoop to sex with Jimbo, and believe me, he tried."

"Oh, thank goodness," I said.

"What? Did that redneck say he'd done it with me?"

"Yes, but I didn't believe it. Hey! I bet Dean said that mean stuff to you just to impress Jimbo. I bet he really likes you, but Jimbo was mad because you wouldn't do it with him, so Dean couldn't admit it."

"Maybe," said Carleen. "I don't know. Whether that's true or not, I've about had it with Jimbo and Kimberly Ann and all their crap."

"Make that three of us," said Doug. "We were just talking about that when you came in. We're hatching a plan to rob Kimberly Ann of her popularity and end her reign as the mean queen of Patriot Christian. If we join forces with you and Jaime and Patti and the rest of your crew, we can make it happen by Christmas."

Carleen held out her bottle, and we all clinked. "Merry Christmas," she said.

# Twenty-Six: High Five

WHEN I WOKE up on Monday morning, I opened my eyes and said out loud, "I can't do this." Dread was in the pit of my stomach, and I made a list of fake symptoms to tell Momma so I could stay home. Jimbo would be at school waiting to kill me. But Doug would be there, and I couldn't let him face Jimbo alone. Plus, Carleen and I were friends again. So I got up and got ready.

I was glad to see Carleen and Doug out front when Momma dropped me off. I wouldn't have to face Jimbo alone.

"Hey, guys, I'm so glad to see you." I gave Doug a totally butch punch on the arm when I really wanted to kiss him on the mouth. The three of us headed to the gym for assembly, and I noticed there was a ton of weirdness going on. First, I didn't see Jimbo anywhere. Second, everybody seemed friendlier than ever. Jaime and Patti came running up.

"Hey, wait up," said Jaime.

"Hey, Timmy. Hey, Doug," said Patti. "How y'all?" She even gave me a little hug like we were best friends or something.

When we got into the gym, all heads turned toward us. Practically every kid in school smiled or waved. At me. When we got to the bleachers, a bunch of kids scooted around to make room for us, as if it was a competition to sit next to us. Even some of Jimbo's redneck friends nodded at me, and not in an "I'm gonna rip your guts out" kind of way. Instead, it felt like respect. Kimberly Ann ignored us, of course. But the Anns cracked tiny smiles at me, and Kathy Ann even gave me a little wave.

At precisely eight thirty, Mrs. Holt took the stage. "Good morning, Christian Soldiers. Today is the kickoff for the annual competition for All American Teen sponsored by the Daughters of the American Revolution." All the kids applauded. I'd completely forgotten it was time for the annual popularity contest. Kimberly Ann had won for the past two years, and I hadn't bothered to enter. No doubt, she would win again.

"In order to qualify as a candidate, you must first do an oral presentation at next week's assembly on a historical figure who has influenced your life. A panel of representatives from the community and the UDC will then choose the top five candidates to run. Then, from now through November, there will be a table with a collection box for each candidate. The candidates who collect the most money for Christmas Seals are the winners. One boy and one girl. Now, with a new twist this year is one of our local businessmen who has generously offered to help judge the competition—Mr. Maurice Moray from Boutique Moray. Mr. Moray?"

In walked none other than Mr. Maurice. I had no idea he was coming. He was beautifully dressed, of course, in a blue blazer and a crisp, white shirt. He was so handsome, even though he was probably forty. He walked up to the microphone and caught my eye. I waved.

"Good morning, young ladies and gentlemen. I am so pleased to be part of the Outstanding Teen competition this year. As part of the festivities, the winner will ride in the Christmas Parade in my very own vintage Cadillac convertible." The crowd gasped. "Good luck to everyone."

Walking back to class after assembly, Carleen was full of herself.

"This is it!" she whispered. "This is how we destroy Kimberly Ann and rule the school."

"How?" I whispered back.

"Do I hear talking?" said Mrs. Morgan at the head of our line of students. I sighed. Like always, she heard me and never Carleen.

"We'll talk at lunch," said Carleen. "It's all coming together in my mind."

At lunch, Doug and Carleen and I sat together and were quickly joined by Patti and Jaime.

"Here's the plan," said Carleen. "We all enter the Outstanding Teen competition. We'll each write a kick-ass presentation on somebody from history and make the final five. We all know Kimberly Ann will make the finals because all the adults love her. That's four out of the five finalists."

"I could be the fifth," said Patti. "History's my best subject."

"Perfect," said Doug. "We make this a group effort. We pick historical figures, then we write out a rough draft, then we get together this weekend and rehearse."

"But we all know who the most popular girl in school is," I said.

"Oh, really?" said Carleen. "Don't be so sure. Look around."

I did and saw that Kimberly Ann and the Anns were sitting at a table completely alone. Usually, there were cute boys and girls buzzing around them, hoping to find a seat at their table. But today? Nothing.

"And look who's coming to sit with us," said Carleen. It was Dean with several of his JV football buddies.

"Hey, Carleen, are these seats taken?"

"Do they look taken?" she said.

They all sat, and Dean turned to me.

"Hey, man, I heard what happened on Saturday with Jimbo. Shit, that was heavy."

"Yeah. Heavy," I said.

"Did you really rip his nuts off?"

I blushed at this language in front of the girls.

"He ripped them off and stuffed them down Jimbo's throat," said Carleen.

Everybody laughed.

"Jimbo had a ball crunching coming," said Dean. "He's such an asshole. I never would have thought you'd be the one to deliver it." He reached his hand up and pressed his palm toward me. I had no idea what he was doing. Doug slapped it with his palm.

"High five," said Doug. I copied Doug and high-fived Dean, and then every member of the football team took turns high-fiving me.

When we were leaving the cafeteria, Carleen put her arm around my shoulders and said, "Still think you can't beat Kimberly Ann?"

I smiled. So this was what it felt like to be popular.

"Stick with me, Timmy. We're in it to win it, and we're totally going to ride in the Christmas Parade," Carleen said.

"You're dreaming if you believe that," said Kimberly Ann, appearing out of nowhere. "I'm the obvious choice. My mother shops at Boutique Moray, unlike your mothers who couldn't afford to walk in the door. He'll choose me, and he'll ask me to model for him in his fashion shows. Won't he, girls?" She turned to the Anns who didn't say a word.

"Well?" said Kimberly Ann.

"I'm sure you'll win," said Kathy Ann, without conviction.

"Your momma doesn't shop there, you liar," said Carleen. "She's always bragging about buying all her clothes at Tapp's in Columbia. And who cares anyway? Timmy and I will raise the most money and kill it at next week's assembly, so you can stuff it." Carleen grabbed my arm and pulled me on to class. Kimberly Ann stood there steaming, and nobody came to her defense.

# Twenty-Seven: Christian Dior Me

ON SATURDAY, CARLEEN, Doug, Jaime, Patti, and I all met at Doug's house to make our presentations perfect. Doug's momma said we could have the living room to ourselves all day. She'd laid out a big platter of that disgusting hummus stuff. Doug was the only one who ate it.

"I've just squeezed some fresh carrot juice. Who's in?" asked Doug's momma. Doug said yes, of course, and the rest of us said we weren't thirsty. Luckily, Carleen had planned ahead and brought Cokes.

We each revealed our choice of historical figure. Carleen announced she was going to do Mama Cass Elliot, the plus-size Mamas & the Papas singer who had died a few years before.

"She was a fat girl who made it big, and she didn't choke on a ham sandwich. That's a lie told by skinny bitches like Kimberly Ann to make us big girls feel bad. Cass was big and beautiful, and so am I."

"Sounds great to me," said Doug.

I wasn't sure if Cass Elliot really qualified as a historical figure, but I wasn't going to butt heads with Carleen again.

Jaime went next. "I've chosen Robert E. Lee."

"Boooring," said Carleen. "Everybody chooses Robert E. Lee or Jeff Davis or some other fella from the War Between the States. Can't you come up with somebody original?"

"I promised my grandmother," said Jaime. "She says we're descended from the Lees of Virginia."

Carleen rolled her eyes. "You and everybody else in the South. How about you, Patti?"

"I chose Francis Hugh Wardlaw who wrote the Articles of Succession of South Carolina. He was a true patriot."

"God, what is it with you people and the Civil War," said Doug. "He rebelled against the United States, and you call him a patriot?"

"He was a patriotic South Carolinian," said Patti. "You're a Yankee, so you wouldn't understand."

"Doug is not a Yankee," I said. "California is in the West, not the North."

"It's okay, Tim," said Doug. "I'd rather be a Yankee than a rebel. Our side won."

"Well, we're gonna rise again," said Patti.

"Okay, okay, people," said Carleen. "This ain't Fort Sumter, and the war's over. Doug, you go next. And for God's sake I hope you didn't chose Abe Lincoln."

"Nope. I chose someone who truly inspired me. A great American named Duke Kahanamoku."

Carleen practically spit up her Coke.

"Duke Kahanawhatku?"

"Duke Kahanamoku. He was a native Hawaiian who popularized surfing. He died, like, ten years ago. He competed in the Olympics in swimming but became really famous as a surfer. He's why people surf in California. He's been a real important influence on my life."

"Only you would know who that is," said Carleen. I smiled with pride. Doug was so smart.

"That leaves you, Timmy. Who'd you choose?" asked Carleen.

I stood and paused for effect. "My choice is..." I paused again, looking around the room. "Monsieur Christian Dior."

Doug applauded.

"Who's that?" asked Jaime.

"You've got to be kidding," said Carleen.

"I certainly am not kidding," I said. "Christian Dior revolutionized fashion after World War II and made Paris the fashion capital of the world. I intend to be a fashion designer when I grow up, and he has been a huge influence on my life."

"Well, there goes my plan for being popular," said Carleen.

"Why?" I said.

"People are just starting to respect you because you fought back against Jimbo. Now you're going to ruin it all."

"I don't get it," said Doug.

"He might as well walk into assembly with a sign saying 'I'm queer bait. Kick me in the butt,'" said Patti. She and Jaime laughed.

"Don't you have to pick an American?" asked Jaime.

"The rules don't say so, and, besides, two years ago, Kimberly Ann won with Marie Antoinette," I said.

"Get serious," said Carleen. "Choosing a fashion designer is, like, super homo."

"Maybe he could wear a pink cape," said Jaime.

"Hey," said Doug. "The word is gay, and, yeah, Tim and I are. We're a couple of big old gay, pink-cape-wearing, super homos and proud of it. You already know this, Carleen."

Patti and Jaime looked at Carleen, wide-eyed. "You knew and didn't tell us?" asked Patti.

"Sure, I knew. Hey, guys, I'm happy for you. You're a great couple. But this is Edgewood, South Carolina. You can't just flaunt it, even if it is 1980."

"Well, maybe this town needs a jump start," said Doug.

"Oh, my God, I've never met a real, actual homo—I mean gay," said Patti, eyes still wide. "So, what do you do?"

"What are you talking about?" I asked.

"You know, in bed. Who does what? Is one of you the woman?"

"Does it hurt?" asked Jaime.

"That is so rude!" I said. "Why don't you tell me how you do it with whatever random football player you hook up with."

"Hey, hey, we are *way* off target," said Carleen. "The whole purpose of meeting here today was to rehearse our presentations. Now, Patti, you go first. Tell us all about this Wardlaw fellow."

The day went on with no more embarrassing questions from Jaime and Patti. All four presentations were solid, even Jaime's predictable choice of Robert E. Lee. We met again the next day for a final run-through, and by Sunday night, I felt good about our chances.

At Monday's assembly, Carleen, Doug, and I were ready to win. I had hopes for Patti and Jaime, too. The panel of judges was assembled. There was Mrs. Holt, Mr. Moray, an old lady, Mrs. Means, from the DAR chapter in Columbia—for some reason—and Pastor Earl Don.

My hopes of a sweep were dashed when Kimberly Ann stepped up on the stage and announced that her presentation would be about Lottie Moon. Nobody would vote against Lottie Moon, the famous Baptist missionary who died tragically while trying to save the souls of the Chinese. I'd heard this speech from her before because she gave it at Sunday school, Sunbeams for Jesus, Vacation Bible School, and everywhere else she could stand up and get attention. But it was good, and she knew it. When she finished, she waited expectantly for applause. The entire school just looked at her in silence as she left the stage and sat down.

Whoa. No applause for Kimberly Ann?

Carleen went next and did her presentation on Mama Cass. Carleen worked it. She wore a Pucci-inspired caftan that her momma had stitched up over the weekend (I helped her pick out the fabric) and, once and for all, dispelled the myth that Mama Cass died choking on a ham sandwich. She even brought a record player and recreated her moment from the lock-in. Jaime and Patti joined her onstage, and, together, they became the Mamas & the Papas, lip-synching while swaying rhythmically to "California Dreaming." They even had choreography. They put their clasped hands by their cheek every time she mouthed the word "dreaming," as if asleep. It was hokey, and Kimberly Ann laughed out loud. She looked around for people to join in, but nobody did. In fact, several people, including both Anns, were copying Carleen's choreography. She really had the crowd hooked. Everybody applauded when Carleen was done.

Next up was Doug. He talked about Duke Kahanamoku and the history of surfing. As a visual aid, he brought his surfboard. The plan was for him to stand on the board and demonstrate surfing techniques. Over the weekend, we'd all joked that he should strip down to a bathing suit and ride the waves on stage. I didn't think he'd actually do it. But as he put the surfboard down, he quickly kicked off his shoes and stripped off his shirt and pants to reveal a little red swimsuit underneath. Everybody in the crowd gasped.

"I can't believe he's actually doing it!" said Carleen.

Doug was beautiful. His smooth chest was perfect. I looked around, and most of the girls, and maybe a few boys, were swooning. I looked at Mr. Maurice who was clutching his collar, mouth open. Mrs. Means was smiling. Pastor Earl Don actually licked his lips, his eyes locked on Doug's pecs. Maybe that explained all those Sodomy sermons.

Only Mrs. Holt looked horrified.

Carleen wolf-whistled, and Patti joined in. Mrs. Holt stood, snapping her fingers.

"Douglas Appleby! Put your shirt back on!"

"Oh, let him finish, Edna," said the old lady from Columbia. "He seems like a nice boy." She held up a pair of opera glasses for a closer look.

Mrs. Holt sat in defeat, and Doug finished his presentation shirtless.

Several other kids took their turns and talked about various Confederate heroes, just like I'd predicted. Jaime's Robert E. Lee presentation was good, but she was, like, the fifth one to do him, and I could tell the judges were bored. Patti's went better because Francis Hugh Wardlaw wasn't super famous, so people were hearing something new. But it was hard to follow a sexy shirtless guy.

Dean did a cool presentation on somebody named Walter Camp who apparently invented football.

I went last. I stood on the podium and looked out at the crowd. Was I really going to do a presentation on a fashion designer? Outside my family, only Doug, Carleen,

Patti, and Jaime knew about my dream of a life in fashion. I looked at Mr. Maurice, who'd helped me with the research and provided some beautiful pictures. That probably broke the rules, but it was our secret. He nodded and smiled. I looked at Doug, and he winked. I plunged in.

I turned on Momma's carousel slide projector, and an image appeared of a wasp-wasted model in a huge full skirt, standing by the Eiffel Tower.

"This is the New Look, and it revolutionized fashion in 1947. It was the creation of the great Christian Dior."

The crowd was silent, and everyone was focused on my slides. I explained Dior's place in history and his role in reestablishing Paris as the world's fashion capital after the war.

I swallowed hard and pressed the button for the next slide. It was the purple gown I'd designed for Ann-Margret.

"I intend to have a career in fashion, and Dior is the designer who has most influenced me. This is one of my designs."

It was out. Everyone knew I wanted to be a fashion designer. Nobody laughed. Nobody even snickered. Instead, there were a few oohs and aahs. I pressed forward with more of my designs. I showed my entire Emmy collection, pointing out Dior's influence on each gown. I ended with the Bette Davis *Jezebel* red. I looked out at the crowd. Mr. Maurice was smiling broadly. There was a pause, and everyone started clapping. Doug, Carleen, Patti, and Jaime all stood, and everyone else followed. I got a standing ovation! Even Mrs. Holt and Pastor Earl Don stood. The only one sitting was Kimberly Ann, who was so mad she looked like she could spit. I returned to my seat, bathed in love.

The judges deliberated for just a few minutes before they announced the five finalists who would progress in the All American Teen competition. Mr. Maurice made the announcement.

"Our first finalist is Miss Carleen Hightower for her very original choice of Cass Elliot."

I stood and cheered as she took the stage. "Yay, Carleen!"

"Our next finalist is Miss Patti Jenkins for her presentation on Francis Hugh Wardlaw."

"Way to go, Patti," screamed Jaime.

"Next up is Mr. Doug Appleby for his rather unconventional demonstration of surfing."

I jumped up in excitement and hugged Doug before I could control myself. He took his place on stage next to Patti.

"Just two more names left. Next is Mr. Dean Monroe for his informative presentation on football."

Wait a minute. There was only one name left, and Kimberly Ann hadn't been called yet. I wasn't going to make it. I'd thought I was so smart choosing Dior because I knew Mr. Maurice would appreciate it. But I hadn't counted on how the other judges would react. Of course, Mrs. Holt and Pastor Earl Don would vote against me. What a dunce I was.

"The final name I'm going to call is…"

I looked over at Kimberly Ann. She met my eyes with a smug smile. She was sure to be the last name called. In fact, she was beginning to stand when Mr. Maurice handed the microphone to the DAR lady from Columbia.

"I asked if I could make this final announcement because I was so impressed by this young student. One person truly understood that the purpose of this assignment was to honor someone who influenced you, not just a historical figure you admire. In that regard, I am pleased to announce the last finalist is Mr. Timothy Thompson for his lovely presentation on Christian Dior."

Everybody stood and clapped. Kimberly Ann froze. I walked to the stage in a daze. Was this really happening? Carleen gave me a big hug. Doug was beaming.

Mrs. Holt took the microphone. "Thank you to all the participants. You were all wonderful, but, unfortunately, only five may progress."

I looked over at Kimberly Ann who was still standing, looking confused.

"Wait!" she called out. Everybody turned. "You forgot a name. Look at your card again. I should be on it. My daddy promised."

"Kimberly Ann, dear..." Mrs. Holt began.

"Do you mean to tell me you chose a fatty, a nerd, a homo, and his Yankee boyfriend over me?"

"Kimberly Ann, sit down," said Mrs. Holt.

"I will not sit down. Just wait till my daddy finds out! My daddy gives more money to this school than anybody!"

She looked around at all of us on stage. "This bunch of freaks is your idea of an outstanding teen? Seriously?" Nobody moved. She looked at the Anns. "We're outta here. Come on, girls." She started to walk out, but Kathy Ann and Lisa Ann kept their seats. She turned back to them. "What's the matter? I said come on."

"We're done with taking orders from you," said Kathy Ann.

"Yeah, we stand with Timmy and Doug," said Lisa Ann, taking Kathy Ann's hand. Kimberly Ann looked on in horror.

"Timmy stood up to that bully, Jimbo, and we're standing up to you," said Lisa Ann. And with that, she took Kathy Ann's face in her hands and kissed her full on the mouth. The crowd went crazy.

"Gay power!" said Kathy Ann.

"Gay power!" said Doug, punching the air with his fist.

"Holy shit," said Carleen.

The crowd began chanting "Gay power! Gay power!" over and over, even though I was pretty sure most of them had no idea what it meant.

I thought Pastor Earl Don would have an aneurysm.

Mrs. Holt dragged Kimberly Ann to her office, telling her she would be expelled.

"Is every kid in this school gay?" asked Dean.

"Not me," said Carleen, "but what do I know? I'm just fat and easy, according to you."

Dean flushed deep red. "It was mean of me to say that. I was being a real jerk."

"You were being way worse than a jerk."

"Okay, I was a moron."

"Closer."

"An asshole?"

"I was going for sexist pig, but an asshole's basically the same thing, so I'll take it."

Dean looked down at his shoes, trying to project contrition, but he couldn't stop himself from smiling. "You're actually pretty cool."

"Way cooler than you'll ever be." Carleen took his arm. "Let's cut class so you can buy me a burger. I'll tell you all the ways you can make it up to me."

FOR THE NEXT two weeks, there was a table set up in the hall at school with collection boxes with each of our names on them. Kids could drop pennies and nickels and dimes in the boxes of whomever they wanted to win. Even after getting a standing ovation, I found it hard to believe anyone would vote for me. But then something interesting began to happen.

The popular kids started asking to sit with me and Carleen and Doug and Patti and Jaime at lunch. First were the Anns, who were going by Kathy and Lisa again. Dean and lots of his teammates joined us. Carleen flirted with him outrageously, and he seemed to love it. This one teammate named Chip, who was quiet and built, always made an effort to sit next to Jaime. The cheerleaders followed the football players, and, pretty soon, we had to move to a bigger table, while Kimberly Ann was forced to sit at the end of the teacher's table. Alone. Carleen's prediction at the beginning of the year had come true. We were the popular table. We really did rule the school.

On the last day before Thanksgiving break, we had another assembly, and Mr. Maurice was there to announce the winners of All American Teen. I was so nervous. Kimberly Ann was supposedly out sick that day. Faker. Doug was totally calm, and Carleen seemed confident.

Mr. Maurice began by calling out the amounts of money that Patti and Dean had raised. It was impressive, and everybody politely clapped. They came on stage, and each got a certificate. Then he continued.

"The amounts raised by the final three, Doug Appleby, Carleen Hightower, and Timothy Thompson, far exceeded expectations. In fact, Doug, Carleen, and Timothy each raised over two hundred dollars! Add in the collections by the other two candidates and that brings the grand total to $803.45 for Christmas Seals!"

The crowd burst into applause. "And the winner of the Outstanding Teen Competition is Timothy Thompson, who raise two hundred and forty-seven dollars!"

Everybody cheered, and Carleen and Doug pushed me up onto the stage. I was in a daze as I looked out at the crowd.

Mr. Moray continued.

"In light of the amazing efforts of Doug Appleby and Carleen Hightower, the committee has decided to name them as runners-up, and the two of them will ride with Timothy in my Cadillac in the Christmas Parade!"

I was so excited I jumped up and down as Doug and Carleen joined me on stage. We hugged each other tight, and I didn't even try to stop the tears.

The crowd went crazy as Mr. Maurice put sashes on each of us, giving my shoulder a squeeze when he placed mine over my head. The three of us stood there, "All American Teen" written across our chests, soaking up the applause of the entire school, all of them on their feet. Carleen grabbed both our hands and pulled them up in victory, *Rocky*-style. Cameras flashed, and that picture was in both the newspaper and the yearbook.

# Twenty-Eight: Santa Claus Is Coming to Edgewood

THE EDGEWOOD CHRISTMAS Parade was always held on the Saturday after Thanksgiving. The day dawned clear and bright. I was up and out of bed with the sun after hardly sleeping from the excitement. Momma got up when she heard me banging around in the kitchen.

"Lord have mercy, Timmy. The birds aren't even up yet. You must be excited about your big day."

"We have to be at the town hall parking lot extra early to set up—you know that. We can't be late."

"Don't worry, honey, we have plenty of time. They can't start without you."

"But they can, Momma, they can. If Santa Claus and the high school band and the mayor and Junior Miss South Carolina are all there and ready to start, then they're gonna start. Nobody's going to say 'Oh, wait, Timmy's not here yet. Everybody stop what you're doing while we wait on Timmy.' Nobody's going to do that."

"Darling, for goodness sake, I promise you won't be a minute late. Now, reach in the pantry and hand me that sack of grits. I can't have you starting your big day without a proper breakfast."

While Momma cooked grits, eggs, toast, and bacon, I showered and carefully blew my hair dry. I gave it a tiny spritz of Momma's Aqua Net just to keep things in place. I'd be riding in a convertible, after all. When I came into the kitchen, I was surprised to see Daddy sitting there.

"Hey, Daddy."

"Hey, son."

"Your father wanted to wish you luck on your big day. I'm going to leave you two alone for a minute." She left the room, and there were a few moments of silence before he spoke.

"I heard you stood up to Jimbo."

"Yeah, I guess I did."

"I heard you stood up to him twice. Is that right?"

"Yes, sir."

"You know he's gone off to live with his grandmomma in Georgia somewhere, don't you?"

"No, sir, I didn't know that. He hasn't been in school lately, but he's always skipped a lot."

"You won't be seeing no more of him."

"Good."

More silence.

"Well, I just wanted to tell you I'm real proud of you, son. You stood up to the bully and you won this big contest and now you're riding in the Christmas Parade. You're a good boy, and you're going to make something of yourself. I know it."

"Thank you, Daddy." I was starting to get choked up.

He reached into his jacket pocket and pulled out a velveteen box. He handed it to me without speaking. I opened it: it was an old watch with a twisty metal band.

"It's real gold. My pa got it for working twenty-five years on the railroad. I got it when he died, but I can't wear no watch when I'm working on cars. It'd end up in somebody's transmission or something."

"Thank you, Daddy."

"It's got that old geezer band on it 'cause Pa's hands were screwed up from the arthritis. You can switch it out if you like."

I set the time, wound it up, and put it on.

"I love it, Daddy."

"Good. I'm right proud of you."

"I love you, Daddy."

"Yeah, okay. Good. Me too."

Mom came back in, and Daddy said he had to leave.

"Are you going to see the parade?" I asked.

"I'll be there, son." And he left.

Momma smiled and served me a plate full of eggs and grits. I showed her the scratched old watch.

"We'll get you a better band for it," she said.

"It's a real man's watch. I like it the way it is."

After breakfast, I pulled out the amazing, beautiful clothes I would be wearing. Mr. Maurice had provided outfits for the three of us. For me, he'd chosen a dark-brown tweed blazer that worked beautifully with my coloring. He told me I was an autumn, so I looked especially good in earth tones. He paired it with a bright-red bow tie that I didn't want to wear at first because it was so flamboyant, but Momma and Aunt Melanie talked me into it. It was my favorite part of the whole look.

When I was dressed, I slipped my feet into a pair of tassel-tie Bass Weejuns. Momma had bought them for me, and I knew they cost a fortune, but I loved them. They were just the right sophisticated touch for the new, popular me. I walked into Momma's room where she was finishing getting ready, and she burst into tears when she saw me.

"Oh, Timmy! You're so handsome." She wrapped me into a big hug. "You're growing up so fast. Oh, honey, have I told you how proud I am of you? Winning this title and all is a huge deal, and I'm so proud I may just bust wide open."

Aunt Melanie called out from the front room, and Momma said, "We're back here, Mel."

"What's Chad Everett doing here? Who kidnapped Timmy Thompson and replaced him with Chad Everett?"

I blushed. "Thank you, Aunt Melanie. Have you seen my new shoes? I just love them."

"I was with your momma when she picked them out. She wanted to get penny loafers, but I said to get the ones with a little extra bit of fancy. I thought you'd like that."

"I do. Gosh, I can't wait to see what Doug and Carleen are wearing."

I walked out to the car very carefully because I didn't want to scuff my new shoes. When I got in, I sat on the edge of the seat so as not to wrinkle my jacket.

Momma, Aunt Melanie, and I got to the town hall parking lot with lots of time to spare. In fact, we got there before Mr. Maurice. It wasn't long, though, until he drove up in the biggest, longest, whitest convertible I'd ever seen. When he cruised to a stop, Aunt Melanie draped herself over the hood like a model and said, "Somebody take my picture; this is the life I was born for. Cadillacs and handsome men."

Mr. Maurice got out of the car laughing. "My dear, I predict a lifetime of Cadillacs and handsome men for you. Speaking of which, Tim, you look flawless. Earth tones are your palette. And, JoAnne dear, don't you look cute as a button in that Christmas sweater. Are those reindeer?"

"Why, yes, I knitted it myself."

"It's precious," said Mr. Maurice.

Just then, a car horn honked, and we all turned to see Mrs. Hightower's Dart pull into the parking lot. Carleen carefully got out, and everyone sucked in their breath.

Carleen looked beautiful. She was in a real Pucci dress, not a homemade knockoff like the one her momma had made for her Cass Elliott presentation. It was tailored to her figure and was quite flattering. It was accented with a beautiful red shawl in the softest cashmere. Then, there was her hair. She'd actually had it done. It was cut in layers with soft curls framing her face.

Mr. Maurice took her hand. "My dear, you look like a vision. I believe I was right about the dress, wasn't I?"

"Oh, yes, you were, Mr. Moray," said Mrs. Hightower. "I've never seen Carleen so excited about her appearance."

"Carleen, you look so pretty," I said. She stood stiffly and hardly moved as if it would all disappear if she breathed wrong.

"Carleen, I've admired that dress in the store, but it was made for you. You look lovely," said Aunt Melanie.

I heard a slight tap of a horn and turned to see Doug's momma's Datsun turn into the parking lot. The car stopped, Doug stepped out, and my heart skipped a beat. There was never anyone more handsome. He was in a spectacular double-breasted navy-blue blazer with a bright-green tie that made his Sprite-bottle eyes pop. His hair had been styled with a bit of gel, and he looked very adult.

"Why, Doug, don't you look handsome," said Momma.

"He certainly does, doesn't he, Timmy?" said Aunt Melanie, nudging me.

"You're almost good-looking enough for me to date," said Carleen. I lightly punched her in the arm, and Doug and I hugged.

With his arm still around my waist, he called to his mother to take our picture. "Carleen, get in here," he said. That was the first of many pictures of Doug, Carleen, and me taken on that magical day.

"Good luck, guys." I turned, and there were Kathy and Lisa, running up, hand in hand. They were followed by Dean, Patti, Jaime, and Chip. Jaime and Chip were holding hands!

"We're so excited for you guys; we just had to see you off," said Patti.

"All right, people, it's time to get in the car." Mr. Maurice took the wheel, and the three of us sat up top as the big, old Cadillac glided down Main Street in the bright winter sun. On the side of the car was a sign that read: America's Outstanding Teens of Patriot Christian Academy, and then, in small print: Sponsored by Boutique Moray.

We were right behind the high school marching band, and between the music and the cheering, the noise was deafening but joyous. We waved, and everybody in town seemed to be on the sidewalks waving back at us. All the kids from school kept running up to get ahead so they could cheer for us. Kathy and Lisa, Patti, Jaime and Chip, and Dean were our cheering section. I also saw Mrs. Morgan, Mrs. Means, and even Mrs. Holt. Nurse Darleen took her cigarette out of her mouth and gave us a real rebel yell when we passed her. When we swung by the pool hall, Daddy was out front grabbing some man by the arm and yelling, "That's my son! That's my son!" Carleen hugged my neck and pulled me to her. I swear she even teared up a little.

When the parade ended, we posed for more pictures for the newspapers, and I even got to meet Junior Miss South Carolina. When it was all over, Carleen, Doug, and I all hugged. We knew it was a moment we would never forget.

THAT NIGHT, THERE was an unexpected knock on the door. Momma answered, and it was Dr. Mingees. He asked if he could speak to Momma in private. She asked me to go occupy myself in my bedroom and took Dr. Mingees into the living room. After about a half hour, I heard him leave, and Momma came back to my room.

"You won't have to worry about Kimberly Ann anymore. Dr. Mingees stopped by to personally tell me he and Mrs. Mingees have decided to take her out of Patriot Christian immediately and send her to boarding school in Virginia."

"Oh my gosh, Momma. Why? And why did he come by here at night to tell you?"

"He said he wanted to personally apologize to me for Kimberly Ann's behavior toward you. He said he was embarrassed and ashamed of her, and he decided the best way to turn her around was to send her away to a totally new environment. They're homeschooling her until Christmas then driving her north to her new school. Come on; let's go to the kitchen, and I'll fix you a snack."

Momma told me to grab whatever I wanted to out of the pantry. I was very surprised to see her pour herself a glass of some of Aunt Melanie's white Zinfandel.

"I hope this gives Kimberly Ann a chance to turn her life around," she said. "I've always liked her. Truth be told,

I always thought you two would make a nice couple. Maybe after boarding school straightens her out?"

I knew this was the moment. I had to come out to her. "Momma. I have something to tell you."

# Twenty-Nine: I'm Coming Out

I REALLY WANTED a swallow of Momma's wine but didn't ask. I looked her in the eyes and decided to plunge in.

"Momma, Kimberly Ann's never going to be my girlfriend."

"Oh? Is that all you have to tell me? Goodness, such drama. If you don't like Kimberly Ann in that way, it's fine. There's lots of fish in the sea."

"But I only like boy fish."

"What are you talking about?"

I took her hand, trying to get my thoughts together. I felt like a dunce for my boy fish comment. "Mom. I don't like Kimberly Ann because I don't like any girl in that way. I'm never going to date girls. Do you understand?"

"You want to be a Catholic priest? Honey, we're Baptists."

"No, Mom. That's not what I'm trying to tell you. I don't like girls in the same way as I like boys."

Her face went pale. "You don't like girls?"

"Sure, I like girls. I like girls fine. But I like boys in a different way, you see?" I sighed. This wasn't going well.

"I'm getting confused."

"Me too. Okay, I'll just say it. Momma, I'm gay."

"Gay as in happy?"

"Gay as in homosexual."

There was a long pause as it sank in.

"You're just being silly. You read something in *Vogue* or *Cosmo*."

"I'm not being silly. I'm being honest. I'm being more honest than I've ever been in my life."

There was another pause as her face hardened, just slightly.

"I tried so hard not to raise you like that. It's your daddy's fault. He was never around. I should never have let Melanie buy you those damn fashion magazines." It was the first time in my life I'd heard my mother use the word *damn*.

"Momma, it has nothing to do with how you raised me. It's not Daddy's fault. It's just how I am."

"You can't tell me that a real male presence in this house wouldn't have made a difference."

"Momma, that has nothing to do with it. I've felt different from the other boys every day of my life, from my earliest memory. I've always known, deep down."

"What does that mean, 'from my earliest memory'? You can't be a homosexual at four."

"Yes, you can."

"Did someone touch you? Oh, my baby, who did this to you?"

"Oh my God, Mom! Nobody! That's not it, either. This is just how I am. It's how God made me."

"Don't bring God into this."

"But it's true."

"How do you know, Mr. Smarty Pants?"

"Because I've lived it every day of my life. And I've been thinking about it a lot lately."

"Everybody has weird thoughts at some time. If you ignore them, they go away."

"This isn't going away."

"You're too young to know all this. This is a phase a lot of boys go through. You'll grow out of it."

"Momma, when you were fifteen, did you know you liked guys?"

"Sure. Of course."

I smiled at her and squeezed her hand.

"Okay, I get your point, but how can you say you don't like girls in that way when you've never, you know."

"Had sex?"

"Yes. That. How do you know you won't like it if you've never done it? You've never done it, have you?"

"No, I haven't. It's not a matter of liking 'it' or not liking 'it.'" I rested my forehead on my palm, trying to come up with a way to express it. Then, it hit me. "Momma, I don't feel passion for girls, and I don't feel romantic about girls. I don't want to kiss girls. I want to kiss boys. I feel romantic passion for boys."

"Have you kissed a boy?"

"Yes."

"Doug?"

"Yes."

There was another long pause, and she began to cry softly.

"I suppose you think you're in love with Doug?"

"I know I'm in love with Doug."

She downed her wine. "Well, at least he's polite and from a nice family."

I laughed. She seemed to be turning the corner.

"This can't be that big a surprise."

"Of course it is!"

"Momma, what have I always wanted to be when I grew up?"

"A women's fashion designer."

I cocked my head and raised my eyebrows.

"So what? Calvin Klein has a girlfriend," she said.

"Seriously?"

"Well, I don't know how serious it is."

"When the other boys started talking about girls they thought were sexy and stuff, I never understood. I always got it wrong. My favorite Charlie's Angel is Kate Jackson, not Farrah Fawcett."

"Kate Jackson is very pretty."

"What was my favorite toy when I was really little?"

"Andie the rag doll."

"The girl doll with the boy's name."

"Why did you give that doll a boy's name? I've always wondered."

"I thought you'd feel better about me playing with a doll if I gave it a boy's name. Dumb, I know."

She put her other hand on top of mine. "Did I make you ashamed of yourself for playing with a doll? Way back then when you were four?"

Now, it was my turn to shed tears. "No. I don't know. Somehow, I thought it was wrong for a boy to play with dolls, but I still wanted to."

"I gave you Barbies."

"I know. Until I was six when you took them away and replaced them with Hot Wheels."

"I did my best."

"You are the best mother in the world. I know I wasn't ever the son you and Daddy expected. That's my point. I've always been gay. There's nothing you or Daddy could have done to make things turn out differently."

"When did you become so smart and wise?"

"I guess you raised me that way."

She laughed. Thank God.

"I remember when you used to play dress-up in my closet. Oh, hey, you're not one of those cross-dressers, are you?"

"No, Momma."

"Okay, just checking. There's only so many news flashes I can take in one day."

"This is it. Nothing else."

"I used to worry so when you'd toddle around in my heels. I thought you'd turn out, well, just like this." She put her hand over her mouth and started laughing. I joined her.

"I'm still the same Timmy I was twenty minutes ago."

She stood and pulled me up. She gave me a big hug. "You'll always be my precious baby boy. I love you, Timmy."

"I love you, Momma." She released me from the hug.

"I don't like it, but at least you chose a nice boy."

"Thank you, Momma."

She downed her wine. "I'm going to bed."

THE NEXT MORNING, I called Doug and told him to meet me at Slave Lake as soon as he could get there. He was already there when I rode up.

"I did it! I did it! I told my mother!" I fell into his arms, and he held me until my breathing slowed.

"Start from the beginning."

We sat on the grass and faced each other. "It happened last night. Dr. Mingees came over to tell Momma he was taking Kimberly Ann out of Patriot Christian and sending her to boarding school in Virginia."

"Wow. When?"

"Immediately. We won't see her again."

"Or miss her."

"Yeah, right. So, after he left, Momma and I were talking, and she said something about how she always thought Kimberly Ann would make a good match for me and maybe after boarding school straightens her out, she and I could date."

"Nothing's going to straighten you out." He smiled.

"Be serious! This was a major crisis in my life! Don't make jokes!"

"Okay, I'm sorry. Go on. What did you say to your mother?"

"I told Momma that Kimberly Ann's not going to ever be my girlfriend. And she said there are lots of fish in the sea and, I can't believe I said this, but I said, 'I only like boy fish.'"

"You came out to your mother by saying 'I only like boy fish'?"

"Yeah. Kinda dumb, I know. I'm such a goofball."

He put his hands on my face, pulled me to him, and kissed me. "I love you, you goofball. Now, go on, what did she say?"

"She asked what I meant, and I stumbled around trying to explain that I like guys more than girls, but that doesn't mean I don't like girls because I do, just not in the same way. I succeeded in confusing us both, so, finally, I just blurted out, 'I'm gay, Mom.'"

"Well, that gets the job done. What did she say?"

"She didn't know what gay meant, so I had to explain it didn't mean happy—although I *am* happy—and then I started getting us confused again, so I just said I'm a homosexual. Then she cried."

"Oh, crap. How long did she cry?"

"She hasn't stopped yet."

"I'm sorry."

"It's okay because we kept talking through the tears. We talked about how I've always wanted to be a women's fashion designer and how my favorite toy was Andie the rag doll."

"The girl doll with a boy's name."

"Right, that one. I told her I never understood when the other boys talked about girls they found hot or sexy—I always got it wrong."

"Like Kate Jackson, who I think is a classy lady."

"Me too! Anyway, I told her I don't feel passion for girls, and I don't feel romantic about girls. I don't want to kiss girls. I want to kiss boys. Then, she asked me if I'd kissed any boys, and I told her yes—you. In fact, I told her I was in love with you."

"Oh, great. No wonder we had to meet in a secret location."

"No, it's not like that. After a whole lot of talking, she seemed to kind of accept it and said, 'I don't like it, but at least you picked a nice boy.'"

"That's a relief."

"Then she called Aunt Melanie at, like, midnight and made her promise to go for shopping and lunch today."

"Mel will set her straight."

"There's that word, again."

"So, how do you feel?"

I took a breath. "I feel really great. Mom will come around. I feel free. No more lies. No more pretending." I lay on the grass and pulled him down next to me. "And no more hiding my love for you."

# Thirty: Goodbye

THE EVENING AFTER Christmas, there was an unexpected knock on the door. It was Doug and his momma.

"May we come in, JoAnne? There's something I'd like to tell you."

"Why, of course, Annette. Timmy, why don't you take Doug back to your bedroom so Mrs. Herlong and I can have a chat."

Doug's momma shook her head. "No, I want Doug to stay with me, and I think Timmy should hear this, also."

Doug met my eyes. They were red-rimmed. I got a bad feeling in the pit of my stomach. Doug's momma turned down Mom's offer of coffee and pie, and we all went to sit in the living room.

"I'll get right to it. I've accepted a job back in Los Angeles, and Doug and I will be leaving right away. In fact, they want me to start in January, so there's no time to waste."

"Why, Annette," said Mom. "I'm thunderstruck. I thought you and Doug were settling in nicely here in Edgewood. Hasn't it been good for you to be near your family?"

"I suppose. You see, JoAnne, I came out here because my divorce turned my world upside down."

"I completely understand," said Momma, taking her hand.

"I didn't know what to do. I suddenly felt stranded a million miles from home, or at least what I thought was home. All I knew was I had to get out of LA. I thought South Carolina would be good for me and bringing Doug to a completely different environment would be a growth experience for him."

"And hasn't it been? I mean, look at what's happened with Doug and Timmy. Doug's, um, feelings for Timmy…"

"Love," said Doug.

"Yes, his love for Timmy has meant so much to him and to Timmy."

"We love each other a lot," I said, fighting back tears and wishing I could think of a better way of expressing it. "We have to be together."

"We're meant to be together," said Doug. "But you know that, Mom."

"I know, dear," said Doug's momma. She looked at me. "Doug and I were up most of the night talking about this. It breaks my heart to separate you two."

"Then don't do it!" I said. "Just stay. You can get a job here. Maybe Columbia or Augusta. They're big cities if that's what you like."

"Thank you, Tim, but I've been offered a wonderful job in my field, and it's what I need to do. I've come to realize that Los Angeles is really my home. Edgewood just isn't anymore. And Doug was born in California. He belongs there. This doesn't mean you two can't ever see each other again. There are airplanes and telephones. In fact, I want to invite you to come out for spring break. Spend the whole week with us."

Spring break felt years away. I couldn't imagine not seeing Doug until then.

"I wanted to tell you all this, JoAnne, because you're really the only person in this town who reached out to me, and you've been so good to Doug. And your sweet Tim has become like a second son to me."

On that, my first tear escaped.

"What sort of work will you be doing?" asked Momma.

"I'll be managing an art gallery. It's very exciting. They feature the most interesting emerging West Coast artists. It's a dream come true in a lot of ways." She looked at Doug and rubbed his shoulder. "They've been trying to get me to come back for a while, actually. I decided to accept the offer when they called and said they were about to give the job to someone else. We leave Sunday morning. Early."

"But this is Thursday," I said. "That only gives us two days."

"I'm sorry, dear," said Doug's momma. "I know it hurts, and I wish I could make it better for you."

When they got up to leave, Mom gave Doug's momma a big hug. Then, Doug's momma hugged me. "I'll miss you, sweet Tim."

"Can Doug stick around a little?" I asked.

"I'll drive him back later," said Momma.

Doug's momma smiled. "Sure. Take all the time you need."

Doug and I went back to my bedroom, shut the door, and flopped onto the bed. We held each other, and I cried into his chest.

When I was cried out, I whispered, "What will I do without you?"

"What will *I* do without *you*?"

We lay there for a while longer. I wanted to memorize everything about him—his smell, his breathing, his heartbeat. Finally, he spoke.

"You'll be great, you know. You're the most popular guy in school. You and Carleen rule Patriot Christian."

Suddenly, all the planning and scheming to be popular felt pointless.

"I don't care about any of it. I only care about you. I want to go with you."

"Your mother would freak out at that idea, and you know it."

"Yeah, I know."

"We'll write and call every day until spring break. Then, I'll take you to the beach and teach you to surf."

"I'd rather make out in the surf." He lightly slapped my butt.

"You bad boy. It's a date."

I paused for a second and continued, "Hey, you're not going to meet one of those surfer boys, are you? Some guy with blond hair and muscles?"

"No way. Who wants some airhead dude when I've got you?"

I smiled. "Spring break seems like forever away."

"I know. I'm not worried about you, though. Carleen will keep you busy. She worked hard for you two to be the king and queen of school, and she's not going to let you slack off."

"Being popular seemed so important until tonight. Now, it doesn't mean anything."

Doug sat up. "Sure it does, man. Listen, when I first got here, you were the one the rednecks bullied all the time, remember? Now, you're the king of the school. Do you think they're going to stop being bullies? Jimbo may be gone, but someone will step up and find some other kids to push around. Maybe some other secretly gay kid from middle school. Maybe that ninth-grade guy with all the zits. Or the skinny girl with buckteeth who's kind of slow. Somebody will be bullied; it's like a high school law."

"I guess so."

"I know so, and you can use your popularity to come to that kid's defense. You can be his friend, and if he's friends with the most popular guy in school, the bullies will leave him alone."

"But then there'll just be another."

"Then, you befriend the other. Pretty soon, all the freaks and outcasts and gays and fatties will be the cool crowd, with you and Carleen at the top. It's revolutionary, man!"

"Wow! That *is* pretty cool."

He lay back down, and I put my head on his chest. Soon, I heard Mom lightly knocking on the door.

"Guys? It's almost eleven. I really need to take Doug home."

That opened the floodgates for both of us. I kissed him hard, and he held me so tight I could hardly breathe. I never wanted him to let go.

The next two days went by in a whirl of activity. I spent every waking minute at Doug's house, helping them pack. We were so busy there were times when I forgot what was really happening, but then I'd catch Doug's eye and the reality flooded back. The movers came Saturday and took everything that wouldn't fit in the car.

On Saturday night, Aunt Melanie and Momma showed up with pizza and two big bottles of wine.

"We brought California chardonnay. We thought you might like that," said Aunt Melanie, pulling a package of paper cups out of the grocery bag. "I thought we'd even let Doug and Tim have some."

"What the hell," said Doug's momma.

"Well, I guess I'm outnumbered," said Mom, looking doubtful.

I wasn't very hungry, but the wine was delicious. It wasn't sweet at all like the pink stuff Aunt Melanie usually drank. Doug's momma said it was "very buttery," and I got it. It tasted rich.

When it was time for Mom and Aunt Melanie to go, Doug's momma asked if I could stay over.

"We'll be in sleeping bags, but I don't think he'll mind."

"Please, Mom?"

She let me. When Doug and I went to his bedroom and shut the door, there was one sleeping bag on the floor. He gave me a naughty grin.

"There's not enough room for the both of us and our clothes, so strip it off, stud."

"What about your mother? She's right in the next room."

"She's not going to bother us," he said, pulling his shirt over his head. "She promised."

We slowly undressed, watching each other reveal our bodies. I'd never seen anyone so beautiful. We gently held each other and began kissing, at first softly then with increasing passion. He laid me down on the bed and got in next to me, pulling me close. I'd never felt full-body contact with a naked man before and was so excited I pushed him away briefly.

"I want to save this," I said. "I want it to last."

He smiled and stroked my face. "We can take it slow."

Taking it slow lasted about two seconds before I pulled him into a passionate kiss. We rolled around on the bed with me on top, then him on top, then me, then him. The feel of his weight on me was intoxicating. I wanted to give myself to him completely; to be united with him.

I lost track of time, but at some point, I had to take a break from the frenzy and catch my breath. He lay next to me and rubbed my earlobe. Looking deep into my eyes, he said, "I love you, Tim."

"I love you, Doug. I always will." He kissed me with urgency, our legs and arms wrapped around each other so I couldn't tell where I ended and he began. In that moment, there was nothing on earth but Doug and me and our all-consuming love. We were one being, connected forever.

# Thirty-One: Farewell

I WOKE UP with a start when Doug's momma knocked on the door.

"It's five AM, boys. I want to be on the road in an hour."

Doug and I were zipped up in his sleeping bag, and he was spooning me. I'd slept soundly wrapped in his warmth, but now that I was awake, I was overcome with dread.

"I don't want to get up," Doug said.

"Me either."

"Actually, I don't think I can get up. We're caught in this sleeping bag, and my arm is asleep."

It was true that we couldn't move, but I didn't want to. He pulled one arm out and managed to unzip us.

"We should probably get dressed before your mother walks in on us," I said.

He stood and began shaking out his arm. He was totally nude and breathtaking. "You're probably right, but I just want one more look at all of you." He kneeled and opened the sleeping bag, revealing my bare body. For once, I felt absolutely no shame or shyness about my imperfections.

"And I want to do this one more time," I said. I pulled him down on top of me and kissed him fully, icky morning breath and all. I couldn't let him go without feeling his weight on me again.

"I love you so much. I'll never forget this night," I said.

"I love you, too. Totally."

There was another knock on the door, this time more forceful, so we got up and put on our clothes.

When we were dressed, we met Doug's momma in the kitchen. She had two little bottles of orange juice for us and a box of Pop-Tarts.

"Pop-Tarts, Mrs. Herlong? I didn't know you ate those."

"I don't, but it's easy. One last concession to South Carolina before we return to the land of tofu and hummus."

They were blueberry, unfrosted. Maybe that was the closest she could get to California Pop-Tarts.

We ate quickly, and I helped Doug carry the last few bags out to the overloaded Datsun. Suddenly, it was time. Doug's momma said she was going to make one last check of the house and left us alone, standing by the car.

We stood facing each other, holding hands. "I'm going to miss you so much. I'll write you every day. I promise," I said.

"I will too, baby. And I'll call all the time. Dad says I can use his long distance when I'm staying with him and his guy."

"That would be great. I'll need to hear your voice."

"And spring break will be here before you know it. We'll have a blast. I'll teach you to surf."

"That would be amazing." We stopped talking and looked into each other's eyes for several minutes. He went first, in a quiet voice.

"I love you, Tim."

"I love you too, Doug. I'll never stop loving you." Doug pulled me to him, and we kissed one last time. Just then, we heard a car honk. We turned toward the sound as Carleen pulled into the driveway in her mother's ancient Dart.

"You didn't think I'd let you get away without hugging your neck, did you?"

"Check it out, Tim; it's Carleen, the queen bee of Patriot Christian. You two have fun ruling the school."

"I am large and in charge, buddy, and don't you forget it." Carleen put her arms around both of us and pulled us in for a group hug. We were all crying when Doug's momma came out and announced it was time to go. I held Doug's hand as he got in the car and reached in and kissed him one last time.

"Y'all drive safe. Bye-bye, Mrs. Herlong," Carleen said.

Doug and I met each other's eyes as his mom started the car and put it in gear. Carleen and I stood in the driveway, her arm tight around my shoulders as they drove away. Doug kept waving until they turned the corner and were gone.

I started crying again. Carleen pulled me into a big hug and let me weep for a while.

"Come on, buddy; dry your tears. You stick with me, and we'll have the semester of our lives. The fat girl and the sissy rule Patriot Christian!"

# Thirty-Two: New Boy at the Academy

"TIMMY, HONEY, GET a move on. Christmas vacation is over, and we've got to be out of the house in fifteen minutes."

I checked my look in the mirror. I liked it. Hunter-green V-neck sweater over a light-pink Oxford button-down, both unexpected Christmas presents from Mr. Maurice. I made one last check of the hair, which had finally grown out enough for me to feather it back. I shut my eyes for a moment, and I could feel Doug's fingers running through it. I missed him so much.

"Timmy? Did you hear me?"

"On my way." I grabbed my book bag and dashed down the hall toward the kitchen.

"No Pop-Tarts this morning, Mom. I'm trying to eat healthy."

"You've got to eat something. At least drink your juice."

I did, and we headed out the door.

"I'll stop by the Bi-Rite on the way home and see if they have tofu Pop-Tarts," Mom said.

"No need. I wrote Doug and asked him to ship us some from LA."

Mom looked at me for a second like I'd sprouted a second head; then she laughed.

We arrived at school and I made a beeline for Carleen, who was surrounded by laughing Anns, past and present.

"Pink and green. Subtle," she said.

"There was a time when you would have called it sissified."

"There was a time when you tried to convince me Kate Jackson is sexy."

"I'm out, so I don't have to worry if people think I'm gay. They already know, so why hide it? And Tom Selleck is the sexy one."

"Ick, he's so hairy," said Jaime as the bell rang.

"That's the best part," said Patti. "That, and the muscles."

We all headed into class.

Doug's seat in first period Good Citizenship class was now occupied by Janie Sue Arostook, a girl I'd hardly ever spoken to. My heart broke again when I realized Doug would no longer be sitting next to me. Janie Sue smiled through her enormous buckteeth, then immediately covered her mouth.

"I know you miss Doug," she said. "I thought you two were so sweet together."

"Thanks." I had no idea she'd ever noticed us.

"But nobody misses Jimbo or that awful Kimberly Ann," she whispered as Mrs. Morgan called the class to attention.

In between classes, a guy named Aaron Goldberg, who nobody really knew because he spent all his spare time playing pinball at the drug store, grabbed my arm. I jerked it back reflexively, thinking a new bully had been born.

"Hey, dude, good job taking care of Jimbo. I'd never have had the guts to do what you did." He pushed his long, uncombed hair out of his face and smiled at me. I'd never seen his face behind his hair before. He was actually pretty cute.

Ernie Jackson, AKA Pizzaface, the guy whose acne had started in third grade and showed no signs of slowing, patted me on the back and gave me a thumbs-up between English and math. I got a high five from Carolyn Connor, who was from one of those Seventh-day Adventist families and wore long skirts and had no friends because everybody thought her people weren't really Christians. Who knew Seventh-day Adventists high-fived?

A weird girl named Ariel, who always wore black and even painted her fingernails black, raised her fist as we were about to go to lunch and said, "Power to the people, man."

"Have you noticed what's happening?" I asked Carleen as we approached the lunchroom.

"It's crazy! We've unleashed the freaks! Did you know we had a ninth grader who apparently won an award from NASA for designing a computer or a rocket or something?"

"No! Who is he?"

"He's the kid with the safety strap on his glasses who, I swear, has never said a word at school. He just asked me to the junior prom. He's like the fifth guy today to ask me. And it's not till May!"

"Are you going with him?"

"Maybe. I'm keeping my options open. Speaking of options, here come Dean and Chip, looking cute."

She was right; they were looking cute. They both walked up to us.

"Hey, you two, let's all sit together at lunch, okay?" asked Dean.

"I think we can squeeze you in," said Carleen, taking both boys' arms and allowing them to escort her into the lunchroom.

When we reached the entrance, everyone turned and looked our way. That must have been what it felt like to be Kimberly Ann. Kimberly Ann always paused, sneered, and modeled her cute, new outfit (and she always had on a cute, new outfit). Instead, I smiled, did not model my new outfit (although it was totally cute), and got in line for a Mountain Dew. Make that a Diet Dew.

Carleen went full sugar. "My beauty secret," she said as we clicked bottles. "Got to maintain my curves."

We got to the table, and Jaime and Patti and Kathy and Lisa were already there, holding our seats at the end. I let Carleen sit at the head, and I sat beside her. Dean sat next to me and talked over me to tell Carleen how much he loved her new denim skirt. Chip sat next to Jaime and shared his Ruffles. I supposed that was his idea of flirting.

"Hey, Tim, what do you hear from Doug?" asked Chip, jamming Ruffles into his mouth.

"I got three postcards from the road—one from Jackson, Mississippi, another from Amarillo, Texas, and a third from Winslow, Arizona."

"Was he standing on the corner?" asked Dean.

"Uh, no. His mother has a car."

Dean punched me lightly on the arm. "Never mind, you goofball. Tell him we all said hey."

"I will. He's in LA, and I'm hoping we can talk on the phone this weekend. His last postcard said he'd call from his dad's place on Saturday night." I was counting the minutes until I could hear his voice.

The long table filled up fast. A few more of Dean's teammates took seats, and then came the new crowd. Ariel was first. She dropped her tray next to Lisa and Kathy and sat without asking permission.

"It's so cool that you two are a couple," Ariel said. "We should hang out sometime." Carleen kicked me under the table.

Next up was Carolyn Connor who politely asked if she could sit at our table and took a seat two chairs away from the nearest football player. She looked at him shyly.

Janie Sue Arostook almost dropped her lunch tray because she was trying to balance it while covering her mouth with the other. "Can I sit here?"

"You can if you stop covering up your mouth all the time," said Carleen. "The only rule of this table is nobody hides and nobody pretends to be somebody they're not, okay? We've all seen your teeth, and none of us care. Ain't that right, people?"

Everybody nodded or said yeah. Ariel said, "Right on." Janie Sue moved her hand away from her face and smiled broadly as she sat next to a football player.

I was proud of Carleen for saying that and could feel Doug's influence in her words.

The ninth-grade science genius walked up. Before today, ninth graders didn't dare approach tenth graders, but this semester, all the rules were changing. "Hello, I'm..."

"Rocket Man!" said Carleen, scooting over. "Sit over here by me. Grab a chair, and I'll make room. You can tell me all about how you invent rockets and stuff."

His face lit up, and he put his tray down. "Well, actually, it's software for rockets."

"I have no idea what that is, but, what the hell, teach me something," said Carleen.

Dean scowled for a moment, then turned his attention to Patti, bumming a carrot stick off her.

The last person to enter the lunchroom was Aaron Goldberg. Without speaking, he took the seat next to Carolyn that no one else had filled, diagonal from me. He pushed back his hair and gave me a half smile.

Carleen immediately pulled on my arm and whispered dramatically in my ear, "Wow! Did you notice how cute Aaron is when he gets his hair out of his face?"

"I know. Who knew?"

"I'll put him on my list right after Rocket Man and Dean."

"Rocket Man? You'd really date a ninth grader?"

"Who do you think is going to end up rich out of this school? The lunkhead football player or the genius who's already making rockets fly?"

I laughed and went back to my sandwich.

I looked around at all these people flirting and partnering up and suddenly felt a stab of sadness. I would give up all my newfound popularity to have Doug back. He had helped create this new world at Patriot Christian, and he'd love to see all these different kids hanging out together. I had so much to tell him when he called.

Patti threw a carrot stick at me and told me to perk up. "You're the coolest guy in school—don't you know that?"

Imagine that. I was the coolest guy in school. I looked around at the growing crowd of people who wanted to sit with us. It was getting so big that tables were being pushed together. There were football players and cheerleaders, science nerds and theater geeks, country kids and townies, gays and straights, and more than a few who were somewhere in between. In fact, it seemed like the whole school was part of our crowd. Gone were the bullies and the prissy girls. "Nobody hides and nobody pretends to be something they're not," Carleen had said. We were all just a bunch of kids from Patriot Christian—all different but, in many ways, the same.

I smiled. It was going to be a great semester.

# Acknowledgements

I owe a huge debt of gratitude to Jaime Olin and Patti Downing. Their unceasing encouragement and pleas for "more Timmy" kept me writing.

When I was a student at the academy that inspired this book, I had one special teacher who encouraged my writing and challenged me to see beyond what I thought was possible. Her name is Phyllis Davis, and I am grateful.

Thank you to Carlos Perkins, Jr. for his time, advice, and encouragement.

Thank you to Elizabetta and Raevyn at NineStar Press for believing in this work.

# About the Author

Sam Hawk's fiction is inspired by his experiences at a private Christian Academy in rural South Carolina in the '70s. He survived his Southern adolescence with his sanity relatively intact and went on to earn degrees from the College of Charleston and the University of South Carolina Law School. He also served in the US Army as a JAG officer for twelve years.

After leaving the service, Sam moved to Dallas, Texas, where he met the man of his dreams and found his LGBTQ family. Sam and his husband, Wes, have been married for over ten years and live with their Corgi and Chartreux cat in the requisite charming old house in a historic district where gay couples are legally compelled to live.

Email: Sam@samueldhawk.com

Facebook: www.facebook.com/WriterSamHawk

Twitter: @WriterSamHawk

Instagram: WriterSamHawk

Website: www.writersamhawk.com

# Also Available from NineStar Press

# Connect with NineStar Press

www.ninestarpress.com

www.facebook.com/ninestarpress

www.facebook.com/groups/NineStarNiche

www.twitter.com/ninestarpress

www.tumblr.com/blog/ninestarpress

www.ingramcontent.com/pod-product-compliance
Lightning Source LLC
Chambersburg PA
CBHW032059180726

48284CB00002B/360

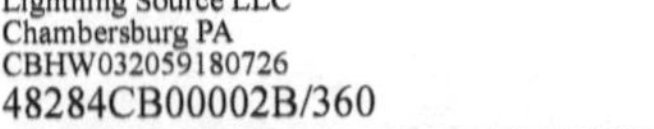